BREAKING HIS LAW

THE BILLIONAIRE HART BROTHERS BOOK ONE

VH NICOLSON

Boldwood

First published in Great Britain in 2025 by Boldwood Books Ltd.

Copyright © VH Nicolson, 2025

Cover Design by Lori Jackson

Cover Images: Ren Saliba, Adobe Stock and Shutterstock

A CIP catalogue record for this book is available from the British Library.

Paperback ISBN 978-1-83678-636-8

Large Print ISBN 978-1-83678-637-5

Hardback ISBN 978-1-83678-635-1

Ebook ISBN 978-1-83678-638-2

Kindle ISBN 978-1-83678-639-9

Audio CD ISBN 978-1-83678-630-6

MP3 CD ISBN 978-1-83678-631-3

Digital audio download ISBN 978-1-83678-632-0

This book is printed on certified sustainable paper. Boldwood Books is dedicated to putting sustainability at the heart of our business. For more information please visit https://www.boldwoodbooks.com/about-us/sustainability/

Boldwood Books Ltd, 23 Bowerdean Street, London, SW6 3TN

www.boldwoodbooks.com

To Sadie Kincaid, you made my dream come true, and for that, I will forever be grateful.

PROLOGUE
ARIANNA—AGE FIFTEEN

A faint hiss of what sounds like high-pressure steam escaping from a tea kettle rouses me from the deep slumber I can't remember drifting into.

My body jerks in response when I let out a staggered raspy cough as the pungent vapor of gasoline consumes my nostrils, filling my lungs and mouth, hitting the back of my throat.

Sharpness spears my shoulder from behind, making me shriek, and I suck in a breath when pain radiates through my shoulder as if a wave of needles is stabbing my skin. I'm unable to stifle my cough, and a high-pitched yelp followed by a long-drawn-out groan leaves my chest.

"Where am I?" I mumble.

Forcing my eyes open, I blink repeatedly, desperately trying to make sense of my surroundings and not gag on the fumes in fear of more pain that may come with even the slightest movement.

The haze lifts, and my vision becomes a little clearer, but it doesn't stop the panic bubbling in my throat because I don't know where I am or why I seem to be lying down on the floor. Or is it a road or a carpet? I glance around the space and silently plead for a clue as to where I am.

The tell-tale signs of being inside a car begin to piece together. Tiny, smashed pieces of glass everywhere, jagged contorted metal poking out in directions they shouldn't, mixed with the smell of burnt rubber and a continual hissing sound I can hear coming from somewhere in the distance.

My body takes a moment to tell my brain that I want it to move, but like a caged animal, I'm trapped with no way out.

With my head to the side, my cheek is pressed against something that feels like metal and I'm unable to lift my neck because something hard is stopping me from above. My breathing labored, it sounds wheezy, and I wince as a throbbing sensation builds across my flattened cheekbone.

The smell of gasoline grows stronger by the second as cold liquid soaks into my clothes, wrapping itself around me like a suffocating fog, thick and inescapable.

Overwhelming my senses, the noxious vapor catches the back of my throat, and I dry heave, my stomach doing somersaults from the high levels of toxicity in the tight space.

My jolting movements have me scratching my cheek against the metal below, making my skin sting from the gasoline seeping into what I can only assume is a wound on my face. It burns like the fires of hell, and when I try to reach up to feel it, my arm won't cooperate. I give it a yank, but I feel nothing, as if it's not there. I know it is; I can see the shocking pink fabric of my gymnastics leotard that's covering my shoulder leading to my arm. I'm numb.

That's when it all hits me at once. I squeeze my eyes shut, praying that it's not true. But when I open them again, it's still there—my pink leotard—and I know I'm not dreaming.

Riley and I were at gymnastics practice, something I've done since I was six years old. I only started because I wanted to be like my big sister, but I absolutely love it and it turns out I'm pretty good at it too, which is a bonus.

Like every Thursday, Mom and Dad picked us up, but instead of going straight home like we usually do, we went for pizza at Franco's to celebrate Riley and me making the finals for the state championship on Beam which we found out at a meet last weekend and were only celebrating now.

We were driving home.

It was late.

Dark.

Foggy.

Then *bang*.

My heart rate spirals out of control as my brain catches up with what happened.

We were in a car crash.

If we hadn't made the state championships, we wouldn't have had a reason to celebrate or be out when it was dark.

Breathing harder, I cough frantically as the agonizing fumes continue to fill my lungs, now making my eyes sting and water as well.

Trying to tilt my head back slightly in search of my family, I let out a scream of horror when my eyes fall on my sister's lifeless body, still in her teal leotard, lying face down on the asphalt outside of the car.

Desperate to get to her, I wiggle my body to free myself, but nothing happens—just more pain, much stronger than before, making the urge to vomit relentless.

Anguish climbs my throat. "Riley." Her name comes out of my mouth with a crack, my heart mirroring the same physical pain.

"Mom? Dad?" Searching around the inside of the car, I sweep the space, assessing my dire situation. Unable to find my parents because my head is restricted, I call out again in frustration. "Mom? Dad?"

No response.

"Help," I call out as best as I can.

Through the fog and over the sound of what I think is the car hissing, I hear quick footsteps.

"Help me, please," I try again, praying someone, anyone, will hear me.

The footsteps run closer.

"I'm in here." Making sure they can hear me this time, I shout louder. "I'm stuck; please help me," I plead. "And my sister." My emotion bubbles over, and I sob hard. "Can you help her? Can you see my mom? Is that you, Dad? Please. Help." My words fade out as I weep.

"Shit," a weak and wobbly whisper of a man's voice utters, followed by, "Shit. Shit. Shit." The fear is evident in his hurried cuss words.

Tears wet my face, the fat droplets mixing with the fuel that's gathered around my cheek like a puddle. I look at my sister's motionless body again. "Please help my sister," I helplessly beg as the sound of the man's footsteps begin to run away fast and disappear, my hope fading with them.

"No," I bellow as loud as I can into the ether. "Please come back." Panicking, I jolt my body upward. Instantly, I'm hit with searing white-hot pain in my back, making me feel like my shoulder is being ripped open, and I scream into the emptiness.

Feeling woozy, my body goes limp, and as hard as I try to keep them open, my eyes shutter close.

Floating memories dance through my mind. My mom

laughing... Dad dancing with her in the living room... My sister and I chasing each other around the backyard... and laughter... so much laughter... and as I go under, everything disappears into a black hole...

1

ARI—FOURTEEN YEARS LATER

As I run the tip of my forefinger in a circle around the lip of my cocktail glass, a loud roar of jovial laughter from behind me fills the bustling bar, pulling me out of the hypnotizing movement. It's packed to the rafters with white-collar workers, and the noise levels rise as they celebrate the start of their weekend.

In the mirror along the back wall, I cast my eyes down the line of people seated to the left and right of me, chatting, laughing, and catching up with friends.

This time next week, it will be me kicking back, rejoicing the two days away from my new boss: the son of a corrupt man. And while I won't be working for him directly, simply being within reach of his orbit makes me want to scrub my skin raw.

My new job is a means to an end.

I have a plan.

I'm uncertain whether I can accomplish it, but I will give it my best shot. For my family's sake.

Unease runs through my veins, causing me to wiggle on my barstool. To settle my nerves, I lift the cocktail to my lips, enjoying the bittersweet taste of my Manhattan, the herbal undertones filling my mouth with full flavor and making me hum in response. I rest my glass down on top of the hammered copper-topped bar.

That hit the spot. I already feel better.

"Can I get you a drink?" A man appears next to me.

Here we go. Cheesiest pick-up line ever.

Letting out a dramatic groan, I twist my neck in the direction of the man who the cocksure voice belongs to, and recognizing him instantly, I look away.

Predictable.

"I'm good, thanks." I rest my hand over my now empty glass.

I wondered if he would have the balls to talk to me. After all, he's been watching me in the mirror for the last half hour.

Far from subtle, he's been checking me out, making eye contact, then looking away, smirking, then looking back. He's an incorrigible flirt.

So cliché.

Just, no.

Flipping my long brown hair over my shoulder, I survey him once again.

I swear this guy, in what looks like a suit that costs more than my entire shoe collection, must do this every Friday night. He's not specifically interested in me. Nope, not at all.

It's because I'm a new face and have never been in this bar before.

I'm fresh meat and judging by the length of his incisors, he wants to eat me alive.

Eh, no thanks; I'd rather chew off my own left arm.

"Are you sure I can't buy you a drink? Because it looks like you could use a refill." He lifts his hand to get the bartender's attention.

I shake my head in response. "I'm fine, but thank you." I push the glass away from me.

Resting his forearm on the bar, he stares at me, turning the awkward dial up to a solid ten. "It's like that, is it?" he asks.

I don't follow. "Like what?" I gesture with open palms.

"You want to cut out the niceties and just come back to my apartment?" He tilts his head to the side, and his hooded eyes drop down my body before his mouth shapes a smug grin.

Presumptuous asshole.

Knowing exactly what he's implying, I ask, "I'm curious; what led you to believe that?"

He moves closer to me, his mouth finding the shell of my ear. "Because for the last thirty minutes you've been eye-fucking me in the mirror." His words feel like ice chips being poured down the back of my dress, and I shiver in disgust.

The delusional prick.

Since I arrived, he's been undressing *me* with his eyes, not the other way around.

I lean out of his closeness that I don't appreciate and pull a fake smile. "Sorry, I didn't catch your name."

He flashes me his teeth, looking pleased with himself, as if he's already assumed he's won me over. "Chase," he answers.

"Well, Chase." I twirl my hair around my finger playfully. "You see, I don't know what your wife would say if I went home with you, do you?"

He flinches, snapping backward as if I'd slapped him. "My wife? Shit, how do you know her? Is this a set-up?" His voice trembles, brows growing worried with lines, and his gaze darts around the bar.

Coolly, I reply, "Here's the thing, Chase. Guys like you are so easy to spot. Your wedding finger has a clear indent in it as well as a tan line." I point to his left hand as I turn to the side on my barstool to face him full on.

I slowly cross my black stocking-covered legs and continue. "Your wedding ring is now wrapped around the ring finger of your other hand, but it's too big for it, and that's why you keep fiddling with it." He stops immediately, tucking his hands into the pockets of his dress pants. "It doesn't feel right on that hand, does it? Because it doesn't belong there."

Red blotches grow across the skin of his neck, while his movements become agitated at my directness.

Satisfied that my observation was correct, I add further, "Also, I watched you take it off and switch its position twenty minutes ago." Dumbass. I raise my finger in the air to make my point and wag it at him. "Be careful not to lose that, or your wife will start asking questions."

Chase flashes his teeth as if he were about to say something, but I stop him in his tracks. And partly because I can't help myself, I go on to say, "Let me take a guess." I feign overthinking, looking up to the left, then tap my fingers against the bar. "You have an apartment in the city for the nights you're working late, but it's really a fuck pad to cover your illicit affairs while your wife is sitting in an obnoxiously oversized house in the suburbs." I stop for a beat. "With one child?" I wait for him to give me an answer, but he doesn't. I guess again. "Two children?" He remains stoic while I take another guess. "Three kids?"

"Are you a witch or something?" His hand nervously runs through his slicked-back hair.

"Three? Wow. You have been busy."

He spits venom my way. "Fuck you."

"You wish." Swiveling round on my ass to face the bar again, I deliver a parting farewell with a finger wave over my shoulder, dismissing him. "Have a great night, Chase. And please do your wife a favor and divorce her already. She deserves better."

I hear him muttering under his breath, which sounds a lot like *Fucking frigid bitch*, as he storms off, and I laugh to myself as I signal to the bartender I would like a drink. "Another Manhattan, please." Smiling, I point to my empty glass.

"I'll get that." A one-hundred-dollar bill is slapped down, then slid across the bar by a strong tan hand in the direction of the bartender. "And a Macallan single malt on the rocks, please."

For a beat, we stare at each other in the mirror before slowly turning to face one another.

As if in slow motion, I'm hit with a wave of energy, like a pure shot of electricity, that awakens something deep in my core, and I hate it.

Because it's him.

Nathaniel Hart.

San Francisco's top personal injury attorney.

Billionaire playboy.

And the son of the man I want to destroy.

2

NATHAN

"I can buy my own drink, thank you though." The feisty woman who gave Chase "Jerkoff" Torres the virtual middle finger rejects my offer to pay for her drink with a dismissive wave of her hand. Her fiery glare pierces through me, as if daring me to challenge her.

But instead of being annoyed, a grin tugs at the corner of my lips. There's something intriguing about her. She's refreshing, and oozes confidence that most people spend a lifetime trying to master.

"Well," I say, resting my elbows casually on the bar, "it seems like you've got everything handled. For the record, I wasn't trying to get you to come home with me. I just thought you might enjoy a drink with some company that doesn't fall into the douchebag category."

Her lips twitch, almost betraying a smile, but she quickly masks it. "Nice try, but I don't need company."

"Noted," I reply, raising my hands in mock surrender, then I reach to unbutton my navy suit jacket. "However, I would like to buy you a drink to congratulate you on sending Chase back to his wife. I like a woman with strong morals." It's a lie by omission; I spotted her as soon as I entered the bar. All legs, dark hair, curves for days, and snarky as hell. She's a fucking smoke show and I immediately wanted to know everything about her.

"You know him?" She points her thumb in the direction Chase left in.

"And his wife," I confirm. "You were right. Suzanne deserves better."

Her voice sounds hopeful about her suspicion when she asks, "So I was right about the three kids?"

"Right on the money."

"Knew it," she says triumphantly with a smug grin before she draws her lips into a thin line again.

Something about her tells me she doesn't let her guard down very often, if at all, and doesn't trust me, or anyone. Not easily anyway.

The only reason I know this is because I recognize a lot of myself in her.

Guarded. Takes no bullshit and can smell a rat a mile off.

I guess that's what makes me the top personal injury lawyer in the city. I'm a skilled listener and can read between the lines, hearing what's *not* being said, and I have an innate ability to analyze client nuances. It's what sets me apart. My success isn't just built on knowing the law, it's also knowing people and how to read them. Which I'm an expert at.

For instance, right now, I know the woman with the tempting mouth who was quick to reject my offer to buy her a drink is now reconsidering. The slight tilt of her head, the irritated way she's tapping her fingers on the bar, and the subtle softening of her posture give her away.

She's unaware of her body leaning closer to me. It shifted by only a couple of inches, but *I* notice. And the way she's licking her lips while staring at mine as if she's imagining what it would be like to kiss me is a sure sign that she's attracted to me, and I bet she hates herself for it.

As she continues to assess me, I can sense a question lingering on the tip of her tongue, but she's holding back. So I say what I know she's eager to hear, because she's trying to figure out if I'm a gentleman or a sleaze ball. "I know Chase because he's a lawyer, like me, but please don't mistake us for being friends. My friends are faithful, and loyal to a fault." Unlike Chase. He's a shitty lawyer with a shitty reputation.

"I wasn't asking," she bites back.

"You didn't need to."

The bartender puts our drinks down on the bar, and I slide the one-hundred-dollar bill his way, instructing him to take it. "Keep the change."

"Thank you, sir." The bartender tips an invisible hat and smiles appreciatively before he walks away.

"You are not buying me a drink." The stunning woman whose name I've yet to find out scrambles through her purse, pulls out a fifty-dollar bill, then attempts to hand it to me, but I refuse it.

"Keep the money. Your company is priceless." I shoot her a grin while lightly pushing the bill back toward her. "If you insist, you can get the next one, but I'd rather you tell me your name as payment for the drink."

"Who said I'm accepting this one?" She points at her glass, and I almost believe her poker face.

"Because I told you that you are." And she'll have another drink with me, trust me. The curiosity flickering in her emerald eyes makes it obvious. She wouldn't still be sitting here if she wasn't drawn to me.

Letting out a defeated sigh, she tucks the fifty back into her purse. "I'll get the next one."

I swivel around on my barstool to face her, grab her seat and pull her closer to me, making the wooden legs screech against the floor, my legs now on either side of hers. "Good girl."

My words make her pupils dilate as she sucks in a breath.

It's the confirmation I needed; I do affect her.

"Now will you relax? You're so uptight." I place my foot on the footrest of her seat.

"What are you doing?" The confidence in her voice slips away.

"You were too far away." I hold her gaze. "Is that okay?"

"Eh, yes, I guess so, and if you're this close no one will try to hit on me again." She surveys the bar, biting her bottom lip between her teeth, looking less self-assured than a few minutes ago, and I bask in the effect I am having on her because I'm a sick bastard and know I'll have her coming all over my dick before the night is through.

I pick up my drink and swirl the amber liquid around the bottom of the glass, making the ice chime against the tumbler before taking a sip of the spicy whiskey.

I'm incapable of taking my eyes off her. She must sense me watching her because when her eyes hit mine, she gulps hard and stares back, completely motionless. And fuck me if she isn't the most beautiful woman I've ever seen. Where the hell has she been hiding?

"I'm not sleeping with you," she blurts out.

She's lying to both of us, because her right eye twitched, giving herself away, but I let it slide, for now.

"How about a name, then? Or is that off the table too?"

She clears her throat, shifts in her seat, then formally holds her hand out and introduces herself. "Ari."

I slip my hand into hers, noticing how soft her skin is. "Nice to meet you, Ari. I'm Nathan."

Batting her doe eyes, she snaps, "Just because I gave you my name doesn't mean I'll be going home with you tonight, Nathan."

There's not an inch of believability in her snarky comment. "Are you sure about that?" I continue to hold on to her hand and give it a squeeze.

"I can assure you that's never going to happen."

3

ARI

"I hate lawyers," I pant as Nathan Hart, the man I finally came face-to-face with—the man I wanted so desperately to hate but instead found myself undeniably drawn to at the bar tonight—fucks me to the edge of oblivion.

"Your pussy disagrees. You are fucking soaked, Ari." Thrusting his hips, he slides his cock in and out of me, much faster than he was before, teasing my inner walls, his balls slapping off my ass, and I know I won't last long as pleasure builds between my thighs.

"How the hell did I end up in your penthouse?" I moan, my breaths coming out in short, stuttered bursts, my tits bouncing up and down with the force of his powerful movements.

"Because after only two drinks you couldn't keep your hands off me." His words escape in quick breaths.

Shit. I don't just hate lawyers, I hate myself right now, because he's right. What the hell am I doing? I'm going to hell for this, and having sex with Nathan Hart was never part of my plan.

He charmed me, I swear he did.

Nathaniel "Snake Charmer" Hart. That should be his new nickname.

Maybe it is already.

And maybe this is his strength: making whoever he meets feel at ease, hypnotizing them with his charm and good looks to get whatever he wants.

His dry humor and air of power about him are all part of his performance too. He's a showman in court; well, that's what the tabloids say because he fights for clients who have been wronged by megacorporations: medical malpractice, catastrophic injuries, wrongful death; he plays big and plays to win. He's a show trial lawyer.

Articulate.

Assertive and compelling.

Persuasive.

So persuasive. I'm convinced that's how I ended up in his bed.

Although, I rack my brain for evidence of that and come up short.

Nothing.

He never asked me to come home with him.

Instead, he challenged me when I said I wouldn't sleep with him.

Are you sure about that? His words whizz around my head like a washing machine on full spin.

Shit.

I came here on my own free will. I *do* want this.

I want him.

Which is bad. Terrible.

I feel like a stranger in my own life.

Back at the bar, before I could unpack my thoughts, I kissed him. I made the first move because I wanted to feel his lips on mine. I couldn't resist the way his lips tugged at the edges of his mouth, like he knew exactly what he was doing to me. Infuriating, really. Every syllable out his mouth kept me hanging on every word and rolled off his tongue like honey. His confidence had me captivated. I felt every cadence and inflection in his pitch and tone that sent shivers down my spine. It was too much, the pull toward him, like an atomic handshake or elemental attraction I don't fully understand. I'm drawn to him, and I know he feels the invisible force between us too.

The tension, the flirty banter, every look he gave me told me he wanted me. It became unbearable, and I had to have him, needed to feel his hands on me. The ones that briefly brushed against my thigh, then my hand. And before I knew what was happening, my hand was laid over his as the next drink flowed, then I was pulling him outside. I didn't stop him when he pressed me against the wall and he cupped my face with those big strong hands of his, all sinewy and dominating, and it was game over. His kiss was like nothing I've ever experienced, filled with passion and longing. The way his tongue touched mine with gentle dominance, like a maestro leading the orchestra. A perfect balance of control and emotion, igniting a thunderous crescendo of notes humming through my body. It was electrifying and left me breathless. With one flick of his tongue it was like he suspended time, holding me in place, building the anticipation.

While we waited for his driver to pick us up, I begged him— yes, begged, which is most unlike me—for him to take me home. I've never wanted a man as much as I want him. My clothes were off the minute I stepped inside his obnoxious penthouse, and I had my legs wrapped around him and was riding his cock before we even entered his bedroom.

There is something seriously wrong with me. It's like I threw my morals off a cliff and waved at them as they crashed into the ocean below.

Who am I right now?

Oh, I know, I'm Ari "The Hypocrite" Donovan.

But this isn't a romance. There will be no happy ending after I do what needs to be done to bring his family down.

For tonight, I'm choosing to be here. It's just one night. And I'm guessing I made the first move because I figured that being in his apartment would work to my advantage, two-fold. First, I get what I want because it's been far too long since I had sex. Second, being here means I'm surrounded by everything him, and I can maybe learn more about the man behind the power suit, possibly gain insight into his weak points, then use it to destroy his family's law firm.

And, okay, having sex with him wasn't part of the plan. It's unexpected, and my shame clings to me like a vice, pressing against my skull, threatening to crack it open, and yet, I'm not leaving.

Can't, because he has so much control over my body right now, I'm defenseless.

I should leave.

Stay; the sex is great.

My inner sinner wins.

That's what I will do. I'll use him for sex and to get what I want, nothing else, because I'm the one in control here, I'm behind the wheel, pushing forward at full speed.

Although it feels like the other way around by the way he's controlling my body, and every glance, every touch, every whispered word chips away at my resolve, making me question if I truly have the strength to see this through.

But I have to.

I can't afford to waver. My family deserves justice, and his family deserves to pay for what they did. No matter how much I *want* and *don't want* to be here, no matter how much I crave him, I can't forget why I came in the first place.

So I'll take what I need tonight, then I'll ruin him.

Which is a pity because he's fucking amazing in between the sheets, and I swear his long cock is trying to puncture my cervix, teasing pleasure from my body and awakening every visceral nerve ending. I'm certain if there was an award for having a beautiful cock, he would win.

I can't stop the flapping of my heart, it's as uncontrollable as the tide pulls to the moon, magnetic and unescapable.

"Oh God," I cry out as my back arches off the bed and the heat between my legs grows hotter, coating his cock in my arousal.

"Not God, baby, it's Nathan." He punctuates every word with a hip thrust. "My." *Thrust.* "Name." *Thrust.* "Is." *Thrust.* "Fucking." *Thrust.* "Nathan." *Thrust.* "Got it?" he says through gritted teeth as he delivers another punishing drive of his hips. "Fuck, Ari, you have to come, your pussy is so tight, it's squeezing my dick." Digging his fingertips so hard into the skin of my ass I know they will leave an impression, he holds himself deep as if trying to stop himself from coming.

"Don't stop," I beg. I really dislike who I am right now. "Feels so good." My words come out breathless and needy.

He wraps his hands around my wrists and flattens his muscular tan body against mine, his skin rubbing against my nipples, making them pebble. His abs should be illegal, and I can't stop looking at his unbelievably handsome face. With his dark hair, piercing blue eyes, and muscles for goddamn days that I want to explore more of, he's like the poster child for billionaire playboys, which I can't stand. Beneath all the money, power suits, and private jets, I bet he's just another spoiled daddy's brat. But I love how he's filling me up, pushing my hands above my head, about to give me one of the best orgasms I've ever had. I know he's going to ruin me for every other man.

I crumble like a cookie under the weight of my own thoughts and arch my neck back when he licks it, causing a shot of scorching heat to run down my spine.

"Be a good girl and come for me," he mutters against my skin, pressing my wrists into the mattress.

Nathan crashes his mouth over mine, slipping his tongue between the seam of my mouth, and I inhale sharply when he slams his cock in and out repeatedly, teasing my orgasm out of me.

There's nothing romantic about this—not even close. It's rough and carnal. I crave it. I want more.

It's one night only.

Our tongues touching, they twist around each other, tasting, licking, exploring. It's sinful and illicit in every way as he pummels his hips into mine. I wrap my legs around his waist to pull him closer to me, because I can't seem to get enough of him.

It feels so right, so good, when it shouldn't.

It's so wrong.

Wrongfully right.

"Come," he mutters against my lips.

My orgasm hits me with force when he commands me to, and I come so hard I see black mixed with shimmering lights flashing behind my vision. It corkscrews around my body, unwinding tension and replacing it with intense pleasure, the feeling so euphoric it feels like it's setting me free. He comes with me, emptying himself inside of me. I'm grateful he wore a condom because I'm sure I would be pregnant otherwise as he keeps coming, shuddering, roaring my name as if he's said it a thousand times before and wearing it like a badge of honor. It's hot and hellish in equal measure because I know I'm not special and he probably does this every weekend, each notch on his bedpost mentally recorded in his brain.

"Fuck. Shit. Fuck. Your pussy is..." He grits his teeth together and touches his forehead against mine, his hot breath dusting my face, and he douses me in his spicy scent I want to know the name of.

No, I don't; he smells like poor choices and bad ideas.

I clench my inner walls around him, pulling every drop of cum out of him, as he jerks and slides himself in and out of my body, much slower now as if he can't stop. I don't want him to; he feels incredible inside me.

He kisses my forehead, then my temple, before moving to my cheek and then kisses my lips again. It's intimate and makes my heart feel like it's galloping faster than a racehorse about to cross the winning line.

It's too much.

"Still hate me?" he asks, staring down at me, sounding pleased with himself. "Even after I gave you one of the best orgasms of your life?"

Looking up at him, it takes every piece of self-restraint within me not to smile. "You're an arrogant asshole." My tone is snarky and brat-like. There is no way I'm telling him how earth shattering my orgasm was.

"The way you screamed my name tells me it was the best orgasm you've ever had."

Oh shit, did I scream his name? This is terrible.

He can read me like a book, and I hate that.

I regret everything that has happened tonight.

But not really.

A little perhaps.

Not enough to stop.

"I've had better," I lie, and he knows it when his mouth shapes a devilish smile.

"You're a terrible liar." He captures my lips with his and kisses me breathless, turning me into a puddle of liquid gold. His touch makes me feel as if I'm glowing like pure molten heat, and it's running through me like a river of fire. "And you're too beautiful for your own good."

His confession makes a place inside my heart and settles there for safekeeping, but the embers of his words feel like hot barbs scraping against the inside of my throat.

Words I shouldn't like but do.

Sliding himself out of my body, I moan from the loss of him and instantly miss our closeness as he slowly releases my wrists.

Resting back on his haunches, he rolls the condom off carefully and ties it before he tosses it on the floor.

"Keep your eyes on me, baby."

He doesn't need to tell me twice; I haven't stopped looking at him.

"So, you hate lawyers?" he asks. Resting his hands on top of my knees, he spreads my legs he's kneeling between wider, then runs his hands down my inner thighs, causing goosebumps to scatter across my skin, every hair on my body standing to his attention.

"I do," I answer much quieter now, and I'm unable to tell him I love how he makes me feel although he'll know how turned on I am by my juices dripping out of me and from how hard my nipples are.

And I don't hate all lawyers, just *his* family. But I keep that to myself.

I lose all logic when his fingertips reach my pussy. The way he's touching me has me questioning everything I ever thought about sexual chemistry. The air is humming with it, his touch like crackling static electricity on my skin.

He pushes my pussy lips together, pressing my over-sensitive clit, then runs his thumbs between them before gently pulling them apart. "But you like me doing this? Even though I'm a lawyer."

"Yes." My body betrays me, and a whimper slips from my mouth when the pad of his thumb rubs my clit before he sinks a thick digit inside of me, followed by another. His pupils turn darker with desire when I cry out his name, something I seem to be incapable of keeping under wraps.

My nipples tighten when he curls his fingers against my inner walls, as if beckoning me to come again.

He wraps his other hand around his hard-again cock and fists himself.

"You're so good at that," I admit, because there's no denying he's experienced. My hips move, riding his fingers as if they have a mind of their own. "How old are you?" I already know how old he is, but I want him to tell me.

"Forty-four," he replies, fucking his cock with his hand. My mouth waters as precum leaks from his slit. I want to taste him and run my tongue up the thick vein of his shaft.

And wow, at forty-four he's got better stamina than my last boyfriend, and he was only thirty years old.

"Are you asking because I'm in my forties and you think I can't fuck all night, Ari?"

"I bet you can't last all night, old man." I push buttons I know I shouldn't be pushing.

"Fucking smartass." He pulls his fingers out of me, slaps my pussy, and inserts them again. The mix of pleasure and pain has me piercing the air with a cry, as if I'm a wolf under a luminous full moon.

"Is that all you've got?" I tease him breathlessly, making him repeat his action, and he spanks my pussy much harder this time, giving me what I wanted. "I need to come," I moan, moving my hips quicker to chase my release.

He stops stroking his cock and holds my hips still at the same time he stops moving his fingers inside me. "You will come when I say you can. Now, be a good girl and tell me how old you are, Ari?"

I respond faster than a bullet out of a gun, desperate for him to let me come. "Twenty-nine. You can be my sugar daddy." I'm messing with him, and he knows it. He moves his fingers in and out of me again, much faster this time, as if he likes my answer.

"Make me come again, please." I fling my head back into the mattress as he teases my inner walls, rubbing my G-spot, and I grab onto his hand, urging him to go deeper.

The sound of my wet arousal combined with my moans and him fisting himself join to make our own symphony of ecstasy.

"Look at me when you come," he demands.

As if under his spell, I obey without question, unable to tear my eyes away from him.

"Good girl."

I quiver at his praise-filled words, which is not something I thought I would like but do.

Our bodies work together so well, it's weird and wonderful, and at this point I have no control over my actions. I'd do anything he says as he expertly pulls another orgasm from my body. Pleasure shoots through every part of me, robbing me of all my senses. My toes curl into the bed, and my fingers dig into the skin of his hand as the intense orgasm leaves me trembling and shaking, soaking his fingers with my juices.

"You are fucking beautiful, Ari." His eyes pierce my soul as if he's searching through it, unraveling my thoughts.

Unsettled by the emotions stirring within me—ones I'd rather not confront—I look away, unwilling to let myself feel anything more for him than the attraction of tonight.

I want to feel nothing when he looks at me, and when he lowers his voice, I don't want my pulse to stutter in my veins the way it is now either. He's an arrogant man with too much charm for his own good. But my body isn't listening, and my thoughts are betraying me. Regardless of how many reasons I stack against him, I crumble the moment he tells me how beautiful I am again.

Does he really mean that?

Who cares? It doesn't matter.

Giving me no time to recover, he removes his fingers from inside me, and I jolt at the loss. Too tired to move, I watch him lick my cum from his fingers.

Holy shit, that's hot.

Then he's reaching for another condom on the nightstand. Tearing it open with his teeth, he rolls it on his hard cock while I'm still lying completely boneless. My breathing hasn't even had a chance to return to normal, and faster than my brain can keep up with, he lies down on the bed, and making it seem effortless, his strong defined muscles flex as he pulls me on top of him.

Lining his cock up with my entrance, I widen my legs as he slides in easily because I'm so wet. For him.

"Now fuck me like you hate me, Ari." He thrusts upward, making the thick tendons in his neck bulge with tension.

Well, that's easy.

No, it's not.

"Okay." Being this agreeable is completely out of character for me.

Shit, I'm in massive trouble.

But I'll stay the night and have a snoop around his fuckboy penthouse in the morning before the sun rises.

That is my endgame, after all.

4

NATHAN

The San Francisco sun blazing through the vast panels of glass in my bedroom is what wakes me up.

I'm slightly dazed, and then it hits me at once with the force of a tornado.

Ari.

The phenomenal woman I spent the night with.

Patting the other side of the bed, which is cold, I quickly roll over and confirm I'm alone. Disappointment washes over me like a rain shower on a sunny day. It's unexpected and I'm unprepared for the thick emotion building in my throat.

I wish she hadn't snuck out.

Grabbing my cell off the nightstand to check the time, I scrub a hand over my face to wake up. Eight o'clock. "Shit." It's the latest I've slept in years, which is likely due to the siren that screamed my name until the early hours of the morning.

For someone who said they hate lawyers, she sure didn't complain when she was sucking my cock. She even told me how good I tasted and how perfect my dick was. That is the first time a woman has ever told me that, and I didn't miss how she mumbled to herself about how it was made just for her, then told herself to shut up, which I found amusing.

Maybe she's right, because it felt like it was made for her.

But that can't be right, can it?

As weariness set in, she seemed perfectly content nuzzling into me before falling asleep in my arms.

One, I never have women stay over, and two, I'm not someone who snuggles, but with her, it felt good.

Right, even.

I'm drawn to her not just for her beauty or because I lack anything in my life, but her energy and that fucking smart mouth of hers drives my dick wild.

She's different.

Forget her—you don't have time for a woman in your life.

I throw back the comforter and storm across the room, then pull on a pair of boxers before heading out of my bedroom to search for the woman I hope is still here and who I appear to have a new obsession with.

Moving into the open space of the living area, I stop in my tracks then hide behind a pillar and watch in amusement as Ari struggle to find her clothes.

"Where the hell are my panties?" She hops up and down on one leg as she puts on one of her heels and then the other, her long dark hair swishing everywhere as she runs around. "Pull yourself together, Arianna."

I roll her full name over my tongue, testing how it feels. "Arianna." It's pretty, like her.

I'm fascinated by everything about her and I watch on, mesmerized as she comes to a standstill and holds her hands out on either side of her. Taking a deep breath, she surveys the space before smoothing down the fabric of her red dress that kisses her sinful curves. "Screw it. Who needs panties anyway?"

She shakes her head, grabs her purse, and makes her way to the elevator, making her heels ricochet off the marble floor. "Shit," she curses before walking on her tiptoes.

Oh, she clearly does not want to be caught sneaking out.

Normally I struggle to get rid of the women I choose to keep me company, not that I do that very often. In fact, it's been so long since I have, I can't even recall when I last had sex, and Ari creeping out is a complete surprise to me.

Not one I like. In fact, I fucking despise it.

It's Saturday, which means I'm playing tennis with my brothers this morning then working later but I'd rather cancel my plans and spend the day with her, because I want to get to know her better.

Wishful thinking? Maybe.

A pipe dream? Definitely.

I've never had these thoughts before.

Odd.

I don't think I like them.

There is no time for a woman in my life; that's why I never got married. I didn't even come close. I never found someone I could see myself committing to.

She would have to be something kind of wonderful to put up with my manic hours and enormous workload and possibly raise children by herself.

I never wanted to inflict that on anyone and that's why I vowed to stay single forever, despite what my mother expects. I watched her raise me and my three younger brothers single-handed while my father worked his ass off to build the law firm we all now work for. We employ hundreds of lawyers, making us one of the largest law firms in the country, but he made sacrifices and was never around. He missed every baseball and football game my brothers played, and he never once made one of my tennis matches.

Since I took over running the firm alongside my three brothers, I understand why he was never home before midnight and only took one vacation a year: the firm demands your time; all of it. Between cases, I barely have the time to sleep. There's no space for anything else, let alone a wife.

Working long hours is how kings are made, and I don't need a queen.

Although, weirdly, settling down with someone is something I've been thinking about a lot lately, which is stupid of me, when I know it's not an idea I should entertain given my career; however, having been invited to more weddings than I have digits in the last year, I've started to wonder recently if I'm missing out on something. If all my friends are getting married to their soulmate and finding love, maybe there is something more to the whole marriage thing they have become obsessed with.

It doesn't matter because that's not meant for me. *It can't be.*

And I'm not a sheep—I lead and don't follow.

Remaining silent, I hang back in Ari's blind spot, carefully watching her.

"Come on." She presses the call button repeatedly as if that will make the elevator come quicker. While staring at the digital counter, she shakes her knees back and forth nervously. The whirling sound of the elevator signals its arrival, and it chimes before the doors open. "Silence," she hisses, her finger motioning toward the elevator doors. "You're going to ruin my escape."

I curl my lips. Without even knowing it, she's funny.

The doors whir open, revealing my three brothers standing

inside, and their loud and overlapping voices instantly go quiet as they have a stare-off with Ari.

There's a beat of silence and I see the power she has over them. She's breathtaking and one look from her can render you speechless. Something that happened to me several times last night. Specifically, when she was sucking my cock like she couldn't get enough of me and looked up at me with those big eyes of hers. She wasn't just doing it to please me, it was because she was enjoying it and needed more as she turned herself around and sat on my face and sucked me until I couldn't see or think straight before she came all over my tongue.

What a rush.

Why the hell am I letting her leave?

Because it was only one night, you fucking asshole.

I do not and will *never* do commitment.

"Fantastic," Ari mutters under her breath before she says a polite "Morning." Nodding her head in the direction of the elevator, she points to it. "I was just leaving."

Eventually, Max, who is younger than me by four years, is the first to jump into action and exit. "Right, yeah. Good morning." He coughs.

Then my youngest brother, Cole, awkwardly steps out of the elevator, following Max and avoiding eye contact with Ari. "Sorry. We, were just..."

"Please ignore my brothers' bad manners." Eli, who is seven years younger than me, trails behind them, apologizing for their stunned awkwardness. "Morning, ma'am." I don't miss the way his gaze drifts over her curves.

"Oh, these must be yours." Sounding surprised, Max hooks his finger into a pair of panties hanging from the side lamp on the entry table and holds them out for Ari to take, the amusement in his tone evident.

Turning brighter than a strawberry, she whips the sliver of red silk off his finger and scrunches it into a ball inside her clenched fist. "Please pretend you didn't see that." Her gaze bounces back and forth between my three brothers who are looking back at her.

Max holds his hands up in mock surrender. "I have no idea what you're referring to."

"Great." She steps inside the elevator, and I take this moment to reveal myself and say goodbye.

Her face pales as I come to a full stop just outside the doors. I cross my arms, plant my feet firmly, and lock my gaze on her. "Arianna."

"Nathaniel." She holds her chin high, and I take note of the way she checks my physique out before the doors slide closed.

Then she's gone.

Why do I wish she was staying?

"Who the fuck was the siren?"

Max.

"Spill the tea or whatever the fucking saying is."

Eli.

"Please tell me you got her number?"

Cole.

I could do without playing tennis with the three stooges this morning.

Ignoring their line of questioning, I deal with them the best way I know how. "No. No. No." I point at each one of them and walk back to my bedroom. "I'll be ready in ten minutes."

Eli sounds exasperated when he says, "He's a killjoy these days."

"What do you mean, these days? Hasn't he always been a mood vampire? And anyway, at least someone is getting their dick wet," Cole grumbles.

Max jumps in on the defense. "Hey, I have no complaints."

"Man whore," I mutter to myself and walk inside my bedroom that smells like sex, sin and reeks of her perfume that I wish I knew the name of.

I'm never having my sheets washed.

What the hell is wrong with me?

"Enough now." I rub my temples, then push my boxers down my hips and step out of them, and jump in the shower to scrub away my stupidity, instantly regretting it when the scolding water hits me, because for some reason I hate that I don't want to wash her off me.

Maybe I'll bump into her again.

Maybe not.

San Francisco is a big city and I've never seen her before.

I bang my fist against the tiled wall, mad at myself for not asking for her number.

Although she was sneaking off, which tells me everything I need to know; she's not interested in anything more than one night.

And that hurts more than I care to admit.

Oh well, here's to never seeing the only woman I've ever felt excited about.

I'm better off being alone anyway.

And did she just call me Nathaniel?

No one calls me that except my mother.

Though, I guess it doesn't take a genius to figure out Nathan comes from Nathaniel.

5

ARI

Shit.

I rest the back of my head against the mirrored elevator wall and stare at my reflection in the ceiling mirror. I can't even look at myself without feeling sick to my stomach.

I slept with Nathaniel Hart.

The man I wanted to get close to, but not carnally.

I used sleeping with him as an excuse to get into his apartment when what actually happened was I overslept then lost the opportunity to snoop around from fear of him waking up before I left.

Which did happen, but at least our interaction was brief.

My remorse and guilt is palpable, and it's speeding through my body as fast as a lightning bolt. Scratch that; it feels faster. More like the re-entry speed of a space shuttle.

An overwhelming wave of fear crashes over me without warning, the suffocating tightness in my chest making it difficult to breathe.

What am I doing?

Should I call my new workplace first thing Monday and tell them I'm not taking the job anymore?

Because what if he sees me?

What then?

Game over.

Boom!

Everything I've been planning for years will go up in flames.

So why then did I jeopardize everything for one night of sex?

It was great sex.

Life changing.

Possibly not, but it felt like it was.

It was just sex, Ari. Stop trying to convince yourself otherwise.

My inner reasoning flips back and forth between right and wrong, good and bad, success and failure.

It wasn't just sex.

It wasn't.

It was more.

Way more.

It was sex with someone I was drawn to like a bee to nectar and couldn't resist a taste of. All despite knowing I may now have risked everything.

I've been such a fool.

The loud ringing in my ears makes my eardrums feel like they are wired to a fire alarm that's screaming in my skull, and the tightness across my chest almost becomes unbearable. It feels like someone has punched all the air out of my lungs, which makes me clench the fabric of my dress in my fist right over my heart.

Pull yourself together, Ari. Now is not the time to give up.

It's a setback, nothing more.

Or maybe I'm overthinking.

Closing my eyes, I release a deep sigh that's heavy with

shame and regret and silently pray the elevator will stop spinning like a tornado tearing through town.

I feel like I'm losing my mind.

I take another breath in.

Then blow out and hold it for a split second.

I do the same over and over again, until the sense of unbearable doom that was creeping its way through my body backs off, and I imagine myself stamping it underfoot and crushing it to smithereens.

"You're freaking out, stop freaking out." I open my eyes, give my head a shake, still feeling unstable.

Which I am.

It was foolish of me to think that my plan was ever going to work.

Turns out I didn't factor *me* into that plan.

Or how I would react to meeting him. Nathan.

I made myself very visible. Too visible. And recognizable.

I worked out every outcome, strategically made my move like a chess player, and positioned myself into a new workplace like a master plotting the perfect gambit.

And yet the unpredictability of coming face-to-face with him made me pull the pin, blowing it all to pieces. It wasn't even a calculated risk; it was downright stupid of me.

I guess there's no going back now.

I have to see this through.

I'll adapt. Adjust to this mini hiccup.

And I will win.

Feeling stronger, I roll my shoulders back, drawing power back into my body, then stand tall and plant my feet, firmly bracing myself like a warrior before battle.

I can do this.

I will do this.

And no one is going to stop me.

6

ARI

Walking quicker than I can keep up with, Janice, the human resources manager, reels off names of staff, departments, and locations of things I should be taking note of but can't. While I might be in the building I've wanted to be inside of for as long as I can remember, I'm also internally having a meltdown.

Now that I'm here at the beginning of a fresh new week, I don't feel as confident after I decided to forget all about what happened on Friday night and spent the weekend cleaning my apartment, grocery shopping, and binge-watching every episode of *Yellowstone*... for the third time. Then I made another decision. I'm here for a week.

In and out. Mission accomplished.

"And the executive team is on the top floor?" I interject, derailing Janice's induction as I take double the number of steps to her one.

Flaring her nostrils, she shakes her head dismissively and replies, "Yes. I already said that. Now pay attention, Ari."

"I was, I promise, I was just clarifying." The last thing I want is to upset Janice. With over a decade of experience at the company, she's deeply familiar with everyone and everything about the office. Building a good rapport with her could prove invaluable, even if it is for only a week.

As I'll be working in the basement in the records room, I'm relieved to discover that I will not be seen by any of the partners or executive team. There are more than ten floors separating us, which is what I was hoping for. *Whew, what a relief.*

If I have to come in earlier than everyone else to avoid bumping into anyone, then I will. If I have to take the stairs for a week, I will. Eat my lunch at my desk? I'll do that too.

In fact, this week, my middle name will be Avoidance. Arianna "Avoidance" Donovan.

Perfect.

"Janice." A frantic-sounding disheveled girl appears looking like she's already been through the wringer and it's not even nine o'clock in the morning. "She's not coming back." She clutches a laptop firmly to her chest and her knuckles that are wrapped around the edges of the laptop turn white before she tucks a lock of hair behind her ear that's escaped from what I think was once an immaculate-looking bun. "She just called in."

Janice purses her lips before saying, "That man is going to be the death of me. Where is Evelyn?" She shoots her first question at the slip of a girl.

"Vacation."

Janice fires another name out of her mouth. "Jodie?"

"In meetings all day."

Like a tennis match, my eyes ping-pong back and forth between them.

"Jessica?"

"Also on vacation. And everyone else is either in meetings, busy, or unavailable today."

Janice places her hands on her hips and arches her neck

back. Eyeing the ceiling, she lets out a long-exaggerated sigh. "Do I have to do everything around here?" Dropping her head, she pins me with her *takes no shit* glare. "You can take minutes."

"Yes," I reply, unsure of what is going on.

"It wasn't a question. Follow me." Janice spins on the balls of her feet and hastily moves between the sea of desks. "Samantha, pull up the forms."

"Yes, Janice." The girl I now know as Samantha follows behind us as her fingers move fast across her screen. "Here." She holds the laptop in front of me. "Sign the space that says signature with your fingertip. It's a touchscreen laptop."

"What am I signing?" I ask, confused, because I can't see the document heading.

"An employee confidentiality agreement," Janice replies coolly.

Of course, I expected I'd have to sign something like this. It complicates my larger plan, but if I want to avoid drawing attention to myself, I'll comply.

Using the pad of my pointer finger, I sign my name and hand the laptop back to Samantha.

"This way." Janice marches past the elevators to another elevator hidden around the corner. She taps a keycard against the wall, the doors slide open, and she hands me the keycard then whips Samantha's laptop out of her hands and thrusts it into mine. "You'll need this. It has all the software you are familiar with on it."

"Where am I going?" I step inside the elevator, feeling bamboozled.

"Top floor. You'll take the minutes for the meeting as no one else is available for today."

Holding the door open to stop it from closing me in, I

exclaim, "What? No." Sweat beads across my top lip. "You hired me to be a records clerk." I applied for that job for a reason.

"Which is ridiculous given that you were a legal secretary before this position and have an impressive résumé, Ari." Face stern, Janice doesn't back down. "The meeting requires you to take down the exact wording of all resolutions, decisions reached, and outcomes of motions or proposals. I'll call Joseph, our top-floor receptionist, to tell him you are on your way up. Congratulations on your promotion."

Promotion?

No!

This can't be happening.

My heart drums faster than a heavy metal band against my ribcage. Unconsciously, I throw my hand up in the air, removing it from where they were keeping the door open, causing it to begin closing. "I can't do this." My voice rises a few octaves as I step forward but I'm too late and the doors slam shut, sealing me inside.

"Welcome to the company, Ari." Janice's voice fades behind the doors, muffled as it penetrates through the thick barrier.

"Shit." I run my hand through my hair.

This wasn't what I had in mind.

I hold my hand over my thumping chest as panic like I've never felt before threatens to strangle me.

If I have a heart attack right now, it wouldn't be a bad thing; at least this way I could die in an elevator without ever having to come face-to-face again with the son of the man who ruined my life, or the man I had earth-shattering sex with. It was amazing. Unforgettable.

My strategy started going off the rails on Friday, and my carriage is careering down the track and I'm losing control.

Nothing is going according to plan.

I miscalculated all the what-ifs.

7

ARI

I brace myself for impact when I reach the top floor—derail and explode on impact—I'm minutes from that happening, I'm sure of it.

"Hey, I'm Joseph, lovely to meet you." I'm instantly greeted by the top-floor receptionist who gently cups my elbow and walks us with urgency to the door of the boardroom.

"Why can't you take the minutes for the meeting?" Like a doe caught in the headlights, I'm startled and so far outside of my comfort zone, my mouth has gone drier than the Sahara. "I need a drink."

"There's water inside." Joseph juts his chin in the direction of the room.

"I might need something stronger."

"We'll save that for after work, sweetie." He smiles warmly. "And I can't take the minutes, I'm just the receptionist. My job is to look pretty." Running his manicured fingers over his perfectly styled wavy locks, he adds, "And keeping everyone happy is a full-time job, then there's being nice to clients, making the coffee, screening calls and keeping them to a minimum. That aside, reminding everyone not to talk to Mr. Crankypants unless instructed to is exhausting."

"Who the hell is Mr. Crankypants?"

Joseph winks. "Technically they all are on this floor. But one is worse than the others. You'll see."

Shit. Shit. Shit.

What the hell was I thinking? *I can't do this.*

"Yes, you can."

I must have said that out loud.

"My oh my, you are pretty." Joseph takes a step back and hums in approval at my outfit. "You are damn fine, girl."

Nervous laughter leaves my lungs. "Any words of advice?" It's too late for that; I'm in way over my head, and it will blow my mission apart before it's even begun if I flee now.

"Listen. Type fast. Don't let Crankypants get to you because it's not personal, he's just, well... you'll see. And lastly, be invisible."

I let out a long exhale; I can do that. "Got it. And don't pee myself on the first day."

Joseph chuckles. "I like you and I can see us being friends." He gestures to the space between us. "I hope you last longer than his previous secretary."

Friends? No way. Someone that could come in useful? Yes.

"Great, let's go for that drink after work one night." I accept his earlier invitation.

Deception is most unlike me, but it's a small step on the path to my destination.

"It's a date," Joseph confirms, reaching past me as he pushes the door open and grabs my shoulder with the other, urging me to enter the room. "See you in two hours."

Two hours? Is that how long the meeting is? I should have used the bathroom first.

I ask him over my shoulder, "I'm the new records clerk." I can't believe Janice was being serious when she said I got a promotion—I don't want it. "What did you mean when you said I'm his new secretary? Who is *he*?"

"You'll meet him soon." He pushes me fully into the room and I stumble clumsily into it, making everyone around the table turn to look at the calamity that is me as the door closes behind me.

World, swallow me up now.

I'm drawing far too much attention to myself.

Coming to a standstill, I clutch the laptop to my chest and inhale a deep breath that's filled with dread then quickly study the faces. Oh, thank God. I exhale in relief as unfamiliar people stare back at me from around the boardroom table.

I drop my shoulders and summon all the confidence I haven't felt since walking through the doors of the building this morning and try my best to hide how flustered I feel. *Okay, maybe I can do this...*

"Good morning." I give them a hint of a smile, walk around the table, then take a seat at the end of it while they mumble polite greetings and go back to talking amongst each other.

"We will begin in five minutes," one of the women informs me as I make myself comfortable.

"Thank you," I reply, unable to comprehend how I ended up here. This is a curve ball I wasn't prepared for.

You've got this, Ari.

Be invisible. Joseph's words of advice swirl around my head, my nerves settling down a little.

I make myself busy, locate the software on the laptop to take the minutes, and set up a new document in the same way I've done hundreds of times before.

Focused on the screen, I jump when a raucous roar of

laughter from what sounds like a rowdy group of frat boys comes from behind the door then bursts into the room.

I snap my head up in the direction of the noise and quicker than the crack of a whip, my blood turns cold.

Oh no.

This wasn't supposed to happen.

It takes what feels like seventy hours for the men to say their hellos, although it's only seconds, but it's enough time for my stomach to turn into a pit of unease. It feels heavy and sour with anticipation, as if a viper is coiling through my gut.

It all happens in slow motion; one after the other, their gazes land on me, making them fall silent.

"Hello again," one of them, who I know to be Cole, greets me.

I know each one of them because I've spent hours studying the company's website and each one of their cases.

"Oh, wow," another chimes in, his tone laced with subtle humor. *Eli.*

The third, Max, flashes me a shit-eating grin. "Well, this is a nice surprise."

But standing at the forefront is the man who looks as though he's been sculpted from the finest marble—sharp and chiseled. Rigid and unmoving, he could pass for a statue if not for the faint twitch in his jaw.

I feel a pang of anguish inside, mixed with an unwelcome spark of desire—completely inappropriate under the circumstances.

Because it's him.

Nathaniel Hart.

The man I shared an unforgettable night with.

And the man I had fervently hoped to avoid until absolutely necessary.

"Everyone out. Now," he barks, and the air between us turns frosty. "Except you." He points at me, and I let out a small whimpered noise that sounds like a cocktail of shock and fear.

Everything is going to shit. This was never part of my plan. And now I'm really screwed.

8

NATHAN

I wait for my colleagues and brothers to leave before storming to
the door and slamming it shut to make my point when the last
person forgets to close it behind them, muffling the smug
laughter of delight from my brothers. They are loving every
minute of this awkward situation I find myself in.

Assholes.

Shoving my hands into the pockets of my dress pants, I
steady myself before turning back to face my beautiful
nightmare.

Why the hell is the woman who spent the night in my bed
and ranted about how much she *hates* lawyers now sitting in my
goddamn boardroom like she owns the place? Acting like she's
my fucking secretary or something. And why can't I stop looking
at her? I don't get it. I don't want to get it. But damn, she's
beautiful.

"Explain," I shout, the words ripping out of me far louder
than I mean, and I can see her flinch—her face turning a shade
of white proving I've crossed a line.

I didn't mean to sound so harsh, not with her.

Arianna replies but she's so quiet I don't hear what she says.

"Speak up," I urge, because she sure as hell didn't hold back when she was screaming my name the other night.

Crestfallen, she bows her head and shakes it. "I started working here today but as a records clerk."

"What the fuck are you doing in the boardroom then?" I snap, clenching my fists tight inside my pockets.

"I'm here to take the minutes. I was the only person available."

I hate that she isn't looking at me, when all I want is to feel her eyes on me. "Look at me," I demand.

When her eyes hit mine, she looks terrified, but screw it, she should be because she's irritated me and whether she likes it or not she's no longer in my personal space but in my place of business. I never mix the two.

This is Hart territory, and I own this fucking firm.

My laws, my way.

"Did you know who I was the other night?" I ask, irritated with myself for being too captivated by her to see through her honeytrap. She must have.

"Yes," she replies, sounding stronger, her brows furrowing, as if she's as confused about our situation as I am. Or maybe she's regretting what happened between us.

At least she told the truth, but her honesty irks me more than I care to admit.

Was I a premeditated target? I need to know.

"Was it a happy accident that you were in the bar I sometimes drink at on Friday night or was that part of some screwed-up plan to bed the boss?" Something I have always avoided; I don't make a mess in my own backyard. That's something my brothers have never agreed with me on.

"Bed the boss?" She screws her face up as if she just licked a thistle, sounding appalled by my accusation. "I already had the job. Trust me, I do not need to sleep my way into a position, and you were not someone I was expecting to bump into. My job here is to work in records as a clerk and I am guessing you have dozens of staff to run around after you to fetch records, so I was never expecting to see you. I genuinely didn't think our paths would cross. Records is in the basement, and you are up here on the top floor. There was never any possibility of seeing each other again. And I most definitely would not have come looking for you."

In my head I had accepted we were perfect strangers, and now it seems that isn't the case. If I knew she was here working for me, I would've sought her out because since Saturday morning all I've wanted to do is see her again. Although I can't make any sense of why I would want to do that.

She keeps blurting out more words I can't stand. "Sleeping with you was a mistake, one I've regretted ever since. It was a lapse in judgment, and I promise you it won't happen again."

It *can't* happen. Not now she works for me.

And it was never a mistake.

She's lying to me and herself.

Working under the same roof as her every day will be a massive fucking problem for me, and my dick. It's also going to be difficult to focus given I now know what she tastes like: sweeter than sugar. And the things she can do with that smartass mouth of hers; it makes my dick hard just thinking about it.

It stings that she feels remorseful about sleeping with me so I'm spiteful when I bite back. "I'm sorry you made the *mistake* of falling onto my cock and riding it all night." My voice sounds sinister and drips with sarcasm. "You and I both know it wasn't a mistake. You wanted me as much as I wanted you."

Her cheeks fill with color. "I never expected to like you as much as I did."

She likes me?

"Because you hate lawyers?" I ask.

She closes the laptop then holds it against her chest as if trying to use it to protect herself. "Only some of them." Her top lip curls up in disgust.

Interesting.

"Who did you work for before you got the records clerk position here?"

"Am I on trial?" She points at her chest.

"It's a simple question, Arianna." And yes, she is.

"It's Ari."

"I pay your salary; I'll call you whatever the hell I want."

"You're impossible," she huffs.

Angry has never looked so beautiful.

Stop it; she's staff.

If she thinks I'm being impossible now just wait until I'm mid trial; that's when I really do become an impossible fucker. "Who did you work for before you got the position of records clerk here?" I repeat the question, desperate to know why she loathes lawyers so much.

"Williams and Jones."

That explains everything. Nick Williams is a low-life piece of shit. A smiling knife to be exact, and he would imprison his own grandmother if it achieved his goals. Word on the street is he's helping to grease the wheels of criminal gang activity in the city. Something we at Hart Law do not tolerate.

I pull my hands out of my pockets, unbutton my suit jacket, and locate my cell from the inside pocket then call Janice, who picks up immediately.

"Talk to me."

As if she was expecting my call, Janice calmly lists a multitude of reasons why Arianna is a suitable replacement for yet another secretary of mine who decided not to come back because they couldn't handle the fluctuating workload and overtime.

"Send it over," I bark down the microphone after Janice suggests I read Arianna's strong résumé, then I end the call and wait for it to drop into my emails.

Arianna slams the laptop she was holding on to like a lifeboat down on the table. "What are you doing?"

"Due diligence, Arianna," I reply. "All breakages must be paid for." I point to the laptop, slightly amused by our encounter. Her salty attitude gives me a thrill, and not one of my secretaries has ever challenged me the way she has.

"This is bullshit." Her voice is even stronger now. She sounds more like the woman I spent the night kissing and licking every inch of.

She adds, "I didn't apply for the position to be your secretary. I don't care if you think I'm suitable or not, just let me go back to the position I was hired to do." She pushes herself to her feet, reminding me that she is much shorter than I am by at least a foot. "Working under you would be a nightmare."

I like her. Far too fucking much and she has no idea how much of a nightmare I can be.

I grin wickedly. "Oh, I don't know about that. I didn't hear you complaining when you were under me the other night."

Her mouth drops open in shock before she folds her arms in front of her and taps her right foot against the floor like a cute but disgruntled bunny.

Engaged in a standoff, we share a charged unblinking stare.

"You know I'm right," I say at the same time the sound of an email whooshing into my inbox breaks our face-off. I hold my pointer finger in the air. "Don't deny it."

"You're intolerable and bossy." Her tone is cold and disapproving.

"Because I'm the boss." I'm not being cocky; it's the truth.

Tapping the email, I open the document named *Arianna Donovan Résumé* that's attached, then skim read her credentials. "You're overqualified for a records clerk," I state, impressed by her résumé.

"I changed positions because I wanted a less stressful role and a better quality of work-life balance."

I quickly glance up to catch her right eye twitching like it did back at the bar, and I know she's lying.

"And a drop in pay?" I ask. That makes no sense.

"It's not about the money," she snaps back.

From her address, she lives in a decent neighborhood in the city, the kind of place where many buy their first home. It's less about survival and more about taking the first steps up the property ladder. She's ambitious, she just doesn't know it.

"You completed a law apprenticeship, worked your way up and passed your legal secretary exam first time." With a ninety-seven percent pass mark. She's remarkable.

"Yes. I continually study and work my ass off."

She doesn't need to tell me that, it's all here in black and white. I close the résumé and click on the recommendation letter Janice attached from Williams and Jones.

It's faultless, and I hide my smile when I read the last line of their letter.

If Arianna was a lawyer, I would make her a partner.

"Explain it to me again. Why did you apply for a position at Hart Law that you could do in your sleep?" I slide my cell back inside the concealed pocket of my jacket. "And this time try to sound convincing." Something isn't adding up, but I can't figure out what it is.

"I told you already." Sounding exasperated, she places her hands on her hips to make her point, the skin on her neck flushing redder by the second.

Slowly, I move toward her and she tracks my every step until we finally come toe to toe.

As I look down at her, she cranes her neck back to meet my six-foot-five height.

Relieved that she doesn't flinch when I do something completely out of character, I push a lock of her hair behind her ear and get lost in her big, beautiful eyes. "If I find out you are lying to me, I will make you regret ever thinking you could fool me."

"Okay." Her reply is softer than I expected but there's a slight crack in her voice, and when the frown she's been wearing since I entered the room deepens, I get the feeling that she doesn't believe me, or she doesn't believe her own reply. But then there is a shift in her demeanor, a sort of deviance washing over her as she squares her shoulders, and lifts her chin. "I understand," she says.

She steps back dropping her arms by her side but I follow her and don't let her get away and when I move my mouth to the shell of her ear, I whisper, "And I bet you won't last the week anyway." I set her a challenge, knowing that it will put fire in her belly.

"You're wrong about that." I don't miss the way her breath hitches in her chest when my lips touch her jaw.

Why do I feel like my chest is going to explode when she's near?

This isn't like me.

With my actions on autopilot, I run my nose down hers,

because I'm unable to resist touching her. Hiring Arianna is either going to be the best or worst decision I've ever made. "I work very long hours," I state. Everyone knows this. I work harder than anyone, even my brothers.

"Most lawyers do."

"Which means you will too, and I don't take breaks."

"I'll bring snacks to your desk. And lunch. Dinner too, if you want."

My previous secretaries have never suggested that. "I take my coffee black with no sugar." I rest my forehead against hers and cup her face with my hands, something I shouldn't be doing.

"Noted." Her eyelashes flutter against my cheek and I imagine it's what the wings of a butterfly would feel like on my skin: soft and delicate.

"I only take calls between ten and eleven o'clock on the days I'm not in court."

"Okay."

"Whatever the records clerk salary we offered you was, I will triple it if you agree to take the position of being my secretary." If she's looking for more balance in her life, she won't find it working for me.

"I accept."

I knew she would. Work-life balance clearly isn't her priority. I'll uncover what really brought her here—and why she stepped down to a lower-grade position.

"Good girl."

Knowing how my praise affects her, right on cue, she shivers and bites her bottom lip between her teeth.

She places the palm of her hand on my shirt, and her touch has me reconsidering my next admission, although now is the time to set the record straight. My mouth hovers over her tempting pillowy lips. "I don't date staff."

A faint "I understand" falls out of her mouth, and her sweet breath dusting my skin makes me want to claim her in the same way I did the other night.

"And that's why nothing can happen between us again." My hands drop away from her face, and I immediately regret stepping away from her when I watch her face falling in disappointment.

Believe me, baby, no one's more frustrated about this than I am.

I smooth down my tie, tighten the knot around my neck and jut my chin. "Welcome to Hart Law, Ms. Donovan," I say, before abruptly storming out of the boardroom.

"Meeting cancelled," I announce as I race past my stupid grinning brothers who are standing in the corridor. "Assholes," I mutter under my breath. "Sorry, everyone." I apologize to my colleagues, who look confused. "I'll have my new secretary, Ms. Donovan, reschedule."

Arianna Donovan.

The woman who has consumed every thought I've had since she left my apartment.

Who the hell are you and what the hell are you doing to me?

Let's hope she only lasts the week.

Why is that suddenly not what I want either?

9

ARI

I proved Nathan wrong.

Three weeks later and I'm still here.

He set me a challenge, and that's why I tore up my one-week tolerating plan at Hart Law into shreds, and it's now burning in the fires of hell.

Which is what the last three weeks have felt like. Hell.

Truth be told, it's been three weeks of suffering the insufferable man I'm unable to stop staring at or fantasizing over, recalling our first night together.

It's the worst kind of torture imaginable.

I stare at the screen of my laptop and let my mind wander, remembering the way he touched me, kissed me, and how he made love to me. It wasn't love, it was sex, but at some points that night, it sure felt like he was making love to me and held intense eye contact with me, as if he could see deep into my soul. I can still feel his hands on me, everywhere.

I snap myself out of my memories of him as heat pools at the apex of my thighs, which is becoming a ridiculous reoccurring problem, and return to reorganizing Nathan's schedule, which I've spent the last half an hour rearranging.

Something he asked me to drop everything for and do urgently.

He's so demanding.

And annoyingly sexy.

Clever, and I'm learning so much from him.

He's also headstrong and... powerful, bossy... and I hate that I find myself drawn to him and utterly addicted to his crankiness.

I find it amusing.

If I didn't, I don't think I would have lasted this long.

The bottom line is, if I didn't *have* to be here, I would have told Nathan Hart where to stick his job because sometimes his abrupt nature comes across as hurtful. But having watched him work for the last few weeks, I've seen another side I didn't think Hart men were capable of. I know he's on edge ninety-nine percent of the time and it's only because he's hard-working and fights for the justice of his clients. He's under a lot of stress and pressure as the court date looms closer on a high-profile case he's been preparing for months, and the weight of public scrutiny and the stakes involved are starting to take their toll.

Easton Forbes, the top stunt double in LA, is one of ten stunt people who were injured in a controversial on-set accident. He's personally suing the movie production company, the stunt coordinator, and the special-effects team for poorly planning an explosion that was mistimed. Easton suffered life-changing injuries and severe burns. If Nathan wins the case, the other victims will sue and there will be a high probability the production company will settle out of court so as not to bring more negative attention to the movie they are still currently filming and damage the movie before it's even released.

One thing for sure: Nathan is a force to be reckoned with. He's the best because he's dedicated, never gives up, and has the highest track record, winning ninety-five percent of his cases. Is this because he uses shady ways to win them? I don't think so because everyone at Hart Law follows strict protocol, which is all they ever harp on about, meaning I could be wrong about Nathan and his family. Which sucks.

Since becoming his secretary, I have discovered that Nathan is not only ethical, but he's also not a quitter.

But neither am I.

I'm only here because I have a mission to complete but some days, I have considered telling Nathan where he can shove his demands.

Like a rabid dog, when Nathan is stressed more than normal, he barks instructions at me, Joseph—everyone.

With ladyballs of steel, I do not let him see how much he bothers me. Any small chink in my armor is like an in for him and I will not allow that to happen.

Not now.

Not ever.

I know his moods aren't a personal attack on me. It's like something comes over him when he steps through the doors of this building because the night we slept together I saw the other side of him.

He was kind.

Thoughtful.

Tender, even.

Which I find perplexing.

I still want to stick hot fire pokers in his eyes while at the same time nurse them back to health so he can see me again. The real me.

The one he saw glimpses of at his apartment.

My mind frequently drifts back to our night together, remembering the way he made me feel. There has been no better feeling than the way he held me, like I was precious cargo, and then waking up in his strong arms that felt like home.

How is that even possible? I want to hate him, but I can't.

Maybe I do, just a smidge.

But he's like a spell that pulled me under and into his dangerous charm.

He's the kind of man I want to open a door for me with one hand and spank my ass with the other.

Sadly, I won't ever get to sample that ass-spanking side of him again, which I'm fine with.

Not really.

Because every morning, I find myself daydreaming, imagining our hot night, but he blows it all to hell when he appears in the office like a bear with a sore head and then has me praying his inner ogre will go into his cave and stay there until my time here is over.

But that's wishful thinking.

When Joseph informed me Nathan's mood is even worse when he's mid-trial, my shield of armor grew even thicker.

Gee, I can't wait for those days. I think I'd rather have a root canal.

I'm ready though, because I won't let him see me falter.

Fingers crossed I only need to put up with Mr. Crankypants, Joseph's nickname for him, until I get my hands on what I came here for. Until then, I'm trying to be patient but it's wearing thin, and I still haven't achieved what I came here to do. It doesn't help that Nathan continues to test my patience daily.

Although, I shouldn't complain. The salary he's paying me is more than compensating me, and I'm going to take whatever I can from him and his family while I can. The Hart family are my enemy and that's never going to change.

And with the raise, I'll finally be able to make the down payment on a house in the area I have wanted to move to.

My very own *family* home.

A deep painful abyss lives inside of me. It's like I am empty without my family—not me, not completely whole—and I loathe the Hart family because they have each other when I have no one.

For me there are no family dinners, celebrations or vacations.

Are my family resting in peace, or unsettled, restless even, like I am about their deaths?

Because that's all I ever feel, and I plan on uncovering the truth surrounding their deaths. The unknown is burrowed under my skin, writhing like a parasite.

And I will find what I am looking for because the evidence I need is under the very roof of the building I am in, and I need to stop Nathan, and everyone, from distracting me.

Until I find what I am looking for, I will use him, play the dutiful secretary; I'll smile, play the game and use my time here to get what I want.

Accountability, truth, and atonement.

Soon, Ari, soon.

I open the last email Nathan sent me and reread it to double-check the meetings he wants me to change. It's to the point. Blunt. Zero airs and graces.

While Joseph's nickname for Nathan is a bit tame, I much prefer Bosszilla. It fits him perfectly, but he's nothing I can't handle. After all, I worked as Nick Williams' legal secretary for years, and if I have anything to thank him for, it's the way he taught me how to deal with difficult people because he was one.

When I questioned Nick about meetings with a few unmention-able characters, where he agreed to defend them, I began to suspect that he might be involved in some shady dealings with the local cartel. While I can't prove it, the signs were there, and it left me uneasy. It's the reason I knew it was time to leave Williams and Jones.

I used my time at Williams and Jones wisely, and once I had gained all the knowledge I needed to help aid me in uncovering the truth I've been searching for my entire life, I knew it was time to leave. I'm finally ready to act. It may take me longer than I first hoped now that my role has changed within the company and I find myself not having daily access to the archived records I thought I could get my hands on quickly and easily.

At least I'm inside the walls of Hart Law though, and no matter what obstacles arise, or how hard Nathan pushes me, I'm here to stay until I achieve my goal.

Breathe, Ari… Inhale patience… Exhale any hint of doubt.

I click save on another calendar appointment I have rearranged and skim read Nathan's hectic schedule to see where I can squeeze in another client consultation. I have one spot left should we have an emergency.

This afternoon, one of Nathan's clients decided to settle out of court, but part of the agreement is that it's done face-to-face tomorrow. So for the last hour I've been shoehorning a day's worth of meetings into any free time he has, which isn't much. Williams and Jones was busy; Nathan is busier solo.

"Are you ready to go for a drink at The Golden Spirit?" Joseph asks, pulling my attention away from rearranging Nathan's calendar.

"I'll inform Mr. Hart I'm leaving," I reply and pull a face.

He laughs at my reluctance to ask. "You can't avoid him

forever, sweetie." Joseph points his head in the direction of Nathan's office, implying that *he's right there*.

"Watch me," I reply confidently.

Although I have done a very good job of avoiding Nathan as much as I could all day because he's been in a level-ten super-tornado mood since lunch, I'm sure he's trying to destroy my own good nature from its very foundations. I even made use of the times he left his office to sneak in and leave a coffee on his desk, which means there has been a very limited amount of physical interaction between us today.

Which I hate.

And enjoy in equal amounts.

I'm still floating between heaven and hell; between worlds.

It's a truly hellish place to be and I don't know how long I can stand it.

Avoidance is something I am failing at daily. With each day that passes it's becoming impossible because we seem to have more and more to discuss.

Or maybe that's just my imagination.

It's stupid of me to think I can avoid him, given that I'm his right-hand woman, but I think we're both in shock that I'm still working for Hart Law after he challenged me that I wouldn't last the week. Combine that with spending an unforgettable night of sex with him, then throw in the curve ball of me working directly for him, it's probably best I try to stay out of his orbit as much as I can.

We're both navigating how we work this close together.

I've been meditating most nights to prepare myself for each day.

It's not helping; he still continues to piss me off most days. Then there are days when I'm around him, I feel myself faltering and can't help watching him move those tempting lips of his as he talks to clients, me, everyone, and all I want to do is kiss him.

Which is so wrong.

But I've been tempted. Too many times.

Still am.

I drop my voice and answer Joseph. "Let me double-check I have confirmed all the calendar changes." I peer through the open doorway of Nathan's office to find him looking out over the bustling city below to see if he's eavesdropping into our conversation.

"He does that a lot." Joseph studies him.

"What?"

Joseph replies, "Stares out of the window. It's like he's mentally piecing parts of his case together."

"That so?" I've noticed he does it too and thought the same thing.

"Yeah. I guess that's what makes him the best." His voice sounds full of admiration.

"Like *The Mentalist*?" I ask.

"Much grumpier than him, and way more handsome."

"You think?" I know he is. I'm trying to put Joseph off my scent because I swear one whiff of my pheromones will expose how attracted I am to Nathan.

Why the hell did I say yes to becoming his secretary?

To gain greater access to confidential files, of course with a higher chance of success. Triple the pay... that's another reason why. But the bigger overarching reason is to get my hands on any evidence I can find. Plus there's also pulling the down payment for a house together faster than I had planned.

"Sweetie, are you blind?" Joseph snaps me from my wandering thoughts, and his mouth gapes open. "That man is fire."

Staring at the back of Nathan's head, I pretend to think about it, then say, "I'll give you that, but I'm not into older men."

Oh, I am totally into older men, one specifically.

The one that dresses in the finest of Italian tailored suits, has solid abs I want to climb like a tree, can fuck all night, and more importantly, told me I was *beautiful* and made me feel special.

But I can't go there with him again.

It was just a one-night stand. I'm delusional to think it was anything more.

Which he made abundantly clear on my first day, and I'm fine with it. I'm working directly under him now, and having sex with him would complicate everything.

I'm lying to myself; sex with him only made me want more.

I have to keep reminding myself how much I hate him.

Ambivalence has never felt so unfair. The inner conflict between the positives and negatives is enough to drive me up the wall as the hatred I felt so strong at the beginning is wavering. Too fast for me; it's as if I have no control.

Seeing him at work, helping people and supporting them, is the worst curve ball the universe could have thrown me.

Joseph leans forward, then looks over his shoulder to check if Nathan is listening in on our conversation before lowering his voice to an almost inaudible whisper. "The things I would let that man do to me." He fans his face with his hand as if trying to cool himself down. "Shame he doesn't swing my way." Joseph pulls himself out of his fantasy and stands to his full height. "So, drinks at The Golden Spirit?"

I chuckle and ask him to give me a minute to check with Nathan first.

"You finish up and I'll go freshen up." Joseph walks off to the restroom, leaving a trail of his citrus aftershave behind him. Wow, that is strong, and the last thing he needs is to freshen up.

He's groomed, moisturized, and fragranced within an inch of his life. I love him already and under different circumstances, I could see us becoming firm friends.

I shake the thought from my head and push my chair away from my desk before I walk toward Nathan's opened office door. As I tap on it with a knuckle to alert him, he spins around on his seat to face me.

He gives me a hard stare. "Yes, Arianna." He addresses me abruptly, confusion causing a thick bump to form between his eyebrows.

I can't work him out. One minute he's nice and the next he's... well... Nathaniel Hart. A grouchy volcano ready to explode.

With confidence I enter his office. "I've been asked to go out for drinks with Joseph and a few of the others from the floor below, and I am leaving for the day." I come to a stop when I arrive at his desk. "I've rearranged your calendar," I inform him, then list everything he tasked me with to do today and which I completed. "And tomorrow I will prepare the court forms for the upcoming Walker case. I can archive those for you too." I point to the stack of boxes behind him that need cataloguing.

"We have someone who does that for us," he replies dryly.

Shit. I knew that. After all, that is the position I was originally hired for. I need to figure out a way to gain access to the archiving, although I've been waiting for so long, another few weeks won't make any difference.

"You may leave." Nathan rolls his seat under his desk, his focus instantly back on his computer monitor.

I hate that he dismissed me without looking at me. "Thank you, and thank you for the promotion you gave me." Maybe I'm a glutton for punishment but I'm enjoying my new job but the words get stuck in the back of my throat, and I'm annoyed at myself for being grateful for the pay rise.

My conscience is at war with itself, because the last thing I want is to feel grateful. I'm far from grateful for what his family did to mine.

I repeat my new mantra in my head... *Get the evidence, take the pay rise, secure a deposit for a house.*

"I didn't hire you," he states firmly.

I flinch.

He adds, "You were forced upon me."

"Forced?" I question, feeling as if I've been slapped across the face. The sting of his words hurts.

Narrowing his eyes to slits, he leans closer to his screen, reading whatever is on it, practically ignoring me altogether, which is maddening when he couldn't take his eyes off me the night we had sex and demanded me to look at him when he made me come all over his fingers.

What a fool I've been to think it might have meant something to him.

At the time, it sure felt like it did.

"Yes, Arianna, forced. I didn't have a secretary, I needed one, Janice filled the position with you. End of story."

He's lying, he had the final say and he knows it. I got the job because I'm qualified and he knows it. That's why he hired me. He wanted me here, but he's too stubborn to admit it.

Screw him, I'm not lowering my manners to match his. "Regardless, thank you."

"You may go."

"See you tomorrow." I try to sound cheerful about that.

"We'll see."

"What do you mean?" I ask, confused by his response.

He taps his fingers against his keyboard and replies without warmth, "Like I said before, Arianna, I gave you a week. And now I'm just waiting for you to hand me your letter of resignation. It's only a matter of time." Resting back in his chair, he lays his elbow on the arm of it, and with the other hand he smooths down his tie, which I've noticed he does a lot.

Sounding more confident than I feel, I say, "Well, I've lasted three weeks which I believe has broken a record, because according to the gossip I heard around the watercooler, I'm the only secretary that has put up with you for this long because you're impossible to work for, rude to everyone, and have a habit of barking orders to get results. So if I do last another three weeks, then it will be longer than the last four secretaries you've had. I win." Just watch me prove him wrong.

"You're overstepping, Ms. Donovan."

"And you're an arrogant asshole who needs a lesson in manners, Mr. Hart." I turn to leave but then spin back around. "Oh, and your first lesson is adding please and thank you into your vocabulary."

My courageous words have him quirking a brow and I swear his mouth twitches at the edges as if he's desperately trying to disguise a smile.

"Is that so, Ms. Donovan?" A playful glint dances in his eyes.

"Yes, and you can even join those words together with other words like thank you very much, please may I have, I was wondering if you could please... You get the idea." I nod my head.

He runs his forefinger across his bottom lip before asking, "Anything else to add to my lesson?"

"Nope, I think that covers it." I head out of his office, and I swear I hear him calling me a smartass under his breath, which makes me smile.

Another three weeks? Just watch me last longer than that.

If I was fired up before, it's nothing in comparison to how I feel now and I'm more than ready to prove him wrong. He'll soon discover I'm not one to back down.

Challenge accepted, Mr. Hart.

I give my ass an extra wiggle, because I know he watches me when he thinks I can't see him. But I see him in the reflection of the glass panels, through them too, following my every move.

He's forgetting who has the power here. It's me.

And I bet he's imagining what it would feel like to place his hands on my hips and down over my curves again.

Tempted, Mr. Hart?

I look back over my shoulder to find his gaze lowered and eating me up with his eyes.

I think that answered my question.

10

NATHAN

"Fucking smartass," I mutter to myself as Arianna steps out of my office, wiggling her hips in yet another figure-hugging dress that kisses every inch of her in all the right places.

I swear to fuck, if no one was around, I'd be storming after her, bending her over her desk and giving her ass a good spanking for speaking to me the way she just did.

Manners?

Is she for real?

There is no way I'm letting her get away with that.

I pick up my phone and send a text to the group chat with my brothers.

ME

Finish up, we're going for drinks at The Golden Spirit.

It's where everyone in the building seems to go after work to decompress and it's where Joseph said he is taking Arianna. I know this because not only am I a master at working people out, I can also hear a pin drop from a hundred meters away.

The words she said to Joseph make my grip around my cell tighten.

Not into older men.

I'll show her old.

COLE

Are you sick?

ME

No.

MAX

Has someone died?

ME

No. Stop asking questions and meet me in the foyer.

ELI

Well, this is a first. When was the last time you left the office before six o'clock?

ME

I do. Sometimes.

I never do.

COLE

Liar. Count me in.

MAX

No can do. I have a date.

ME

Celeste?

MAX

No, Juliette.

ELI

Who the hell is Juliette?

MAX

The fire chief's daughter *smiling devil emoji*

ME

What happened to Celeste?

MAX

She wanted more.

COLE

Babies?

ME

Engagement ring?

ELI

Marriage?

MAX

All three.

COLE

You're a commitment-phobe.

MAX

I think Nathan wins that title.

ME

Fuck off.

He's right, but at least I'm obvious about it, and I've never given anyone I hook up with false hope or left room for interpretation.

I'm married to my business. Simple as that.

I've never told my brothers before but being the eldest, and with Dad the way he is now, I feel like the business is my responsibility. Even though they all work hard, and we make decisions about the company together, the burden of success rests heavy on my shoulders. I don't want to let our father down.

Covertly, I watch Arianna and Joseph gather their belongings then leave their desks before heading to the elevator. My feet are itching to follow her.

ME

Eli, are you joining us?

COLE

Why are we going to The Golden Spirit? We never go there.

MAX

Has your new secretary got you rattled yet again?

ME

No.

Liar.

I may have talked—sorry, complained—about her one too many times.

Something I have no control over.

All her little quirks and things she does for me don't annoy me. I fucking love them, but I will never admit that to my brothers.

ELI

You're a terrible liar. I'm in.

Eli's strength is sniffing a bald-faced lie a mile off, and at this point I'm reeking.

ME

Meet you in the foyer.

> **COLE**
>
> I've already shut down my computer.

> **MAX**
>
> Have fun… You should introduce your new secretary to the new guy in finance. Evander. All the women think he's hot.

I grit my teeth, making them grind together from the pressure. Evander better stay the hell away from her or I'll fire him. Not that I can or ever would because he'd sue my ass.

But if push came to shove...

An influx of texts fly into our group chat one after the other.

> **ELI**
>
> I bet he's already thinking of ways to fire Evander.

> **MAX**
>
> Or imagining all the ways he'd like to kill him.

> **COLE**
>
> Don't say that because he'll ask for our help to dispose of the body.

> **MAX**
>
> He's on his own. I'm an upstanding member of the community.

> **COLE**
>
> We all are.

I smirk at Cole's message. Us Hart brothers have principles. We avoid lying in court and falsifying evidence. We also avoid activities including bribery and fraud, and we never take clients on that we don't believe. And that's what sets us apart from other lawyers: we prioritize cases that morally and ethically align with us. If it doesn't feel right, then we don't represent clients. Something my father drilled into us from an early age.

MAX

Later, losers.

ELI

Have fun.

COLE

Enjoy.

ELI

So, when are you asking your one-night stand, sorry, your new secretary, on a date?

ME

She's staff. Remember that.

ELI

Is that all she is to you?

MAX

He'll never admit he likes her.

ME

Foyer in ten minutes.

MAX

Avoidance... Nathan's greatest strength.

COLE

Stronger than his volley at Saturday morning's tennis match last weekend.

ME

Fuck.

ME

Off.

ELI

How long can we keep this up until he breaks?

MAX

Months.

Years more like.

Assholes.

I close my messaging app then open my email on my computer.

Desperate to discover everything about Arianna, I open Janice's email and read Arianna's résumé in detail for the millionth time.

Meets deadlines, ensures compliance, confidential, adaptable... All the usual suspects are listed, but what I didn't expect to read under extra-curricular activities is that she volunteers at a charity called The Connecting Kids Foundation, helping children to overcome grief, specifically those dealing with trauma and the loss of a parent.

Does she have first-hand knowledge of that?

I hope not.

If she has, I feel deep empathy for the pain she must have gone through. No one deserves that.

Even though my father is no longer the man he used to be, I'm lucky that my parents are still here, and I can't imagine what she must have gone through if she did lose one as a kid.

Suddenly wanting to know everything about Arianna and to protect her, my chest tightens with the need to get to her faster. I close my computer down, grab my jacket, and storm toward the elevator.

Whatever has happened to her in her life, I want to make her feel better.

Arianna Donovan.

The strong tempting woman who, at fifteen years my junior, is much too young for me, but if I don't see her again tonight to make sure she's okay, I might lose my shit.

11

ARI

The Golden Spirit, the bar Joseph invited me to, is filled to the rafters, but lucky for us, several of my new colleagues have arrived already, securing a large circular booth for us all to sit around.

On arrival, Joseph introduced me to everyone, and within minutes I was laughing, which instantly made me feel like part of the team but also dreadful. I should stay away from them all because I can't be their friend, and I don't even know what made me say yes to coming here tonight.

"Incoming," Joseph says, peering over his glass, dropping his mouth to the lip of it.

I follow his gaze and quickly realize *who* he is referring to.

Nathan. Alongside two of his brothers.

They look like they just stepped off a photoshoot.

Collectively they are handsome, but for me Nathan is devastatingly, pantie-soaking gorgeous and all day I've found it difficult to tear my eyes off him. Specifically, his strong hands that expertly typed on his computer keyboard, which had me imagining what it would be like to feel them running over every inch of my skin again.

The same feeling I get when he's close by flutters low in my belly. It's like a mix of jumping beans and butterflies, and who the hell knows what it is, but it's something.

Nothing.

It's nice.

No, it's not, it's awful.

Why is my body betraying me?

Why him?

"Prepare yourselves." Libby, who is our law librarian, speaks up, causing some groans and a ripple of bodies to shift restlessly around the table.

"Joseph." Nathan greets him with a curt nod.

Just the sound of his voice has my mouth turning drier than sandpaper and I have to lick my lips to wet them. He's just so... hot.

Ridiculously so.

"Good evening, Mr. Hart," Joseph replies.

"Call me Nathan from now on, *please*, Joseph," he says in his usual smooth and steady voice, but there's a warmth about it this evening.

The extra emphasis on the *please* has me stifling a chuckle. Maybe he paid attention to my lesson in manners from earlier.

Joseph nods to acknowledge his instruction, but I can tell by the way he scratches the back of his head, brows pinching together, he's as confused as everyone else around the table.

Nathan is being... nice.

"Arianna," Nathan addresses me next, and I feel his stare all the way down to my core, the heat growing there making me feel both aroused and irritated.

Mainly irritated. And, okay, I can admit that I'm attracted to him, but between his gravelly voice and devilishly handsome face, it's difficult not to be.

"Ah-ha, it all makes sense as to why we are here now," Cole says, as if amused, rocking back on his heels.

He's much cheerier than the other three brothers and roguish looking too. Handsome though; there's no escaping how handsome they all are.

But Nathan's chiseled jaw and ocean eyes give him a mysterious edge I seem to have a thing for.

This new infatuation I have with him is getting out of hand.

And what does Cole mean?

Nathan motions to his brother, formally introducing us. "Cole, meet Arianna, my secretary."

"We've met." Several times in passing, so what's with all the formalities?

I remove myself from the end seat I'm sitting on and rise to my feet to take the hand Cole is holding out for me to shake. He surprises me when he leans in and taps a kiss to one of my cheeks and then the other. "I think you might be more to him than just his secretary," he whispers out of earshot. "This is his roundabout way of getting our approval."

What does he mean, more than just his secretary?

My face burns from embarrassment as I remember the first encounter with his brothers. I was still wearing my clothes from the night before and it's where his brother, Max, who isn't anywhere to be seen, handed me my panties.

World, swallow me up now.

The second time I saw them as a foursome was my first day in the boardroom where they struggled to hide their amusement at our situation.

There was nothing funny about it.

Maybe I shouldn't be working for Hart Law. What the hell was I thinking?

"And this is Eli." Nathan waves his hand in the direction of his other brother.

Cole lets go of my hand before Eli shakes it, copying Cole in kissing my cheeks one after the other.

Nathan and his brother proceed to say hello to everyone else.

Despite what I've seen and heard from my new colleagues, the Hart brothers are much nicer than I thought.

Goddamn it, could they not all be ignorant ogres? Which is what I thought they were.

"Welcome to the company, Arianna." Eli smiles when he stands back and surveys me then drops my hand out of his.

Shaking his head with a grin, Cole claps his hands together and casts his gaze around the table. "Who wants a drink? Nathan is buying as he's the one who dragged us here tonight."

Nathan scowls hard, clearly unhappy with his brother for sharing that private information.

Everyone does their best to keep their sniggers under wraps but fail before they all reel off their drinks order.

"I'm not staying." I hold my hand over the top of my glass causing a few people to disagree and beg me to stay, but I stand my ground. "I'm leaving as soon as I've finished my drink." I need to create space between me and Nathan.

Nathan gives Cole his drink order, handing over his platinum credit card. "Macallan on the rocks. And nothing for the lightweight." He points his head in my direction as if goading me.

Does he want me to stay? Surely not. I annoy him, I know I do because his irritation is tangible and bounces off him like a hot summer breeze off a stone cliff most days.

"I'll help you at the bar, Cole." Libby slides out of her seat and Eli follows her.

"Did I tell you about that dating app I downloaded, Libby?" Cole's loud question can be heard over the crowd, raising a few eyebrows because out of the four brothers, Cole is quieter and comes across as a bit of a deep thinker.

I like how Cole and Libby seem close, but I shudder at the mention of dating apps.

I've never tried them before, but my friend Maeve is never off the damn things. She's convinced she will find her future husband on there, and maybe I'm a skeptic, but I don't think she will. However, she's someone who never fails to amaze me, so she'll probably prove me wrong.

Fascinated and slightly confused why Nathan wanted to come here combined with Cole's comment about being "more than just his secretary," I study Nathan's considered movements.

Slowly, as if unsure of Nathan's dominating presence, my work colleagues finally begin to talk amongst themselves again while Nathan unbuttons his suit jacket then loosens his tie before sliding himself next to me.

It's unexpected and he's too close, and yet not close enough.

I reluctantly scooch over to give him space but all that does is make him move closer to me, pressing his firm warm thigh next to mine.

Please go away.

Touch me.

Not a word passes between us, the silence stretching like an elasticated band.

I pick up my glass and finish my Manhattan. I'm glad I refused another drink because I don't trust myself around him anymore.

Although... Manhattan cocktails... followed by more great sex... hmm... Maybe it wouldn't be such a bad thing.

Don't kid yourself; it would be a terrible idea.

"Have you had a good day?" Nathan asks, sounding less than interested.

"Not really. My boss is an ass," I reply deadpan, looking straight ahead, knowing I'm crossing the boundary into unprofessional and we need more balance to the interactions we have. But to hell with it, he is an ass.

"My new secretary is one of those too. I overheard her telling another employee that I was old." He sighs, almost exaggeratingly. "I'm so old now, my heart might not cope with that level of criticism."

His unexpected dry wit surprises me and I burst out laughing. "You heard that?" I cover my mouth to stifle the loudness of my laughter that's also laced with heavy embarrassment.

"Even though I'm practically geriatric now, my eyes and ears work perfectly fine, Arianna. I see and hear everything," he snaps back. I know it's his way of telling me that he's tuned into every aspect of his business.

I shouldn't have said that to Joseph earlier. Nathan is only forty-four.

And he fucks all night with the energy of a twenty-year-old, except his experience eclipses anyone I've ever slept with.

I've said it before, and I'll say it again.

Best.

Sex.

Ever.

"I'm sorry," I say, hoping I sound sincere.

Pleasantries aside, a gruff-sounding *hmpf* rattles his chest. "Accepted," is all he says.

"Great. Well, I need to use the restroom and then I'm leaving."

Resting his back against the seat, he drums his fingers on the tabletop. "So soon? That's a shame because I was just about to show you the brochures I brought with me so you could help me pick out a retirement home," he responds in a sardonic flat tone.

I think I like this playful side of him and if I stay any longer the way his mouth is now curving upward is too delicious to not have me wishing I could taste his lips again.

He's too much of a temptation. And someone I shouldn't be allowing to tempt me.

Flicking my hair over my shoulder, I grab my purse from under the table. "Well, I'm sorry but discussing what brand of walking cane you should buy next is less than appealing." My voice drips with boredom, and I lower it to make sure no one else hears what I say next. "Before I go, would you like me to write a Post-it with your name and address on to make sure you get home safely? Just in case you forget where you live. Now that you're getting older, your memory maybe isn't quite as good as it once was."

His jaw tightens in the same way it's been doing since he spoke to me on my first day and when he goes to reply, I butt in and tell everyone I'm leaving then wave goodbye. With Stephanie from marketing on one side and Nathan on the other, I urge Nathan to let me out, which he does, albeit reluctantly.

I straighten the skirt of my dress and push the handle of my purse up over my shoulder once I'm out and wave goodbye one final time. "See you tomorrow." Then I shift my attention to Nathan. "Mr. Hart." I give him a curt nod, ignoring his death stare, swivel on the balls of my pumps and walk toward the bathroom.

Another day done.
Thank God that's over.

12

NATHAN

If she thinks for one minute I'm letting her get away with any of her sass, she's sadly mistaken.

Covertly, I keep a watchful eye on her and as soon as Arianna is out of sight, I excuse myself and follow the spirited siren I seem to be completely obsessed with through the bar.

Pushing open the bathroom door, I enter, and I'm pleased to find the stalls are empty except for the one Arianna occupies. Satisfied, I quietly walk back to the main door and turn the latch to lock it to stop anyone interrupting us.

I pull a smile at the way she hums to herself contently, enjoying her sweet-sounding tune as she does her business before flushing the toilet.

Resting my ass on the vanity unit, I cross my arms and legs and don't have to wait too long for her to unlock the door to exit the stall, my skin prickling with anticipation.

The door slightly ajar, her eyes blow wide as soon as she spots me, followed by a wide wicked smile that brings an end to her melodic humming. She fucking knows she's been teasing me all day. More than usual.

Her reaction is quicker than a bolt of lightning as she pretends to close the door to seal herself back inside the safety of the stall. But I know she's playing with me, like cat and fucking mouse.

I take two large strides and I'm right there pushing the door open to prevent her relocking it, which she won't. I know she wants this, me chasing after her.

She quickly scampers backward, wedging herself into the back corner as if she's a caged animal, mischief dancing all over her face. When I'm inside the stall, I awkwardly close the door in the tight space, lay my back against it then secure the lock behind my back.

"What are you doing?" she whispers. The little gulp noise she makes doesn't go unnoticed, her eyes almost falling out of their sockets when she realizes we are sealed in and it's just the two of us, something she's been avoiding for weeks, because I get the impression she doesn't trust herself around me. Hell, I don't trust myself. I'm desperate to touch her again.

"Teaching you a lesson in manners, Ms. Donovan." I step forward, rubbing my hands together.

"What?" she asks, sounding confused, lines wrinkling her forehead before she sucks in a breath as if she understands what I mean. She holds her pointer finger up in the air. "Now, wait, just one—"

I don't give her an opportunity to finish her sentence, because faster than a blink of an eye, I'm throwing myself at her. I can't seem to stay away and I've sprung forward, looped my arm around her waist, and I'm crashing my lips to hers.

Surprised at first, she lets out a squeak, then slowly as I push the seam of her mouth open with my tongue, she sighs, sounding blissed out, and gives in to our kiss, dropping her purse to the floor with a *thud*.

It's a kiss unlike any other we've shared yet, because this time, I know her, I know what turns her on, what she likes, what makes her go all dopey eyed and what makes her scream my name. I know every inch of her and I've committed every one of her curves to memory for safekeeping.

There isn't an ounce of rational thought in my brain that tells me to stop as she grabs my tie and pulls me closer, letting me know she wants this too.

I shouldn't be kissing the woman I had a one-night stand with, but I don't care.

I shouldn't be kissing the woman I had a one-night stand with and then who scolded me in my own office today, but I don't care.

I shouldn't be kissing the vixen who has teased me all day in her little black dress, but I don't care.

I shouldn't be kissing my secretary, but I don't care.

And I sure as hell shouldn't be kissing my employee, but I really couldn't give a fuck, because none of that seems to matter anymore.

I want her.

So fucking bad.

Which is ridiculous.

I don't know her, and yet I do.

Every contour, sigh, freckle, and scar.

Specifically, the ten-inch jagged-looking silvery-colored scar that runs down the length of her right shoulder blade.

When I fucked her from behind the night she stayed over at my apartment and ran my finger down it, she refused to tell me what caused the slightly raised scar with the small dots along either side of it, indicating sutures had been placed there. Yelling at me, she told me not to touch it again, which I didn't.

Whatever caused her scar, it looked like it was a deep cut

with a lot of history that most likely required surgery. It's been screwing with my head since then and I wish she trusted me enough to tell me what happened to her.

Invading her mouth with my tongue, hers twists around mine as we lick and taste each other like starved animals. She tastes sweet and bitter, the bourbon from her cocktail both spicy and smooth; the exact flavor of what I imagine temptation and regret tastes like. And she tastes like consequences, really fucking bad ones. Not that I make many bad decisions, if ever, but when it comes to her, I can't stop myself from wanting her and I don't care what the repercussions are.

We explore each other's mouths, and it feels so good to have her in my arms again.

Right.

And also mischievous and sinful.

Perfect.

If someone told me that I had to kiss her for the rest of my life to end all suffering in the world, I'd do it, because even a lifetime wouldn't be enough. And nothing has ever felt so good.

We're sealed to each other, and I move my hands to her ass and give it a squeeze, rubbing my hips against her soft body, making my aching cock leak with precum.

She threads her fingers into the hair at the back of my neck and scrapes her nails over my scalp, causing me to shiver.

"I love the way you touch me," I confess. "I shouldn't want you." Kissing someone has never felt so good.

"I shouldn't want you either," she mumbles breathlessly between our desperate kisses.

"But I do."

"Same."

"I should fire you." Couldn't if I tried.

"You should."

"But I won't." Can't. I don't want to.

I grab her hair and tilt her head back so I can kiss her neck in the delicious spot behind her ear that makes her call my name. Every. Single. Time.

"Nathan." My name falls out of her pretty lips exactly like I had hoped, and I love the way she moans as if I'm her new life anthem that stirs up only the best memories.

But what I really want is to hear her chanting my name in reverence, begging me to fuck her hard as more precum leaks from the tip of my cock in appreciation of her sweet-sounding voice.

With my hands still gripping her hair, I pull her mouth back to mine and hold her tight against me, the height difference between us more obvious than ever.

"Turn around," I order, sucking her bottom lip into my mouth before giving it a gentle bite.

Fucking hell, I want to devour her.

Surprising me, without question, Arianna does as she's told and quickly turns around.

She lays her palms flat on the wall and presses herself against it, and I smile at how compliant she is when I have her like this, wanting me.

I run my hands up her outer thighs then push her dress up, bunching it around her waist, her breathing growing louder with anticipation and my heart thumps in time with each of her breaths, proving I'm feeling the same way.

"I think I should teach *you* a lesson in manners, don't you agree?" I ask, unable to keep the desperation and longing out of my tone. It's impossible. I am desperate, and all I want is to experience again the connection we shared the first night we spent together, in every way.

I chuckle to myself when her body says one thing, a yes, as

she wiggles her tempting ass against my hard length, while her head shakes a no as if in conflict, and she replies, "No," like I knew she would, but the slight crack in her voice tells me she's nervous and gives her away.

"No?" I rub my concealed cock against her ass so she can feel just how hard I am for her and what she does to me. "That's the wrong fucking answer, baby." I force my fingers into her silk pantyhose and tear a hole from the waist all the way down her thighs, exposing her naked ass, causing her to let out a little yelp.

"What the hell are you doing?" She tries to turn around, but I cage her in with my body, which is so much bigger than hers, and rip the nylon some more.

The high-pitched sound of the fabric breaking apart makes me want to tear every shred of clothing from her delectable body.

"Don't even think about moving." I hold her in place. "You, Ms. Donovan, appear to need a little reminder about who is in charge here."

"No, I don't."

Her brattish reply has me removing my hips from hers.

Looking down, I groan at the sliver of black lace that's nestled between her ass cheeks, jealous that it's not my face between them instead.

Smoothing my hand over the soft naked skin of her ass cheek, I ask again, "You don't think you need a lesson, Arianna?"

"No." Her infuriating one-word answer has me slapping her ass much harder than I wanted but I can tell she likes it when she bows her back and moans the exact same way she did when I stuffed her pussy full of my cock.

"So, you didn't say I was old?"

"No." She lies intentionally, and I know she is loving every scorching hot minute of this, so I slap her ass again, this time rubbing the area to ease the sting. "I didn't say you were old." Panting, she struggles to get her words out.

I move my mouth to the shell of her ear. "What did you say then, Ms. Donovan?" I nibble her earlobe between my teeth, and she tilts her neck to the side, inviting me to give her more of what she wants.

Moaning loudly, she cries out when I bite her neck and suck it hard enough to leave a mark, before licking her vanilla-scented skin.

"I said... God, that's so good." She pushes into me, tempting me some more before she finishes what she started saying. "I wasn't into older men."

I tut darkly. "And if I were to sink my fingers into your pretty pussy to check just how wet you are, I think I'd find that you are lying and are most definitely into older men, don't you?"

"No."

This stubborn woman has my dick so fucking hard I might come in my goddamn boxers any minute. And I haven't done that since... well... I was a teenager.

She's scrambling my brain and my bodily functions.

Using my foot to widen her legs, I push one of her feet out, then the other, spank her ass then slide the lace fabric of her panties to the side. Moving my fingers between her thighs, I push a thick digit inside of her dripping pussy.

"Fucking knew it." I lick the length of her neck and move my finger in and out of her wet heat.

"Nathan." Desperate to fuck, she rides my finger, and I slide another one inside of her, giving her exactly what she wants, making her juices drip down my fingers and onto my knuckle.

"You like that, baby girl, but you wish it was my cock filling your pretty cunt, don't you?"

"No."

I hum in her ear as if considering what I say next. "Liar." I add another finger, stretching her greedy hole. "Admit it, you don't hate me."

"I do hate you."

"No, you don't." I think she hates herself for liking me.

"I hate your grumpy ass." A long groan fills the empty space as she tries to tighten her inner thighs around my hand to chase her release, the walls of her pussy tightening around my fingers.

"That's such a shame, because I quite like my naughty little secretary and for most of the afternoon, I've been imagining all the ways I would like to bend you over my desk and fuck you into oblivion."

Much quicker now, I finger fuck her. She removes one of her hands from the wall to between her legs to rub her clit, as if to get herself there quicker, but there is no way I'm allowing that, so I slap her hand away with my other hand. "No fucking way, Ari. Just me."

My words only make her whimper some more.

"Tell me you like me," I order.

"No."

"Say. It." I force my words through gritted teeth. "Or I won't let you come." I rub her inner walls, willing her orgasm to come out and play.

"No."

"Fine." I pull my fingers out of her slick center, causing her to let out a frustrated whine.

Almost sobbing, she begs, "Don't stop."

I don't feel like being a gentleman tonight. "No." I flatten my front to her back, pressing her firmly against the wall. "Like I said, it's you that needs a lesson in pleasantries, not me, and you didn't say *please*."

"Go to hell." Huffing, she tries to push back but I hold her firmly in place with my broad body.

"Already there, baby." Because I know how sweet her pussy tastes, and working with her every day is like living in Satan's den of iniquity without being allowed to play if I never get to taste it again.

When she turns to face me, I lift my fingers that were just inside of her, then rub the tips across her bottom lip. "Taste," I command.

The way she flicks her tongue out and licks my digits sparks memories of the way she sucked my cock three weeks ago as if I was the best thing she'd ever tasted, and all the blood rushes to the end of my dick, making it pound harder.

"Good girl." It's the second thing she's done without protest.

And the way her pupils dilate confirms to me that she likes my praise. She liked it the other night and she is most definitely into me.

I wonder how long she'll keep denying it.

"See you tomorrow morning, Arianna." I back away, palm my hard cock, readjusting it to ease the pressure, then unlock the door and yank it open, leaving the stall quicker than her brain can keep up with. It's also the last thing I want to do, but to hell with it, she's not the one in control here. I am.

"And don't even think about playing with yourself." That's my job. "Or I will know," I call back over my shoulder.

What the hell am I saying? This is messed up.

Arianna yells from behind me as I take long strides toward the exit. "You can't leave me like this," she squeals. Fucking squeals like a woman on the edge, which she is.

Oh yes, I can leave you, baby girl, oh yes I fucking can.

Because I just know she'll be screaming the word *please*, and admitting how much she likes me, before the week is through.

When what I should really be doing is staying away from her like I promised her I would.

But some part of me just can't help myself.

"Nathaniel," she calls after me, but I ignore her as I unlock the main door and exit the restroom with unshakable confidence.

Walking past a line of women waiting to enter, I ignore their stares and gasps of disapproval.

Smoothing down my tie, I rebutton my suit jacket, and stretch out the tension in my neck, moving it one way and then the other. I'm going to have blue balls until I get home, but fuck it, I have a new memory to jerk off to tonight; spanking Arianna might just be my new favorite thing.

Guilt and disappointment coils around my gut like a boa constrictor suffocating its prey.

Add self-loathing to that list for wanting someone I shouldn't be wanting: my secretary.

Why is this happening to me? And why can't I stop?

I know I'm playing with fire, only I think I'm going to be the one that burns to ashes.

13

ARI

Annoyed and frustrated that Nathan didn't let me come, I slam the stall door shut with a loud bang when high-pitched chatter, from what sounds like a dozen or so female voices, suddenly fills the empty bathroom.

I slip off my heels before removing my ruined pantyhose.

"Asshole," I mutter to myself under my breath and scrunch them up before throwing them into the trash can.

I still for a moment when a voice swoons words of admiration for the infuriating man I'm learning likes to play games. "Wow, Nathan looks hot tonight. Whoever got to sample his goods is one hell of a lucky lady."

No, she's not. She's more frustrated than an author with writer's block.

Flustered, I quickly and quietly compose myself, slipping my heels back on and tugging my dress down over my hips.

I'll wait for everyone to leave before I make my exit—otherwise, they'll know it was me who was the lucky, or perhaps not so lucky, girl who was with Nathan.

My skin is still flushed and the burning in my core lives on as does the incredible feeling of him stretching me.

Arousal is quickly replaced with annoyance. *Don't play with yourself or I'll know*. Who the hell does he think he is? He's nothing special and nothing my vibrator can't sort as soon as I get home.

I'm lying to myself. It can never replace his electrifying touch and the way he makes me feel: adored and worshipped.

Bile rises in my throat when the women on the other side of my cubicle continue talking about Nathan. "Why is he still single?" one of them asks, and another replies, "Since his father retired, he's committed to his work."

"I heard his dad took early retirement because he's sick but I don't know how true that is."

This is new information to me. What's wrong with his father?

"I don't know anything about that, but I do know Nathan Hart will never settle down." Another woman jumps into the conversation. "Which is such a shame because according to Vivienne Cavendish he has the stamina of a mountain lion on the hunt."

"Relentless," one says.

"Powerful," another adds.

"Unstoppable until the job is done." Someone else interjects and they all burst into cackling laughter, making them sound like a coven of witches.

God, that makes me feel sick, but they aren't wrong. Nathan's body is built for the long game. And whoever Vivienne Cavendish is, I'm jealous that she has first-hand knowledge of what Nathan fucks like all night.

I hold my hand over my stomach at the mention of him being with another woman, hating that she knows him like I do.

Maybe I'm just another accomplishment for him, or another challenge. And maybe I mean nothing to him at all.

But there is no denying the chemistry between us. Every time we touch, sparks fly, causing warmth unlike anything I've ever felt to tingle everywhere. It's exciting.

Maybe I'm delusional.

What seems like a lifetime passes and finally, when the commotion of people using the facilities finally subsides, I tentatively make my way out of the stall and thank the Big Man above at the sight of the empty space.

Walking over to the sink, I lay my purse on it and clean my hands, while my brain revisits the conversation between the women.

I shudder at the idea of another woman's hands on Nathan's body. It fills me with such intense jealousy, it feels as if I could tear the skin from my own.

The unease I'm experiencing makes me question everything about who I am. What *we* are. What we've become.

We aren't exclusive; hell, we aren't even friends. I'm his secretary, nothing more, but why do I feel like we are?

And I need to remember my big overarching why. Why I am working for him.

It's temporary.

Being with him or getting close to him is inappropriate. It's unethical and I need to put a stop to whatever is happening between us, immediately.

I finish drying my hands and dig my cell out my purse to ask my journalist friend, Julie, if she's uncovered anything new.

JULIE

Not yet. You?

ME

Nothing. I'm hoping to have some information soon, though.

JULIE

I have a couple of leads on the traffic officer and detective who investigated the case but weren't called to give evidence.

Is she sure about that? I swear the two investigators involved gave evidence. Strange.

ME

Great, let me know as soon as you have anything.

JULIE

Will do.

I tuck my cell inside my purse.

Staring hard at my reflection in the mirror, I find it difficult to look at the woman I've become.

It's time to focus my energy on the true reason I applied for a position at Hart Law: to uncover the truth and gather the evidence that Nathan's father is a corrupt lawyer and the man who helped get my family's killer acquitted in his trial.

I slept with the enemy.

And I liked it.

I had sex with the son of the lawyer who defended a criminal and got him out of a prison sentence.

Which makes me a traitor.

I'm as guilty as his father and the man who killed my family.

And I can't sleep with him again.

Tomorrow, I'll set the record straight with him.

14

ARI

I run across the hall in my stockinged feet to my front door, surprised that someone is ringing my doorbell so early in the morning. I haven't even had my first cup of coffee yet.

"Just a minute," I call out, tucking my cream silk shirt inside the waistband of my black pencil skirt.

Grabbing my keys off the entryway table, I stick my key in to unlock the door, then use the thumb turn on the deadbolts, both top and bottom, allowing me to open it fully.

"Good morning, Ms. Donovan, my name is Jenkins." A man dressed in a fine black suit greets me cheerfully.

"Morning," I reply, unsure who he is but recognize him from somewhere. Then it dawns on me. It's Nathan's driver, the one from the first night we slept together. I was like a cat in heat that night. How embarrassing.

"I'm here to drive you to the Logan settlement conference."

"That's a bit unnecessary." I usually make my own way to out-of-court settlements.

"Mr. Hart insisted."

Oh, did he now?

I look over Jenkins' shoulder to discover Nathan's shiny black limo parked up in front of my house.

How flashy.

"Can we stop for coffee on the way?" I ask, excited because I'll be traveling to work in style this morning.

"There is already one waiting for you inside the car."

I feel like a movie star. "Thank you."

"And a banana and caramel muffin," Jenkins adds.

They are my favorite. I ate one at my desk yesterday for lunch.

Did Nathan notice and tell him what I liked? Surely not; he had his head stuck in files for ninety-nine percent of the day. I swear a bomb could go off and he wouldn't notice.

I recall Nathan's words from last night. *I see and hear everything.*

Of course he told Jenkins what to order for me this morning.

Which is sweet of him, and awful; mostly awful. But it also shows his caring side. Why does he have to be so nice? Or is this all part of his game? Because after last night, he left me desperate for more and he knew what he was doing. He's not a nice guy. He's the devil in the flesh. The worst kind of temptation. A tease. *Goddammit.*

Pushing my thumb over my shoulder, I inform Jenkins, "I'll just grab my things."

He nods his acknowledgment.

Excited, I skip along the hallway and enter my bedroom. Slipping my shoes on, I put on my favorite black blazer with the big gold buttons, then check my appearance in the mirror one last time. "You'll do." I comb my fingers through my hair to fluff it out before lifting my work bag off the floor, and I'm out the door, ready to face another day in record time.

Hands behind his back, standing waiting for me as rigid as a soldier, Jenkins only breaks character to open the door for me when I get closer and his mouth breaks into a gigantic smile. "Ms. Donovan." He nods.

"Thank you, Jenkins, but please call me Ari." I make my request before sliding into the back seat and get the fright of my life when I realize someone is already inside.

Nathan.

Softly closing the car door, Jenkins seals us inside before getting into the driver's seat then proceeds to raise the glass divider between the rear seats and the front of the car, giving us some privacy.

"Good morning, Arianna." Nathan's voice is smooth and sultry, every word steady and wrapping around me like melted golden honey; rich and irresistible.

I nod, my mouth refusing to cooperate, anxiety creeping in as I realize I've found myself once again in a situation where I'm far too close for comfort. And alone with him.

When I place my work bag on the floor, he hands me a to-go cup. "One grande flat white with extra hot steamed oat milk, one pump of cinnamon dolce syrup, and a double shot of espresso."

Holy shit.

He must listen to every conversation I have.

Nathan places a brown paper bag between us on the leather seat. "And a banana and caramel breakfast muffin."

As if hypnotized, I wrap my fingers around the to-go cup, unable to take my eyes off him, or control the rapid beat of my heart.

He shakes his head and mutters something under his breath I don't catch then opens the lid of the laptop that's resting on his knees. "Are all the settlement documents ready for today?" he asks firmly, getting straight down to business.

"Yes," I reply. "I have the settlement agreement drafted which includes all the terms you discussed with the opposing party." I typed them up when I went home last night. "I also have the waivers and confidentiality forms ready for everyone to review and sign once we finalize everything. I read the opposing party's latest offer and we're all on the same page."

I look over at him to find him staring at me as if in awe.

He gives me a curt nod, which is a complete contrast to how he was with me last night when he spanked me, something I never thought I would enjoy, but did.

"You're efficient, thank you, Arianna."

"I've done this before." Many times. "This isn't my first rodeo." I take a sip of my coffee, the strong caffeine increasing my energy levels in a flash and warming my throat, which always seems to go drier than a box of crackers when I'm around him.

He breaks our gaze, his concentration returning to his inbox. "We could be in this meeting all day." He lets out a long sigh, knowing our day needs our full attention.

"I know." It's all part of the negotiation process and if they fall through then we go back to square one. Sometimes clients change their minds and decide to go to trial even during negotiations. I hope that doesn't happen for Nathan today.

Keeping his head bowed, tapping his fingers against his laptop keyboard, he asks, "Can you keep an eye on everyone's responses today? I'm tempted to push for more settlement money depending on those."

"Absolutely, and I called James"—our client—"early this morning, and he had already arrived for the meeting."

James' wife was killed when the brakes failed on their new car. I was up most of the night reading the case file, and after months of denying it, the motor company finally admitted liability.

Nathan stares at his laptop screen. "I know James is desperate to move forward. After today, maybe he can finally get some closure following the death of his wife. Not that ten million dollars will ever bring her back."

"No money in the world will ever bring my beautiful family back." As soon as I've said those words, I instantly regret it, but I just couldn't help myself. To me, their lives were priceless, as are all the future memories we could have made together but which can never be anything more than a wish for me now.

If only things could have been different.

But they're not, and there aren't enough miracles in the world available to bring them back.

I jump, making my coffee slosh about in my cup, when Nathan slams the lid of his laptop shut then slides it onto the seat opposite us. "What happened to your family, Arianna?" he asks, his voice full of curiosity and determination, his face mirroring the same. He looks... concerned... sorry for me... like he cares?

Which he shouldn't. I don't want his sympathy.

"They died." It sounds so clinical when I say it like that, but there's no dressing it up and putting a pretty bow on it. It happened.

His eyes narrow, crinkling at the edges, and I can almost hear the next question he's desperate to ask running around his brain, because it's always the same one that follows every time I tell anyone that my family died.

"In a car crash," I answer his non-vocal question. "I was fifteen. I survived." My grip around my coffee cup tightens, and I turn away to focus on the scenery out the window before swiping away a tear that's rolled down my cheek. "They didn't."

Sometimes, like now, my emotions get the better of me and I can't stop them from overwhelming me.

There's a huge stretch of silence that rolls by until he finally says, "I'm so sorry, Arianna." The warmth of his hand on my thigh makes me want to lower my defenses and allow him to leave it there because I find it comforting, but I can't. Instead, I swivel my legs away from him and his hand disappears.

"Is the scar along your shoulder blade from the crash?" he asks slowly.

When he touched it, I begged him not to. But if only he knew that sometimes even I can't look at it. It makes me feel guilty; that I lived, and they didn't.

When I don't respond, I think he might push for more detail, but thankfully he doesn't, letting me wallow like a hippo in my own grief.

"Eat." The muffin he bought for me appears in my lap. Much softer than before, he says, "If this case is too close to your heart and you find it too difficult to sit in on the negotiations today, please tell me."

"I'll be fine." I'm not feeling one bit hungry, but I don't want to talk anymore, so I open the brown paper bag, lift the muffin out of it, and take a bite. I almost moan when the flavor of caramelly goodness and banana fills my mouth, awakening my senses.

My stomach groans in appreciation. Maybe I am hungry after all.

"I hate that you lost your family." His husky voice is filled with genuine compassion that makes me want to climb into his lap and curl myself around him, because I know what being wrapped in his arms feels like. Like home. Which they shouldn't.

There's no rhyme or reason to us.

Working for him isn't permanent. I'm here for one purpose, and hopefully, it brings justice for my family and the closure I so deeply need.

"Thank you." I turn away, feeling guilty about my reasons for being here, but I can't let him cloud my emotions.

Time passes and I have almost finished my delicious muffin which has made me feel so much better, pulling me out of my sadness. I cast a nervous glance in Nathan's direction when I feel him staring at me again.

"You're very beautiful," he says out of the blue, then adds, "I find it difficult to concentrate when you're around."

His confession has heat flushing in waves over my skin.

Not only am I a traitor but my body is too. It knows what it wants... Him.

Dropping his attention to my mouth, he sucks in a breath of the heated air between us. The tension is almost too much as heat pools between my thighs, my skin tingling with anticipation.

I push the last bit of muffin into my mouth then lick the sticky caramel topping off my lips. In a heartbeat, his entire demeanor changes, his shoulder stiff as if on high alert.

He points at my lip. "You missed a crumb." His voice is low and dangerous sounding.

When I curl my tongue at the corner of my mouth to get it, he leans over at the same time and runs his finger over my bottom lip, unexpectedly causing the tip of my tongue to hit the tip of his finger, and I swear he growls, which sounds so good.

Holding a prolonged gaze, the intensity of it burns through my soul, destroying any fragment of logical thought out of my brain. I have no control over my senses and before I realize what I'm doing, I'm sucking his finger into my mouth and licking the topping off the same finger that was buried deep inside my pussy last night.

With my lips firmly sealed around his finger, he swallows a deep groan, his Adam's apple bobbing up and down in an audible gulp when I swirl my tongue around his digit, once, then twice. Tasting his intoxicating cologne on his fingers makes my brain glitch, neither of us attempting to end our connection.

"Arianna." He draws out the four syllables of my name, which sounds like a warning that if I keep tasting him, he won't be responsible for his actions. His breathing grows heavier, his chest moving in and out like he's trying to control himself.

What the hell am I doing?

I push his finger out of my mouth with my tongue and shake my head, confused with the effect he has over me.

Why can't I resist him?

"Nothing can happen between us," I whisper, disappointed in myself for allowing things to go too far yet again.

He bares his teeth, almost snarling at me, as if annoyed that I drew a line in the sand, bringing an end to us. Whatever *us* means. There can never be an *us*.

He remains silent, and his movements are jerky when he sits back in his seat, picks his laptop back up again and returns to work.

"Email the settlement agreement, waivers, and confidentiality forms to me," he demands, speaking deeper, his words clipped. Then he bolts on a "Please" at the end.

"Okay."

Well, this is awkward.

Welcome to another day in hell.

15

NATHAN

Another four horrifically painful weeks have passed of working alongside Arianna, the woman who is hell-bent on making my life and my dick as hard as possible.

From her spellbinding perfume to the way she sashays around the place in her tight little dresses that I want to shred from her body. Every night I've jerked off in the shower, but the relief never feels like it's enough.

It's her I crave, every inch of her.

I told her she wouldn't last the week, but now that I know her, I've learned just how stubborn she is. She's going the distance working for me, and I've been forced to watch her every move, and every man who walks by through the doorway of my office which has a direct view of her desk flirt with her.

How can you not like her? She's captivating and beautiful.

Efficient.

Happy. Which irks me because she can barely bring herself to smile at me but with everyone else, she's different. Herself, I think.

With me, she schools her emotions and retreats into herself.

Everyone loves her and for reasons I still can't figure out, she's the person everyone comes to for advice when she's only worked here for a couple of months. She knows everything about everyone, pays attention to the in-depth details about the cases I'm working on, what lawyers are representing who and why. She's memorized their court dates and knows when negotiations are taking place. She even knows who Gloria had lunch with last Wednesday and when Keith from marketing is getting married. She remembers the names of everyone's spouses and children.

How is that even possible? And where has she been hiding for so long?

She's fucking perfect.

Annoying.

But perfect.

Every day I arrive at the office to discover a coffee sitting on my desk, alongside a detailed schedule of tasks that need my urgent attention. My desk is always cleared of any files and paperwork I may have left on it from the night before and for the first time ever, I never need to ask if all the required court documents are prepared, reviewed or filed electronically and physically, because I know they will already be done.

She's magic.

I want to admit that having her in my work life has made work ten times easier for me since she started, but the truth is, I'm more frustrated than ever.

For the first time, I want someone I can't have.

Nothing can happen between us.

I can't shake her words that I have been replaying endlessly in my mind.

Which they shouldn't, because I said them first.

Meant them then. Don't mean them now.

"What's with the frown?" Cole enters my office.

At the same time, Arianna's chipper voice floats into the room like it does every goddam day. "If you send me your court check-in list, I can chase them up for you."

I glare at her through the open doorway.

Resting her phone between her ear and her shoulder, she continues the conversation with whoever is on the end of the phone, doing about a dozen tasks all at once.

"Does she ever fucking sleep?" I ask, annoyed that she runs this place like she owns it.

A vision of her and me running the company together plays out like a movie in my mind. As husband and wife.

What the fuck? Where did that come from?

"Only you can answer that." Cole sits down on the sofa opposite my desk and gives me a hard stare before looking over his shoulder at Arianna and back at me again. "She did sleep that night at your place, right?"

"A little." In between us fucking each other's brains out.

"She's got you rattled."

"No, she doesn't." That's a lie; my head is fucked.

"Yes, she does, and the sooner you admit it, the sooner we can have grouchy Nathan 1.0 back and not this extreme 2.0 version you've been lately. You were unbearable before, but now you're—"

"Needing to get your dick sucked to relieve all the sexual tension you two have." Max interjects, walking into my office alongside Eli.

"Leave," I bark. "All of you." Idiots.

"I'm staying." Eli dismisses me, and I think I'm going to pop a gasket any minute; he can raise my blood pressure in seconds. He further annoys me when he picks up the donut with multicolored sprinkles on top that Arianna left on my desk for me this morning and takes a bite out of it.

"Give me that." I grab it out of his hand, making some of the topping drop off and scatter over my keyboard. "That's mine."

"Did Arianna buy it for you?" He scrunches his nose up and doesn't let me reply. "Aw, isn't that cute," he says in a singsong voice that's playful and exaggerated.

"Fuck off." I hate it when my brothers tease me. "Isn't there a bull somewhere you can wave a red flag at?"

Holding his hand to his heart, he pretends to be offended. "It's going-home time, which you should be doing too and we're heading to The Golden Spirit, are you coming?"

"Can't." I point at my screen. "I have client background checks to review, and I want to look at the previous cases filed against the airline she is suing." I grab a tissue out of the box and wipe the sticky residue from my donut off my fingers.

Max lifts his head from the magazine he's stuck his nose in and asks curiously, "What's the case?"

"Vivienne Cavendish versus Regal Wings," I reply, trying to remain cool. I haven't seen that woman in a very, *very* long time and I'm surprised she wants me to represent her given our history.

"I thought she married that old fucker who owns the television channel, SFCTV?" Eli asks.

"She did, but he died recently during a private flight to Japan," I state. "Nut allergy. The flight attendant failed to communicate the severity of his allergy to the crew, and they served him a stir fry meal where they used peanut oil."

"Holy shit," Cole exclaims in disbelief. "I remember seeing that on the news."

"And she wants you to represent her?" Max asks, stepping into the conversation again.

I confirm with a nod. "Death caused by an in-flight incident and negligence. That's what she's suing the airline for and she's asking for fifty million dollars."

A descending whistle leaves Cole's lips. "She'll never get that."

She won't, but I know she needs it. Her deceased husband left her next to nothing and his children from his first marriage ensured she isn't getting a cent more than was stated on their prenup.

"You underestimate me and my abilities." I shake my finger at him. Depending on how tomorrow goes, because I like to gauge my client's ethics first in a face-to-face meeting, I was going to suggest we sue for more. Although knowing Vivienne the way I do, her values aren't that high, and she's suing because she hasn't got a dime to her name. Nothing more.

"Didn't you fuck her?" Eli asks worriedly, clearly doubting if I should represent her, a thought that has already crossed my mind.

I sit forward in my seat, wanting to punch him in the face. "It was almost a decade ago, and will you keep your fucking voice down?" When my brothers follow my line of sight, they realize I don't want Arianna overhearing that information, but we're all met with a piercing glare.

She heard.

Asshole.

Tapping her fingers against the desk as if annoyed, she glares at me. Arianna gives the person she was on the phone with a curt farewell, slams the handset down, before removing herself from behind her desk, then she picks up a stack of files and storms off in the direction of the elevator.

"Interesting," Eli pipes up.

Then Max. "Oh, yeah, bro, she heard that and is totally into you. She's jealous."

"Are you going to make a move on her?" Cole asks, and the heightening curiosity bounces between all three of my brothers.

"She's my secretary." As if that isn't obvious.

Eli rolls his eyes. "Who you've already slept with. I think your rule about not dating staff has already been broken, don't you?" He tilts his head to the side slightly, a smirk playing on his lips as if challenging me.

He's right; my own law book of sorts was burnt to smithereens the minute she stepped inside this building.

Max adds, leaning over my desk, "And as you know, the clause in all of our employee contracts states, *Should an employee wish to pursue a personal relationship with another employee, they must immediately notify their supervisor.*"

He quotes it verbatim as if he's a walking encyclopedia.

Smart fucker.

Which he is; he wrote the contracts.

Cole chimes in, looking smugger than a fox in a henhouse. "Unless your relationship interferes with her performance, then I see no reason why you can't be together. In fact, it might make you more pleasant and easier to work with. And *technically* we have the final say, and we give you permission to date Arianna."

"I don't date." Well, that was until Arianna made me question everything about my non-existent life outside of work. I have no balance, very little fun, and no one to share my day with, which is something I have wanted to do every day since Arianna parked herself outside my office.

What I wouldn't give to unpack my day and ask about hers over a glass of wine, in the bath, just the two of us.

This obsession I have with her is getting out of hand.

"Do you have a date for next Friday?" Max asks, bursting my dream bubble.

"Next Friday? What's happening next Friday?" I immediately check my online calendar, and staring back at me on my computer monitor are the words I dread every year. *The Connecting Kids Charity Ball.*

I usually accept the invitation, secure a couple of tables for family and friends, then at the last minute make my apologies and use courtroom preparation as an excuse not to attend. Out of guilt, I send a donation toward The Connecting Kids Foundation, a nonprofit dedicated to providing fostered children scholarships, mentorship, and resources to prepare them for life after foster care including housing and business startup grants.

They also provide grief counselling services, something I only know because it's the same charity Arianna volunteers for.

It's a great cause; I should attend this year but attending alone, yet again, sounds... sad... pathetic... which I am.

In harmony, my brothers all rise to their feet and it's Max who delivers their parting thoughts. "Come to the ball. Bring Arianna."

"I'm not co—" I go to reply but Max cuts in.

"That's an order and it's nonnegotiable."

And with that they exit my office leaving me with my mouth gaping open in shock at the size of their balls they've suddenly all grown around me.

I can't ask her.

An uneasy feeling lines the pit of my stomach.

Every day I have tolerated her snarky-ass mouth and brat-like comments.

She's testing my limits.

It's not banter, it's more than that. She's flirting with me and it's annoying as hell. Because I can't do anything about it. Us.

She said she hated me the first night. Numerous times.

But now I feel like something has changed between us since she started working with me. Like she's warming to me.

Donuts.

Coffee.

Takeout ordered before I've even asked, and it's left on my desk.

She likes me.

I'm sure of it.

Maybe my brothers are right. Maybe I should take her.

Show her I'm not always a cantankerous bastard.

In fact, when it comes to her, I want to switch it off, but if I did, would everyone in the office see through me? Would I give myself away that I like her?

I more than like her. I want her.

And I want to unwrap her like a gift, discover everything about her and how she lost her family. It's none of my business, and yet I have this deep need to unearth all her secrets.

The day she told me she lost her family in a car crash, it felt like my heart gave out. I felt the pain in her words, saw it etched over her face, and it gutted me when she cried.

If she ever lets me inside that fortress she's built around her, I think she'd let me see her. The real Arianna. Not the one that pretends to be strong every minute of the goddamn day, but the one that is funny, kind, and helps everyone. She's naturally beautiful inside and out.

Regardless of what she and I both say about nothing happening between us again, her constant stolen glances and body language tell me she likes me and wants to get to know me better. Because I feel the same way too.

The feeling between us has its own life form and it's becoming harder and harder to ignore.

It's unbearable being around her without touching her, threading my hand into her hair and crushing her lips with mine, which I've imagined doing over a billion times since she rolled her seat behind her desk.

How long can we resist each other?

And what if she says no to my invitation?

You told her you didn't date staff, you arrogant bastard, of course she'll say no.

And I've been more of an unreasonable ass and arrogant lately. Preparing Easton Forbes, stunt-gone-wrong case, has been more demanding than I first envisaged. Hollywood is watching and the spotlight is on me. I'm being judged and I'm not sure I like it.

Arianna knows the pressure I'm under. She understands and I think that's why she urged me to go home early last night, which I didn't when I should have taken her advice.

She cares.

Fuck it, she'll say no at first to my invitation to the ball because she likes to challenge me and fuck with me, then she'll say yes.

I'm confident about that.

I see how she melted into me in the restroom weeks ago.

I know the effect I have on her.

But again, I told her I don't date staff. Which I don't. I made a big deal about it. Told her she and I were off limits.

I'll tell her she's going as my secretary. My plus one. Not a date. My work colleague, that's all it is.

Which sucks.

Will she see through my lie?

Because hell, she's been living rent free in my brain daily. I'm a complete mess and I have been doing my best to hide my struggle to focus on anything. I'm even surprised I managed to pull off the Walker case yesterday and win it.

Because I crave her. I know how our bodies work together. As if they were meant to be. Destined to be, or some other radical universal shit which is confusing the hell out of me.

Like caramel and salt; her sweet and me salty, perfectly balancing each other out.

Don't think I haven't noticed her watching me like I watch her.

She buys me donuts. I eye the half-eaten colorful cake sitting on my desk.

She wouldn't do that if she didn't feel something for me.

And she's not just another admirer who wants me for my position of power and money. She's different, full of fire, and someone who's immune to my arrogant attitude and calls me out when I overstep.

And was she jealous when she overheard Eli saying I'd slept with Vivienne Cavendish?

I shudder, recalling my mistake. Hell knows what I was thinking back then.

I clearly wasn't.

Fuck it, I'm going to ask Arianna to attend the ball with me, lie and tell her it's to make up the numbers at our table.

She'll say yes to that.

I know she will.

I head out of my office in search of Arianna.

There's no time like the present.

16

ARI

"Vivienne Cavendish," I mutter under my breath, feeling completely ruffled as I storm out of the elevator.

I already can't stand Vivienne, and I've never even met her. Unlucky for me, tomorrow I will, because I'm sitting in on her initial consultation with Nathan.

Having read the articles online about her marriage to one of the richest men in television, I discovered how her deceased husband's children cut her out of his will when they first got married, ensuring she didn't receive a penny of his inheritance.

Now Vivienne is on her very own one-woman warpath against the airline who she claims failed to follow the allergy protocol, and she publicly made a statement informing everyone that as soon as she's done there, she will be suing her deceased husband's children to ensure she gets everything that is owed to her.

What does she deserve exactly? He built his empire long before she entered the picture, and she was only married to the eighty-two-year-old for twelve months. At forty-two years his junior, she must have thought she'd won the lotto when she met Henry Cavendish, who she claims "swept her off her feet."

Whatever. I'll meet the undeniably beautiful woman who hides her "greed," Henry's son's words, not mine, tomorrow. After all, gold diggers sometimes come wrapped in a pretty package.

I shake off my distaste and paint on a smile, which isn't hard to do as I really like the new girl. "Hey, Leesa." I clutch the files to my chest and give our new records assistant, the one who filled the role I was originally hired for, a broad smile.

"Oh, I was just leaving." Leesa looks around the empty basement, her coat already on.

I wave my hand through the air. "That's not a problem. You head out, I'll file these."

I befriended Leesa the day she started, and I know she trusts me because I've done this exact same thing once a week for the last month, pretending to file at the last minute just to test the water.

"Are you sure you don't mind doing it again?" She tilts her head to the side in question. "It's just I have to get Talia to dance class tonight by six or you know I would stay."

I knew that. On Wednesdays we only have one records clerk and Leesa leaves early to take her daughter to lessons. "I promise, no problem, you go."

She places her hand on her heart. "Thank you."

Leesa turns around and lays her hand against the security panel to open the gigantic records room behind the secure door. "You know the drill," she says, jamming the thick metal fire door open for me with a rubber stopper.

"Get in, file, leave, shut the door and double-check the red light on the panel to ensure it's locked. Got it." I give her a mock salute, confirming the process.

Leesa checks the time on the wall clock then lifts her purse off her desk. "I gotta go."

"See you tomorrow." I wave goodbye.

"Don't work too late," she replies cheerily, running to the elevator that will take her up one floor to the main exit.

"I won't." I turn on the balls of my feet and enter one of the largest record rooms I've ever been in. It has zero windows, and it's fireproofed within an inch of its life; the Hart family take people's personal details very seriously.

On a mission and with intention tonight, I stride along the alphabetized aisles, making my way to the one marked T. For Kevin Taylor. The man who killed my parents and my sister.

Being this close to the information I've waited to get my hands on since I was a teenager, my heart is racing with anticipation.

My heels ricochet off the concrete flooring, every clatter echoing louder than the next, as if mirroring every beat of my thumping heart.

Clutching the files I brought along, pretending I needed them as an excuse, I tighten my grip and finally approach the aisle I'd been eyeing. Unlike previous weeks, when I could only stand and stare from a distance, tonight I felt brave enough to take the next step and search for what I've been seeking.

Inhaling a deep breath, I summon all the courage I can and take my first step into the narrow space that's lined with hundreds of gray rectangular boxes, each with a white label on the end and black writing outlining each case name, number, and date. Walking slowly, looking left and right, I sound out the letters of the alphabet under my breath as I pass by the archive boxes. "Tab, Tac, Tad, Tae." I continue past the Tak's and Tam's, all the way down, and that's when I find what I'm looking for:

Tay. I take another couple of steps and find a gray box labelled "Kevin Taylor."

I read the words in front of me, then I reread the label, double-checking it's the correct file.

Case Name: The State v. Kevin Taylor
Case Number: 10CR07354
Contents: Pleadings, discovery, depositions, correspondence, exhibits
Date Range: June 2010–Feb 2011
File Reference: File #8416 Taylor
Attorney: Daniel Hart
Confidential: Attorney-Client Privileged

"That's the one." I talk to myself, confirming it is.

To free up my hands, I lay the files I've been holding on the floor.

Adrenaline courses through my body, making everything feel more intense, stress and excitement blending together under the weight of the risk I'm taking. I reach up and slide the box out of the space it's probably not moved from in over a decade and clumsily pull it down off the shelf, catching the heavy box in my arms with a *humph*. This is the moment I've been planning for years and yet I feel so unprepared.

My awareness on high alert, I dart my eyes around the space to check I'm alone, even though I know I am. I hug the box close to my chest and walk toward a table at the end of the aisle.

Quickening my pace, every step closer to uncovering the truth, I cradle the box full of information in my arms as if it's precious gold, which it is to me.

Hands shaking, I place the box gently down on the table

when I reach it and curse at myself when I can't make my trembling fingers work to open the closure tab.

I lay my hands out in front of me before drawing in a deep breath through my nostrils and then out through my mouth to steady me.

"You've got this, Ari," I whisper to steady myself.

I flip the corrugated cardboard lid open and push it back to reveal the paperwork documenting the car crash that killed my family and the man who ran off and left us all to die. The memories I have from that night flash through my brain like a picture flip book, the images animated and slightly hazy in places, recreating what it remembers from that night. Which isn't as clear as it used to be. It's as if my brain has blocked out the finer details of that night but I remember the impact of the crash, the ambulance, the ride to the hospital, the fire department, and the police interviews.

The skin on my scar tugs and tingles in response as if recalling what happened that night too.

Pulling the files within the box out, one after the other, I memorize the order they came out in and go directly to the file marked "Evidence," which I have seen numerous times before because the case is available to the public. But I'm not looking for what I already know, I'm looking for the information I suspect Nathan's father Daniel hid to protect his client.

I'm convinced Kevin Taylor was under the influence of drugs or alcohol the evening he killed my lovely mom, dad, and sister, and I don't think the witness that was called to testify was telling the truth. There is no way there was an oil spill earlier that day, or that the foggy weather conditions made it difficult to see. My father didn't miss the warning signs that night. It wasn't his fault.

There just has to be more to it.

I search the names of the detectives and criminal investigators, mentally taking note that it doesn't correlate with what Julie said. Everyone involved was called forward to testify, so what was she talking about when she said not everyone did?

Something doesn't add up.

Twenty minutes pass by, and frustrated, I plonk myself down on one of the chairs around the table and run my hands through my hair, staring at a piece of paperwork before me which has been redacted.

Now that is new to me, but I can't see what's written on it. Even when I hold it up to the light, the black lines don't give anything away.

A feeling I know all too well creeps in, disappointment overwhelming me, and I think I could cry at how devastated I am that I didn't find anything.

I was convinced there would be something to pin falsifying information, concealing evidence, witness tampering, or anything that would uncover the truth that Nathan's father was corrupt. Maybe that's what's hidden within the redacted letter between Nathan's father and Kevin Taylor, but surely not. This letter looks different and is personally handwritten.

Like a letter between friends almost.

As I look at the files, everything I seem to do only makes me hit a dead end.

Assuming that any shady dealings would be in this file was naive of me.

I feel like such an idiot.

Every piece of information is documented clearly and concisely, as the law dictates, making the records I have read several times before perfect.

Which is just like every other file held within this room.

Nathan and his brothers follow the law to the letter, something I didn't think their father did.

I can't be wrong about that; I just can't be.

But maybe I am.

Maybe I'm wrong about it all.

In case I've missed anything, I slide my phone out of the pocket of my dress pants and photograph the information to study again later, specifically the censored letter.

I hope it's the key to uncovering the truth.

It's not as simple as I thought it would be and I'll keep coming back here until I find what I'm looking for.

Just as I am photographing the last document, a voice from behind me asks, "What are you doing?"

17

ARI

I jump out of my skin, then whip around, instantly feeling hot with guilt, to find Nathan with his hands in his pockets, standing with his legs spread wide and looking at me suspiciously.

That man wears suit pants like they were made for him, which they were, and are made from the finest Italian fabric. But there is something about him in a virgin-white shirt left open at the collar that does something to my insides, turning them to goo every time.

"Did you come looking for me?" I was too engrossed in what I was doing to hear him. He's like a ninja or something.

"You've been missing for over thirty minutes, Arianna."

I grit my teeth together, annoyed at him calling me that. How many times do I have to tell him it's Ari? Only my parents and sister, Riley, called me Arianna.

And I didn't think he would notice I was gone. He was too busy talking to his brothers about fucking Vivienne Cavendish.

God, that makes me feel sick.

"I was beginning to get worried," he says. His voice is full of concern, which is unwanted. The way he walks with purpose toward me has panic weaving its way through my veins, and I gather the files back into a neat pile. Files I shouldn't be accessing. It isn't labelled "Attorney-Client Privileged" on the outside of the box for no reason.

Although I've never understood why it is. If there is nothing to hide, why is it labelled as such? And why is that letter between Nathan's father and Kevin Taylor redacted?

What am I not seeing?

"You don't need to worry about me," I say, turning my back to him, pushing my phone inside my pocket, then discreetly place the case paperwork into the archive box. "I'm fine."

The only person who has ever worried about me was my foster mom, Jean, and after she died when I was twenty-one, I've been looking after myself just fine. I don't need anyone's concern.

His steps grow closer. "What are you doing down here, Arianna?"

I close the lid, lift the box, and hold it against my chest before turning around to face him.

Straightening my shoulders, I hold my head high and walk past him to return the box, his cologne chasing me as I float by. *God, he smells good.* "I was digging out similar cases to help with the Vivienne Cavendish versus Regal Wings case," I lie. "I must have taken down the wrong case number; this isn't the one I wanted."

"Right." His footsteps follow me and just as I replace the box on the shelf, he's right there, arms folded in front of him and leaning against the shelving unit. "You're really good at your job."

I feel my cheeks growing hot. "Thanks." I accept the compliment, feeling guilty that he thinks I'm helpful, and I can't even bring myself to look at him so I bend down to pick the other files I brought with me off the floor, stand to my full height then look around. The nervous tension between us growing by the second.

He's right though, I am good at my job. I take great pride in what I do and genuinely love it. Regardless of any suspicions I might have about his father's dodgy dealings, I am committed to upholding the law and strictly adhering to the rules and regulations of my role.

"You're the best secretary I've ever had," he adds, throwing my conscience sideways.

God, I wish my time here was over and I could stop hiding the reasons I'm really here.

I finally manage to look at him. "Thanks," I say again, my body thick with guilt.

There's this huge space of time that's filled with awkward silence before he asks, "Come to The Connecting Kids Charity Ball with me next week."

That doesn't sound like a question.

"I'm busy," I lie, but I would love to go; that charity is very close to my heart but a ticket costs over one thousand dollars.

He looks shocked by my quick response and asks, "Doing what?"

Making an effigy of your father and setting fire to it. "I have plans," I simply reply. I don't have a single thing to do next Friday night.

"Plans?" He questions my vague responses.

"Yes, plans. Unlike you, I *do* have a life outside of work."

"I doubt that. You've been here working until midnight almost every night."

I scoff at his arrogance. "My world doesn't revolve around you, Nathan."

He tuts, shaking his head. "You're fucking wrong about that, baby."

I roll my eyes at him. "Whatever." I feel snarky. "See you tomorrow. Be sure to lock the door. That's if your head will fit through it, it's that big." I don't manage even one step back up the aisle, because quicker than I can comprehend I'm being pushed against the shelving unit and Nathan's mouth is on mine, taking what he wants, anything I'll give him. The files I was holding on to drop to the floor, scattering paper everywhere.

I wrap my arms around him because I've been longing to touch him again.

My gasps of relief and pleasure get swallowed by him when his hands find my neck and he tilts my chin up, thrusting his tongue into my mouth, as if he's trying to crawl inside my body.

I'm defenseless against his intoxicating kisses that have heat pooling between my legs, my skin flushing with desire as it spreads across my skin.

He presses himself flush against me, and with one hand firmly grasped around my neck, the other explores the contours of my body as we breathe against each other heavily, our lips sealed together in the perfect kiss.

When I pull my hips to meet his, he rubs his hard cock against my stomach, and we both groan into each other's mouths at the same time.

Our tongues mouth fuck each other, teeth clattering, tongues sliding, licking, enjoying every single desperate second, working in perfect harmony.

I tilt my hips to ease the pulsing sensation in my pelvis when Nathan deepens our kiss, which I didn't think was possible, my heart racing faster than a bullet out of a shotgun.

Sliding my hands up over his sculpted back, I run my nails

down the cool fabric, feeling every muscle contract as he groans my name.

"Your smart mouth is my fucking undoing, baby," he mumbles against my lips.

If I'd known that I wouldn't have said anything, or maybe I should have been even more brat-like because the little devil on my shoulder seems to like the way he responds to my impertinence.

"Did you touch yourself the other week?" he asks, panting between our illicit kisses.

"No." My body thinks it belongs to him. I couldn't bring myself to touch myself; it's him I want. I'm more frustrated than a romance novel character left on a cliffhanger without her happy ever after.

What am I thinking? My body does not belong to him, or anyone. It's just a trick of my imagination, that's all it is. The chemistry is not real.

And yet I find myself experiencing this infuriating pull toward him, which disgusts me because I like him more than I should.

He gives my neck a squeeze in appreciation. "Good girl." His lips leave mine, before he peppers kisses over my jaw.

My body responds, feeling about a million degrees hotter, loving the way he calls me his good girl every time I do something he approves of.

"Did you jerk off while thinking about me?" I don't know why I'm asking if he touched himself. I gasp when he licks the shell of my ear.

"You're all I can think about, Arianna."

Was that a yes?

His next confession has me wanting to shed my clothes and

ride his face until I'm chanting his name like a tantric meditation.

He admits, "I can't sleep; eating feels pointless. I don't know what is happening to me." Laying much softer kisses than before over the pulse point of my neck sends shivers across my heated skin, my body humming with happiness.

How long can I keep denying the passion and fire that is burning between us?

"Come with me to the ball," he whispers in my ear, sending tingles down my spine and deep in my core.

"I can't." I want to but I know if I accept his invitation, it will be yet another bad decision of mine.

But I want to say yes. So much.

Temptation is messing with my judgment. And karma is playing a cruel game, laughing at me with its wicked sense of humor, and pulling strings I can't control.

I find every thought I have of wanting him completely sense-less, even when a small part of me believes that there is sense to us. But what is it?

Being surrounded by everything Nathan and him heli-coptering around me all day every day in the office is both intox-icating and tormenting.

My mind tells me to ignore this thing between us, forget him, and move on—which I've been trying to do for weeks, but my heart isn't getting the memo.

There's a thin line between doing what's right and what I can't help but want.

In the same way he's caged me against the shelves, I'm trapped.

Every thought of him, every kiss and exchange feels like betrayal. My family would hate the person I have become, and yet I can't stop.

It's like the universe is playing some cosmic joke, dangling him just out of reach and watching me wrestle with the impossible ache of wanting what I can never truly have.

Or maybe the universe is trying to show me what I can't see.

It's so confusing.

"I have to go," I say. I need to put an end to this.

"I don't want you to go," he declares.

For reasons I don't understand, neither do I, but I must. "Nathaniel." I address him by his full name to get his attention, and he stops doing that crazy thing with his tongue behind my ear that pushes my senses into overdrive, breathing new life into them.

Eyes closed, he rests his forehead against mine, his chest heaving frantically. "You do something to me." His determined eyes snap open and connect with mine. "And there isn't a damn thing you could say to keep me away from you. You make me want to burn down the world for you, protect you, and never let you go. I've never seen myself settling down before, but with you..." He stops himself from continuing. "Fuck..."

Holy shit, does he mean that?

His nostrils flare as if angry with himself that he feels this way about me, and I can't help but think that it must annoy him that I came into his life and changed things for him.

Everyone in the office knows he doesn't date.

As if time stops, my heart slows and I inhale a slow breath when the contrast and power behind his words don't match the soft kiss he places on my lips. The butterflies that are fluttering in my lower belly take on a life of their own, making my stomach feel like it's doing cartwheels.

"I'll think about your invitation to the ball." I finally manage to form words.

His grins as if I just threw him a lifeline. "Thank you, and take your time. It's not a date, Arianna, you'd be coming as my secretary." It feels like he just poured ice down my spine, because for a fleeting minute there I thought he was asking me to go as his date.

I slide sideways out of his hold. "I'll see you tomorrow."

Before I've even taken a full step, his firm hand wraps around my wrist, holding me hostage, and I can't look back because I'll cave if I do and say yes to him, but I want to make him sweat a little longer.

I leave on parting words. "I promise, I'll think about your invitation."

Why am I even entertaining this?

He releases me and when he replies I barely hear it. "Please say yes."

I stay quiet and walk across the scattered paperwork.

This must be what it feels like to be caught between heaven and hell.

I'm stuck between truth and lies.

"Come out for dinner with me tonight?" His words stop me in my tracks, and I turn to face him.

"You want to take me out for dinner?" I ask, poking my chest with my pointer finger, completely baffled.

What's with all the confessions and the want to woo me all of a sudden?

What changed?

I look down at the scattered paperwork. I can't believe I was about to leave it like this. His admission has my head feeling like a cyclone is whirling through it.

There isn't a damn thing you could say to keep me away from you.

This is big.

Big, big.

Huge.

He runs his hand over his scruff, and while his words might sound confident, there's an air of uncertainty in his facial expression when he scratches his beard a bit too hard then glances sideways before looking back at me again. "It's just dinner. Not a date," he confirms.

"Just dinner?"

"Yes, it's getting late. You didn't stop for lunch, Arianna. You need to eat."

Paying attention to me seems to have become his new hobby. Same for me too when it comes to him.

When will we give in to the increasing daily tension that is building between us? Does anyone in the office see or feel it, too? They must, because my heart can't take any more. The rapid increase in my pulse is beating with a force large enough to cause an explosion.

It's a date and he knows it, which intrigues me.

"Okay. Just dinner."

"Jenkins will take you home."

"Perfect." I bend down to pick up the still scattered paperwork all over the floor. "Where are we going?"

"The Orchid Dome."

Crouched down, startled by his reply, I look up to find him watching me. "The Orchid Dome?" Isn't that the place to go to be seen? It's the most upscale restaurant experience in the city.

It's definitely a date.

Nathan runs his tongue along his teeth, knowing I can see right through him. He knows I know this is more than dinner.

"Do you have a problem with my choice of restaurant?" he asks, lifting his jaw slightly higher.

"No," I squeak.

In fact, I'm so excited my stomach's doing a giddy dance. I've never been before. One, because it's way out of my budget, and two, you need to book several months in advance to reserve a table. "Will we get a table?" I ask.

"Of course." He pulls his phone from his back pocket.

Before I've shuffled the papers into a neat pile, which I'll file properly tomorrow, he announces, "Done."

"Just like that?" Oh, to be as powerful as Nathaniel Hart. The puller of strings. Or at least that's certainly how I feel around him. Like he's the puppet master and I'm a marionette, I gladly give in too often to him operating me and wouldn't complain if he used me like a glove puppet... The things that man can do with his fingers.

"Arianna, did you hear me?" I'm drawn out of my memories of our night together.

"Sorry?"

"I said, yes, just like that." His gaze drops to my lips, causing me to touch them and him to add, "I ruined your lipstick."

What I wouldn't give for him to ruin me again.

I toss my morals onto the fire and hear them sizzle in my ears.

"Meet me in the foyer. You have ten minutes to freshen up, Arianna."

"I'll be ready in five," I retort, feeling snarky and standing to my full height. "And I might just like the thought of you ruining my lipstick again." My declaration tumbles out my mouth faster than I can catch it and I gasp, making his mouth lift at the corners.

"I'll keep that in mind, Arianna." Pride fills his chest, and somehow he appears broader as he strides past me.

"Forget I said that."

"Not a chance."

18

NATHAN

"Two of the grilled chicken with salad." I hand my menu to the waiter.

Arianna looks across the table as if amused. "And I will have the champagne mussels, please." The waiter takes her menu.

Oh, so she wants to order herself. Stupid me, of course she would. "That's one grilled chicken with salad and one mussels."

"Yes, sir," the waiter replies.

"And a Manhattan, please, for the lady." That was her drink from the first night we met.

"And a Macallan single malt on the rocks, for the gentleman," she counters, remembering mine from the same evening.

"Yes, ma'am." He bows his head in acknowledgment then leaves.

"Is this where you usually eat?" she asks, breaking eye contact with me to look around at the two-star Michelin restaurant.

"No." I've only been here a handful of times.

"So this isn't just dinner for you?" She raises a perfectly plucked brow.

I rest my forearms on the table and lean closer. "Of course it is. It's just dinner." It's not, it's a date, and she can see right through my invisibility cloak.

"Right." She tucks her lips into her mouth to hide a smile.

"What made you become a legal secretary?" I ask.

"Wow, straight in for the kill, just like that?"

"I want to get to know you better."

"Why?"

"Because we work together every day." I shrug.

"Well." She considers her answer. "I wanted to do a job where I could help make a difference."

"Do you enjoy it?"

Her whole face lights up and I believe her when she says, "I do. I love it, actually."

"So why did you apply for the records job?"

"I told you why."

She did, but I still don't believe her, or she never would have accepted being my secretary so quickly. We work long hours, and the paperwork can be tedious, and yet she's never complained. Not once.

Dedication is one of her strengths. She's also tenacious and determined and everything she does for me makes my job easier. Like a dream come true, she's been sent from an otherworldly planet directly to me.

Switching the focus away from herself and onto one of my cases, she says, "I think if you threaten the pharmaceutical company with negligence, deceptive practices for actively falsifying clinical trials and failure to warn, they'll back down and agree to an out-of-court settlement." And while I hate that she doesn't want to talk about herself, I appreciate her passion for my work.

If she had gone to law school, I know she would have breezed through it, because she's capable of being a lawyer herself. She's so fucking smart and clued in. Caring is a huge part of my job, which Arianna seems to understand.

"I agree." For the next hour Arianna and I eat and talk work and tactics. While it might have been my plan to invite her out for dinner, she seems to have railroaded me, and I still don't know that much about her.

I swirl the last of my ice around my glass then ask her, "Do you have many friends, Arianna?"

"Not many. My best friend is Maeve."

"How did you meet her?"

She tucks a lock of hair behind her ear before she answers, "When I was moved to a foster home. Maeve was assigned to me on my first day at my new school as my buddy and we've been friends ever since. She's like family to me."

"Foster home?" How did I not put the facts together? With no family, foster care is where she would have been placed and that makes me feel unsettled. Volunteering for the foster kids' charity makes sense now too. She wants to give back.

She's kind.

I grew up in a loving family home, with three brothers who may have driven me insane, but while my childhood was noisy and busy, it was wholesome. And I was loved. I still am.

She adds, "After the accident, I was placed in care with a woman named Jean. She was amazing."

"You were well cared for?"

"Yes," she replies with confidence, smiling fondly.

I'm relieved; not everyone in foster care has the same experience.

"Is this twenty questions, Nathan?"

She's got me pegged.

I shrug. "I just want to get to know you better, that's all."

"Okay. Well, here goes." She lists dozens of things, giving me an insight into who she is. "I love *Harry Potter*, Coldplay is my favorite band of all time, but I do like old eighties music, the cheesier the better. My favorite color is navy, because it goes with everything. I'm saving up to buy a house in Nob Hill, which is wishful thinking, but it's a dream of mine. I once fell over and flashed my panties to the entire football team in high school, which was the most embarrassing day of my life. I love watching true crime documentaries. I subscribe to every subscription service known to man and watch everything and anything on all of them when I get the time. My go-to karaoke song is Bonnie Tyler's 'Holding Out for a Hero'. I don't have any children, but I would like a family. The first concert I ever went to was a local band from our school and they were terrible. The last book I read was called *Owen* and it was about a runaway groom who meets an aerobatic pilot. She was a badass and I want to be her when I grow up. I can quote *Friends* by heart. I hate liars. My favorite cocktail is a Manhattan, which you knew already, and I think you might just be the smartest person I have ever met." She sounds out of breath as she says her last word.

Wow.

"You?" she challenges.

I reply, watching her closely, "I'm not a fan of fantasy movies; action is more my thing but I can't remember the last time I watched a movie. Coldplay is one of my all-time favorite bands, and I like old eighties music, the cheesier the better."

That makes her smile wide.

I add, "Navy can't be a favorite color of anyone's because it's like black, it's not a color."

"It is. Like I said, it goes with everything," she counters, sounding lighter.

"I did have a house in Nob Hill once but sold it, and had I known that's where you wanted to live, I would have sold it to you. I once fell over in court and split my pants in front of the jury, which was the most embarrassing day of my life. I like watching true crime documentaries but never get the time to watch them. I don't subscribe to any subscription services. I've never done karaoke."

Her mouth drops open in shock at that fact.

"I don't have any children, and it's not something I've ever considered before. But all my friends have family and recently, I've been thinking about it a lot." I clear my throat, as I have never admitted that to anyone. "The first concert I ever went to was a local band from our school and they were dreadful. The last book I read was called *The Regulation of Healthcare Professionals*."

"Sounds riveting."

"Great bedtime reading," I reply sardonically. "And recently someone named Arianna stepped into my life. She's a badass, even though she doesn't think she is, and all the women in the office want to be her when they grow up," I continue, not stopping when her eyebrows lift in surprise as I go through her list because I memorized everything she told me. "I can quote every law and regulation off by heart. I hate liars. My favorite drink is a Macallan single malt."

"On the rocks."

I nod. "And I think you might just be the smartest person I have ever met." I repeat her verbatim.

"That can't be true." She disagrees with me, shaking her head.

"It's true."

"Thank you." The skin of her cheeks pinken.

"We have lots in common, Arianna."

"We do."

And we are fucking great together in bed and I want to take you home and let you fuck my dick raw.

"We're a great team." I back up how good we are together outside of the bedroom because in the office we are the dream team.

We sit in comfortable silence for a while, as if letting the words sink in.

"We don't make sense," she whispers.

"Do we have to?"

"I don't know anything anymore."

Tell me about it, baby.

She taps the screen of her phone to check the time and gasps. "Wow, it's getting late and we have an early meeting at eight tomorrow."

I raise my hand to get the waiter's attention and ask for the check, annoyed that my time with her tonight is ending.

"I'll have Jenkins drive you home," I inform her.

Outside, I hold open the car door for her. "I'll see you tomorrow, Arianna."

"You're not coming?" Sounding shocked, she stops getting into my car.

"I'll catch a cab back to the office. I have some work to do before tomorrow's consultation."

"You work too hard. You should try and get some sleep, Nathan." Reaching up, she cups my face and part of me wishes she was really mine and she could touch me like that whenever she wanted. "You look tired. Don't work too late, okay?"

I had the best night's sleep when she stayed over at my apartment, which I found odd.

I nod and before she slides into the car, she rises up on her tiptoes and kisses my cheek. "Thank you for dinner." Her lips find the shell of my ear. "Goodnight, Nathan."

Ask me to come home with you.

"See you in the morning, Arianna."

19

NATHAN

"And that's everything you need to know." Vivienne Cavendish flashes me a toothy grin that makes her look every inch a wolf in sheep's clothing.

I throw Arianna, who is sitting next to me, a knowing look, mentally informing her that Vivienne has been lying since the minute she walked into the boardroom.

Arianna gives me a slow deliberate nod, confirming she understands.

We have this intangible connection I can't explain; we don't need words to know what we mean. After last night's dinner, it feels stronger today.

I wish I had kissed her again last night.

Why didn't I?

Idiot.

She's here working for me because she wants to, and she wants to help make a difference. That's what she said last night, and I know she means it.

We value the same things.

I look down at the questions Vivienne has left unanswered

and ask the first one at the top of my list. "You said you told a member of the cabin crew about Henry's allergy just before you boarded the flight?"

"Yes." She threads her fingers together on top of the table.

The slight shift in her demeanor tells me she's hiding something. The shaking of her head that said *no* mismatched her words when she said *yes*, is a dead giveaway that she's lying.

I press her for more information. "And yet, the statements from each of the cabin crew all said the same thing." I read out one of the sections I highlighted before today's meeting. "'Mrs. Cavendish did not inform me or any of the crew of any allergy.' That correct?"

"Not true. I did." Her rapid eye blinking combined with the tapping of her fingers against the tabletop confirms she didn't.

And when I feel a slight tap of Arianna's foot against my ankle, I know it's her way of talking to me without saying anything. Vivienne thinks she has us fooled.

I prod her further. "Isn't it standard practice for passengers to inform the airline of any allergies during the booking process?"

"Not always," she replies defensively.

Another lie.

I ask something that's been bothering me that's not on my notepad. "Was it normal for you to book Henry's flights?"

"Not always."

I suspect it was never.

"Who usually took care of booking Henry's flights and organizing his schedule?"

"Um, his assistant."

"But on this occasion, you did?"

"Yes."

I fire a quick question at her, one I've already asked, but I ask her in a different way. "And this is the only one you ever booked?"

"Yes."

Bingo.

"Sorry, I didn't understand the question to begin with, that's not what I meant. I mean, it was one of the many I booked. I liked being involved with—"

I don't let her finish. Her babbling and overexplaining scream "liar" much louder this time.

I push my seat back, indicating the meeting is over. "I think we have all the information required. You'll hear from us in the next two to five days by letter."

"So, you'll take the case." Vivienne looks like the cat that got the cream, a gigantic smile shaping her lips, and it's not a question; it's a presumption.

"Like I said, we'll be in touch."

Her honeyed reply sounds like it's laced with poison; it's unsettling. "You won't regret this. Thank you, Nathan."

I would regret it, and that's why I will not represent her.

Vivienne pushes her designer purse up over her shoulder and walks to the door at the same time as I do so I can see her out.

"I saw your name on the list for The Connecting Kids Ball," she purrs, the saccharine tone making my skin crawl.

I nod, not confirming or denying my attendance.

"If you don't have a date, would you like to come with me?" she asks, eagerness written all over her face. She twirls a lock of blonde hair around her finger, looking nothing like the heartbroken widow she said she was when she entered the room.

Even the sound of her voice sends chills up my spine. I'd rather eat glass than go out on a date with Vivienne. The night I slept with her, I'd had a bad day in court and lost my case. I wasn't thinking straight.

It was a long time ago but the regret I have still lives on.

I ignore Vivienne's question as Arianna makes her way around the boardroom table.

"I'll see you out, Mrs. Cavendish," Arianna informs Vivienne, surprising me as I'd planned to do that.

Arianna elegantly wafts past, and at the same time Vivienne shamelessly asks me again, "I'm assuming you don't have a date, so what time will you pick me up next Friday?"

"I'm his date." Arianna jumps in, sounding strong, confidence bouncing off her, making my brain glitch.

What?

But also, hell yes.

I school my emotions, hiding my surprise at Arianna's outburst.

"Sorry, Vivienne," I say, not sounding one bit apologetic but smug as fuck. "I already have a date."

Vivienne looks Arianna up and down, flaring her nostrils as if envious that she's not as naturally gorgeous as my enchanting secretary.

"This way, Mrs. Cavendish." Arianna ignores Vivienne's death glare, sounding every bit professional, and she side-eyes me sheepishly before urging Vivienne to follow her to the elevator.

Did Arianna not like the thought of me going to the ball with another woman? Is my little siren jealous? Fuck, I think she might be.

"Have a good day, Vivienne." I wish her well. I hope she gets everything she deserves. A prison sentence, preferably.

"See you at the ball," she replies with a flirty finger wave.

I hope not.

I pull a fake smile then turn my back on her, ending the meeting, and my shoulders drop with relief when she leaves.

Gathering up my notes off the boardroom table, I wait for Arianna to return.

If she's coming to the ball with me, I'll make sure it's a night she never forgets.

"That was a good initial consultation." Her sweet voice, which I've become addicted to, fills the room.

"It was." I straighten up, pushing my shoulders back, and stare at her intensely. Her big beautiful eyes are my undoing. If only she knew how much I crave her and how much I want to take care of her, she might change her mind and let me into her life.

She has no idea the effect she has on me and how much I like a challenge, but she can only resist me for so long, and I guarantee she'll be begging me to take her home after the ball.

I told her she was coming as my secretary, nothing more, but I'm sure she saw through my lie. I'm as transparent as a jellyfish in clear water.

For one night, I can be a gentleman, can't I?

"Let me know your decision about Vivienne and I'll draft a letter." She tidies up the cups and saucers and puts them in a neat pile.

"I'm not taking the case, Arianna." I'd rather chew on a hornet's nest.

Her forehead creases as if she wasn't expecting me to say that. "You're not?" she asks.

"She's lying."

Arianna nods her head in agreement. "I know, I just thought that since you know her and you have history, you know, having slept with—"

"Do not finish that sentence. Whatever you heard my brothers and me talking about, it was a one-time thing and it happened a very long time ago. It's not something I'm proud of. I don't represent liars," I add. "Especially one I suspect murdered her own husband." The fucking moxie of the woman coming in here thinking she could hoodwink me makes me sick to my stomach.

My words halt her in her tracks, and she stops mid-reach to pick up her laptop off the table. "I think she did too," she whispers. "And you're not going to represent her?" she asks, clearly needing me to confirm my stance.

"If you don't know by now how we operate at Hart Law, Arianna, you haven't been paying close enough attention. We represent the good guys."

"Not everyone is good. How can you be so sure?" she fires back.

"After a while you get to know people, work out how they operate, read body language."

"Did you learn that from a book?"

"No. From my father."

She scrunches up her nose, the same way she does every time someone says something she doesn't agree with.

"What did I say that annoyed you, Arianna?"

"Nothing." Clearing her throat, she rubs the end of her nose before lifting her laptop off the table. "I just think that you can't say with complete confidence that every person we represent now or even in the past is, or was, a good guy." Slowly, she moves to the door. "Not every time." Her voice is much smaller now and there's hurt in her eyes, and something else I can't quite work out, which I hate.

She hides her pain well and after learning that she lost her family in a car crash, it has been gnawing away at me. I want to know what happened, but I don't think she'll give up the information. Not easily anyway.

I straighten my spine, confident about who we represent. "Every day, when we were growing up, my father would have me and my brothers recite our key values and code of ethics. It was drummed into us. Everything we do here at Hart Law is by the book and we do everything within our power to uphold my father's mission to provide exceptional legal representation with integrity."

I couldn't have been clearer, but the way she's looking at me makes it seem like she's struggling to process what I said—confused, annoyed, maybe both?

I drive home my point. "I would never, not in a million years, take on a client like Vivienne Cavendish. If my father was standing in this room his decision would be the same as mine."

"So what you're saying is that you're a stand-up guy, as is your father?"

It surprises me that having worked here for some time she can't see that.

I reply, "Absolutely. I believe in honesty. I'm dedicated to the justice system and upholding my father's high ethical standards." And I will die on that hill.

"Did your father retire?" she asks, raising a perfectly plucked brow.

"Sort of."

"What does that mean?" She taps her fingers against her lip, her voice thick with curiousness.

"That's a story for another day." I move on, preferring not to talk about my father; it's too painful. "In the meantime, I have two things I need you to do for me."

"Name them."

"Schedule lunch with Deputy Chief Philip Robbins. Tell

him it's to discuss information I may have on a suspected homicide."

"Vivienne?"

"You learn fast."

"But you don't have any evidence that she was involved with the death of her husband."

"That's not my job to investigate, Arianna, but the police department might just need a nudge in the right direction."

She grants me a giant smile and I about melt on the spot. She's breathtaking and I think she likes that I'm a man of my word.

"And what's the second thing you need me to do?" she asks.

I take a step closer to her, bow my head, and move my lips to her ear to whisper in it. "Buy a dress for the ball." Preferably one that's easily removed. "And put it through expenses. I'll pick you up at seven next Friday."

She angles her head, her eyes locking with mine. "I can pay for my own dress, Nathan."

"It's for work. It's an expense. Don't argue with me." It's not for work, it's all for me, because I'm a selfish and devious bastard when it comes to her.

"Well, then if it's for work, I'll accept your offer. I'll buy the most expensive dress I can find." She inches back a bit and studies my face. "I'll be ready at seven next Friday."

Her continual nettlesome jabs make a smile pull at my lips. Verbally sparring has become the thing we do best. Well, sex together is something we'd win Olympic gold at, but linguistic acrobatics we'd win silver for sure, no doubt about it.

"Buy the most expensive shoes you can find too," I counter. "You'll be the most captivating woman in the room." And everyone will know she's with me.

Mine.

I might just be buying her a dress, but I would buy her the whole fucking boutique if it meant I got to see her delectable curves wrapped in the finest material money can buy and show her off to the world.

When they see us together, they'll know who she is to me.

Because I'm the boss, and I can change the rules anytime I want.

My decision.

I'm tired of fighting how I feel, but I'll spin the white lie for a little longer that she's attending with me as my secretary, when in fact it couldn't be further from the truth.

I want her.

All of her.

20

ARI

I scrub my hands down my face as the shower washes away the remnants of my day down the drain. Pushing my fingertips through my soaked locks, I give my scalp an extra massage to ease the lingering tension.

I'm convinced my life is one big test. Working for Hart Law being the most difficult one yet. I'm being pushed to the outer limits in ways I never expected, as if the world is playing a game of Push Me Pull You.

I can't take any more and I have the worst case of emotional whiplash.

Confusion? Tick.

Intense, unstable thoughts about Nathan? Tick.

Like him one minute? Tick.

Annoyed with him the next? Tick.

Feelings of grief for what and who I lost? Tick.

That never subsides.

Euphoric one minute for managing to get a job at the firm that failed my family? Tick.

Anxious the next minute for managing to get a job at the firm that failed my family to unearth the facts? Tick.

I must have had a lapse in serious judgment when I blurted out that I was going to the ball with Nathan earlier today.

No, it wasn't, it was jealousy. Stop lying to yourself.

But it was more than that.

Like the flick of a switch, something changed today for me in that boardroom.

Watching Nathan, listening to him deliver his cleverly crafted questions for Vivienne, it was like watching an artist paint his finest work. He knows what he's doing; he's analytical and creative in searching for the truth.

Something the entire team at Hart Law maintains. It's weaved into every discussion, every case, proving everything I ever thought I knew about them wrong.

Since I started my new role, little by little each day, I've seen with my own eyes how ethical the business is.

Earlier, before Vivienne arrived, Nathan asked me to organize an internal audit, something they do sporadically throughout the year without warning, to check compliance. In over twenty years, they've never failed.

Which means Nathan's father is good.

Or good at hiding lies.

Either way, it's sort of taken me by surprise, because it's not what I was expecting.

The business is diligent.

And Nathan is not just good, but great. Honest.

He defends good people and weeds out the bad, like he did with Vivienne today.

Knowing she was lying, Nathan didn't accept her as a client. He's not after fame, glory or money like I thought he was. He takes on clients who are the best fit because he has a moral compass and prides himself on the strong ethics of the business.

Something he said his father engrained into him.

All signs lead to good, not wicked.

It's a paradox and I'm so tired of feeling conflicted. Maybe it's me who needs to switch up my perspective.

Maybe I'm the one who is wrong.

Maybe there is nothing to find. Either that or I'm looking in the wrong place.

Who knows?

I turn up the heat of the water and let the shower soothe and relax my muscles, cleansing my body and mind from any more doubt-filled thoughts.

For now, I'll buy the dress and the shoes.

And while I'm at it, I'll buy a purse that matches.

I'll hit his credit card hard and attend the ball with Nathan.

As his secretary.

Which almost feels impossible when he does something to me too. His words from the other night bounce around my brain like popcorn kernels in a microwave on the highest setting.

Could we be more?

I think I want that.

Like my mom always used to say, "It's okay to want what you want."

I want him.

The guilt loops endlessly in my mind, like a rollercoaster I can't get off. This journey that led me to Nathan has been beautifully disastrous and unpredictable.

Laying my palms flat against the tiles, I let the water run over my skin and release a large breath of acceptance that I want to be more than just his secretary.

I step into the decision and let it settle in my bones. It's time to shake the hand of unpredictability.

Hello, courage. I think the roads are about to get even more bumpy.

It's Saturday, and instead of walking along the beach like I hoped, I'm standing in an exclusive fashion boutique.

"I don't think I like this one either," I call out to Joseph, who was determined to come with me, along with my best friend, Maeve, to pick a dress for the ball.

"Show us." Maeve encourages me to step out of the changing room.

I turn around awkwardly and hike the trailing dress up to one side then slide back the curtain to reveal the bright teal dress that's much too long for me.

"Nope." Joseph shoos me back into the changing room. "That's drowning you." He takes a sip of champagne that was offered to us when we arrived.

Maeve tilts her head to the side; confusion lines appear across her forehead. "Try on the gold." She points to the one hanging up.

Who knew dress shopping would be so difficult.

"I'm not sure I like the back on the gold one." The plunging cowl back won't hide my scar.

"Kill my curiosity, go on." Maeve makes praying hands, pleading with me, giving me huge puppy dog eyes.

"Okay." I give in and close the curtain again, annoyed that after trying on over a dozen dresses, I don't even have a maybe. They've all been a no so far. "I won't be able to wear a bra with it." I point out the obvious.

"They do those stick-on bras. Let me ask the assistant," Joseph says, eagerly willing to help. "Size?" he asks, and I give him my cup size as I struggle to get out of yet another dress and rehang it, then take my bra off.

"I'm not sure gold is my color." With my hands on my hips, I stare at it. As stunning as it is, I really wanted to wear a dark colored dress, not one that looks like sunshine.

"Here you go, sweetie." Joseph pushes his hand through the small gap in the curtain and hands me a delicate-looking stick-on bra that's slightly padded in a natural color that might actually work.

"Thank you." I take the bra out of his wiggling hand and laugh at him. Joseph is a ball of energy every single second of every day and he's a breath of fresh air in the office.

Even after I leave Hart Law, I hope we remain friends, but he may not want to if I expose my findings.

Not that I've found anything.

I spoke to Julie, my contact at *The Golden Telegraph*, again via email last night and she said she finally has some concrete evidence coming her way and would send it to me once she had it in her hands. She wasn't sure how long it would take, it could be days, weeks or months, but she'd found something, and I've been waiting for years already so another few months won't matter.

Whatever it is, I hope it's enough to finally put an end to the torment I've been feeling since I was old enough to investigate the case myself but have only been able to get so far.

If I'm not careful I'm going to drive myself stupid. My obsession is becoming just that: obsessive. I push the thoughts of my family aside so I can focus on the task at hand... finding a dress.

"Why the hell did I say I would be his date?" I ask out loud, knowing full well it was because the thought of Nathan with another woman curdled my blood.

Joseph replies, "Because Vivienne Cavendish is vile and we don't want her near Mr. Crankypants. He deserves someone much less..."

Maeve jumps in. "Gold digger and murdery."

We all burst out laughing. It seems like everyone knows what Vivienne is like.

"Have you read the statement his family released? They despise her and I swear she killed her husband on that flight." Maeve says what everyone is thinking.

Confidentiality is king in the office; Joseph and I haven't spoken about Vivienne since she left the other day.

Joseph says with confidence, "Karma will get her."

"Amen to that," I agree. It's what I'm hoping for; justice for my family.

Joseph informed me that Nathan's parents are attending the ball, which means I'll finally come face-to-face with his father.

I inhale a deep breath. I might need a whiskey, or maybe even a distillery, to prepare me for that.

Sticking the clear self-adhesive wings of the bra to the side of one boob and then the other, I push the girls up to give them some much-needed cleavage. "This bra is great." I check the sides, then my back, which is completely exposed and will work with the deep cowl back, then jump up and down to check how robust the bra is. "It's even jiggle proof."

"Great, now enough stalling and put the dress on." Maeve urges me to move quicker.

I don't blame her for being annoyed. I thought we'd be in and out of the dress shop within twenty minutes, but two hours later, we are still here.

I slip the golden ankle-length evening gown off the clothes hanger, step into the satin, and slide it up my body. Wiggling it up over my hips, I slip my arms through the holes to place the elegant straps on my shoulders and do up the concealed zipper under my armpit. I catch a glimpse of the draping cowl back in the mirror in front of me, reflecting in another behind me, and I feel a little zing of excitement.

I love it.

Stepping into a pair of gold-colored barely there bow-back high heels the assistant gave me to try on with the dresses and to boost my height, I smile at how utterly perfect they match the gold of the dress and buckle up the thin ankle straps.

"This is the one," I say excitedly, almost squealing when I'm ready. "Look." I push the curtain back quickly, causing it to swish back and forth, and reveal the decadent dress.

"Wow." Joseph clasps his hands to his heart. "You look stunning."

"Gorgeous." Maeve beams, stands up, and walks to me. "Turn around."

I do what she asks, showing them the back that's much lower than I would usually pick, and peek back at them over my shoulder, my face feeling sore from smiling. "It's perfect." Then a little self-doubt kicks in, and I ask Maeve, "Can you see my scar? Is it too much?"

Maeve turns me around then grabs the tops of my shoulders and looks right at me, as if she's staring directly into my darkness I feel sometimes. "Your scar is part of what makes you you.

Embrace it." She releases me from her hold, and I face the giant mirror on the wall at the far end of the changing rooms.

"I feel so glamourous." I bounce my shoulders up and down with glee, feeling giddy.

"It elongates you," Joseph says before finishing his last sip of champagne. "Your tan skin makes you look like you're glowing and your dark hair oozes sexy glam. Everything, is just"—he chef's kisses his fingers—"perfection."

"It screams sophistication," Maeve adds. "Now can we please go get something to eat? I'm starving. And I need to pee." She dashes off in the direction of the restroom.

Joseph's face appears over my shoulder and he stares at my reflection in the mirror, admiring my outfit. "You're going to knock his socks off."

"I don't think so." I can't stop looking at the dress. It's so pretty.

"Oh, I've seen the way he looks at you. And since you arrived, he's been nice to me, and less cranky. And even when he is, you still manage to navigate his moods. You deserve this dress." Joseph catches my eye in the mirror.

"He's not so bad once you get to know him," I say, defending him. He's a man with many layers but when it's just me and him, he's different.

You do something to me.

When he made that confession along with struggling to eat and sleep because of me, I knew he was being serious. Nathan is careful with his words and his feelings, which I'm handling with care, but I'm not sure I am equipped to deal with them when I don't even understand my own feelings for him. Although compartmentalizing and separating him from his father, as well as him from the business, is helping.

When it's just us, it's exactly that, just us, and nothing else matters in those moments. Part of me wishes that I could forget about seeking the truth while the other is determined to keep on looking.

I feel so conflicted, and at this point I don't know what side of the fence I'm sitting on.

His words replay in my mind like looped CCTV footage. *There isn't a damn thing you could say to keep me away from you. You make me want to burn down the world for you, protect you, and never let you go. I've never seen myself settling down before...*

Which has me reconsidering my next move.

Should I halt digging any deeper into my family's deaths and pursue things with Nathan or forget about him completely?

Forgetting him isn't an option. He's already made a place inside my brain and my heart for himself.

I want him to burn down the world for me, but settling down with him? Was he serious?

What if I accept that what happened to my family was an accident and that there was nothing more to it?

What if their deaths were all meant to lead me to Nathan?

A grand plan or something equally universal.

My mind and body continue this inner fight with one another. I love my job at Hart Law, which I also can't understand. It's become more than just a mission for me; I'm helping to change lives and help people. It's a position I would love to stay in.

Nathan, his brothers, and everyone at Hart Law are cleaner than a virgin-white tablecloth.

So why can't I let the unsettling feeling I have in my gut rest?

It's actually beginning to annoy me now.

Joseph breaks me out of my muddled thoughts. "And if this dress doesn't make him fall in love with you, I will. In fact, I might be a little bit in love with you already."

"Don't tell your boyfriend that." I snort, lifting the ankle-skimming silk upward. "I'm taking the shoes too." I show them off. They're the most beautiful shoes I have ever owned, and I have no idea how much they are because none of the items in this shop that Joseph insisted we come to has a price tag.

"Take the shoes and let's find you a purse to match." Joseph pulls a platinum credit card out of his pocket and waves it at me. "It's all on Nathan." He winks.

"I feel like a million dollars."

"Nathan's golden girl." He narrows his eyes, as if deep in thought. "It looks like that gold dress from *How to Lose a Guy in 10 Days*, only you wear it better."

"*How to Lose a Guy in 10 Days*?" I scoff.

Little does he know how accurate that is... How many more days will I be at Hart Law?

The unfortunate truth is that I want more days, more nights, every night with Nathan.

My decision is made. I'm going to stop digging for things that might bring me more pain and put my own investigation on hold to see how things pan out between us.

For now.

Until such a time, and when I'm ready to pick up my investigation again, I'm praying Nathan doesn't find out my secret and my real reason for me switching my job to bring to light the truth behind the car crash.

Because if he ever finds out my true reason for being there, it will kill him and it will make him question everything about me and how trustworthy I am.

He's a loyal man, and my reasons for working for him are in no way loyal and that's why I need to stop my search for the truth. I'm not giving up, I'm just doing things on my own terms.

And I know I will never be able to give myself to him fully, so for now, he'll have to accept whatever I offer.

I mean, it's not like we have a future together.

I've never seen myself settling down before, but with you...

I knew he meant he could see himself doing that with me, and that one sentence tugged at my heart and hurt so bad because a little part of me can see glimmers of that too.

Reality is, we have no future together because since our first encounter, I've never been honest.

"Ready to go?" Joseph asks brightly.

"As ready as I'll ever be."

Ready for anything life throws my way.

Yet another weekend spent working all of it; it's now Monday and I feel like I could go back to my bed for several hours. But I can't do that as I have upcoming cases to prepare for.

"You need to relax." Arianna steps into my office as I slam the lid of my laptop shut.

"What I need is for Hargreaves Pharmaceuticals to admit they had manufacturing errors that led to the contamination of their medication." I drag my hands down my face.

"There's more chance of you going on vacation to Mars. C'mon, let's go."

"Where are we going?" Alert now, I sit up straighter.

"You need something to help you chill out, Nathan."

"I need to work." I can't leave.

"Which you can do later, but first I want to take you somewhere. You don't need your jacket." She exits my office and before I'm on my feet she's telling Joseph to take messages if someone calls and not to transfer any to my cell.

"I'm waiting for Franklin Edwards to call me."

"He can wait." Arianna picks up her desk phone to make a call. "Hey, Jenkins, could you get the car ready, please?" She waits for his reply. "Great. Be down in five." Replacing the handset, she waves to Joseph. "We'll be back soon."

"Soon? How soon is soon?" I can't afford to take any time off today.

"A couple of hours. Maximum."

"Two hours?" That's a long time out of my working day.

"Stop questioning me. Just trust me."

Standing on the other side of her desk, I rest my hands on my hips, eye the ceiling and curse under my breath. Arianna has been sent to me from the big man above to test my patience, I'm sure of it.

"Then I can come back to the office?" I ask, like the fucking pussy I am, because I can never say no to her and part of me is curious as to what she has planned.

"Yes." She winks, fucking winks at me.

How can I refuse? She's irresistible.

* * *

"This is your plan?" I push my sunglasses up my nose.

"Yes, a walk on the beach will help you destress and unwind."

"I'm not making sandcastles."

"Neither am I. What we are going to do though"—she pulls two bottles of water out of the back of the limo and hands them to Jenkins—"is walk, chill, and talk. But not about work. Cell phone." Laying the palm of her hand out flat, she does a gimmie gesture with her fingers.

"I'm not giving you my cell."

"Give it to Jenkins then. Here's mine." She passes her cell to

Jenkins. "We're having a digital detox."

"I'm never without my phone."

"And that's half your problem, Nathan." Head tilted to the side in challenge, she smiles with satisfaction as I hand Jenkins my cell. "You have too many clothes on."

I raise my eyebrows, surprised by her admission. Judging by the way her lips curve up, it's clear what I'm amused at.

"Shoes and socks off, and roll up your pants," she clarifies, pointing to my feet.

"What?"

"Just do it, Nathan. We're going to dip our toes in the ocean."

"I'm not doing that in the middle of the day." Who the fuck has time for this bullshit?

"Yes. You. Are." Before I can argue, she steps toward me then does something most unexpected. She undoes my tie in the same way she did the first night we had sex, only this time she's not sucking my tongue into her mouth.

Pity.

It's as if someone's punched all the air out of my lungs; being this close to her makes me want to kiss her.

"Much better," she says, removing my tie completely then unbuttoning the top two buttons of my dress shirt.

I gulp, remembering everything we did on that first night, feeling hotter than before under the Californian sun.

She bends and slips her shoes off her feet. "I'm glad I didn't wear silk stockings today."

So am I. My mind wanders off, trying to work out what color panties she has on under her pale pink dress today.

White, I hope.

"Thanks, Jenkins." Arianna takes a bottle of water from him, replacing it with her heels and my tie. "Roll your pants up and grab your water." She breezes past me and in the blink of an eye she's walking down over the golden sand toward the shoreline. "Just go with the flow, Nathan," she shouts, not looking back.

"Sir?" Jenkins breaks my mesmerized ogling at the woman who is sliding into my every thought and my heart more and more as the weeks go by. 'Cause she's fucking sneaky like that.

"She's not going to back down on this, is she?" I ask him quietly.

"I would suggest you 'go with the flow,' sir."

This is a conspiracy, I'm sure of it.

Exasperated, I take my shoes then my socks off and roll my pants up, before taking my water from Jenkins and running down the beach to catch up with Arianna.

That's right, I'm fucking chasing after her, at two o'clock on a Monday afternoon, when what I should be doing is working.

What the hell is she doing to me?

I feel like I'm playing hooky.

"So what do we do now?" I ask, almost out of breath. I shove my bottle of water into my pocket so I can free my hands and roll up the sleeves of my shirt.

"We walk."

"That's it?"

"Yes, Nathan, it's called enjoying the view, taking a breather, having a break."

I look out over the ocean. "Were you sent from hell to annoy me?"

"Nope, I was sent to you to show you that there is more to life than working."

There's a lot of truth in that.

In silence we stroll up the long stretch of sand, and I enjoy watching Arianna dipping her toes into the water and rubbing the sand between her perfectly manicured toes.

She loves the beach.

"Do you do this often?" I already feel less tense. She was right; this is exactly what I needed today.

"At least twice a week. We have some of the best beaches in the world right on our doorstep. Are you telling me you don't come down here at the weekends?" She motions to the ocean and the crashing waves that make the sand fizz along the shore.

"Never."

"Well, that needs to change. You need to add more down time into your crazy schedule."

I need to add her into my schedule, and the ball can't come quick enough.

"From now on, I'm going to block out time for relaxation into your calendar," she declares confidently.

"I play tennis on Saturday." Isn't that enough?

"That's an adrenaline rushing activity. What you need is something to help you decompress and sleep better."

She must have overheard me complaining to my mom on the phone earlier that I didn't sleep well again last night.

"Okay. Do it," I agree.

"Great." Her smile has an air of mischief about it.

What the hell am I letting myself in for?

"Besides walking the beach, do you have any hobbies?" I ask. Having spent dinner with her the other evening, I want to unpeel even more layers to her life.

"When I was younger, I was a gymnast and I was great at Beam, and while I can't do it anymore, I still try to go to the gym a few times a week. I'm not into watching sports, but when the Olympics are on, I watch it all."

Interesting.

She adds, "I love watching fantasy movies and reading romance novels. Romantasy is my favorite."

"Romantasy, what's that?"

"Romance and fantasy mixed together."

"Do they have a happy ending?" I ask, intrigued by her love of romance novels.

"The ones I read do, yeah."

"Do you believe in happy ever afters?"

"I believe we all deserve one, only some of us don't believe we are worthy or that we will ever find our one true love." She stops walking, takes a sip of her water and looks out across the horizon to watch the handful of surfers riding the waves.

"Do you think you deserve love, Nathan?" Her voice is full of wonder.

"I didn't think so until recently." That's the truth.

"What changed?" she asks, not looking my way.

"Someone came into my life and made me question everything." It's crazy and it sort of annoys me. It all happened a bit fast and hit me without warning.

"Is she special?"

"Very."

"Do I know her?" she fishes.

"Extremely well."

"Is she staff?"

"Yes."

"Pity, she could have been your one chance at playing out the perfect office romance. However, if you really meant what you said about burning down the world for her, are you also burning your self-inflicted law around not dating staff?"

"I make the rules, Arianna, and I burned it, it's gone. I don't think that way anymore." Not since her. I mentally torched it for her. Only her.

"Really?"

"Yeah." I give her a little head space.

Eventually she says, "She might need some time to think

about his offer of never letting her go, because it all sounded a bit overwhelming."

"I'm an all or nothing guy, Arianna." I love the way her name rolls off the tip of my tongue, and I love saying it. "And what are you going to do, make him sweat first while you consider what he said? Although, it doesn't have to be anything serious, or overwhelming. It could just be a bit of fun?" I backtrack on my loose tongue from the records room. What the hell was I thinking? Clearly, I wasn't. But I feel myself smiling, my heart blooming in my chest. I knew she was playing with me and I know she wants me as much as I want her. But if she needs time, that I can give her. I've been waiting my whole life for someone special like her.

She scares the shit out of me, but at the same time, I see myself with her.

Something I never saw coming.

"I might have been drunk when I said those things." My cover-up is terrible.

"Sure you were." She rolls her eyes at my lie.

And there is no one else I would leave work midafternoon to walk on the beach with.

She's changing me, giving me a different perspective on my life, and I like it.

I clear my throat, feeling a million degrees hotter than I was, and change the subject. "Did you get a dress for the ball?"

"It's gold." She sighs, sounding blissed out. "It's beautiful."

She's beautiful. "I can't wait to see you in it."

"Well, if the rules about not dating staff no longer apply, you might just see me out of it."

Fuck me to hell.

"But first, we have to get back to work. I have some appointments to make for you." She's already five steps ahead of me and strolling back up the hot golden sand toward the car.

"What kind of appointments?" I already hate myself for allowing her to book *relaxing* shit for me to do, but I follow her anyway.

"You'll see."

23

ARI

Relaxing appointments?

No chance, baby.

This is my opportunity to have some fun with Nathan before giving him what he really needs... which is some guidance on how to chill out, something he struggles with.

I overheard him on the phone to his mom earlier today where he was complaining, yet again, about another night of terrible sleep. His brain is permanently firing on all cylinders, with no off switch.

I like him. No. That's an understatement; I *really* like him, and I worry about his well-being. He needs to slow down or he's going to work himself to death.

Deciding to be courageous while I was in the shower the other night wasn't just about going to the ball with him or admitting to myself that if I pursue things with him I would have to put my plans on hold, it was more about stepping into the unknown with someone I barely know, someone I thought I had all figured out but didn't know even half of his story. I still don't.

My new mission is to uncover everything about him.

Beneath the polished power suits he wears like an exoskeleton lies the man I see every day when he's with clients, in meetings, and court—gentle yet strong, patient but relentless, and kind. He fights to right the wrongs.

To truly know him, the first thing I need to do is strip away the layers that shield him from the world. He may hate me for what I have planned though, but it's a risk I'm willing to take.

Well, hell, when he finds out who I am eventually he will hate me anyway.

So, right now, I have nothing to lose.

Just my job, which I need, but I know how busy he is and he needs me, which he'll never admit.

He won't fire me. I know what he wants from me; he's made that more than clear. He wants *me*, which practically makes me untouchable.

To me, before I knew him, he was untouchable.

Then he was my boss.

Now he's so much more.

My motivation changed, my thoughts reshaped what I thought I knew, and now that makes me want to help him find more balance.

Help him see there is more to life than his job.

If I show him how much I want to help him, maybe we can both stop being so guarded. As long as I don't blow us up before we even get started.

Which is just as well that's not going to happen because I have a new plan.

And it's not about Hart Law.

It's all about him. Only him.

And me.

Together.

But I won't tell him that.

If fun is how he spun his twist on the truth, then it's fun I can do.

And we can keep lying to each other for a little bit longer.

24

NATHAN

I walk out of my private penthouse elevator and toward my limousine. "Good morning, Jenkins."

"Good morning, Mr. Hart." He opens the door; I climb in and get settled before pulling out my work bag.

I roll my shoulders to release the tension. This is the way I begin every day and I know I have exactly one hour to prepare for the day ahead.

I enjoyed Arianna's surprise walk on the beach yesterday, but what surprised me even more was when she told me that she was seriously thinking about *us*, which made me feel more settled than the beach walk did.

Part of me wants her to say yes to going all in and the other part of me is fucking petrified. Our dinner date was incredible, and I want more of those, more nights, days, every millisecond in between.

Fuck fun, I want it all.

Twenty minutes later the car stops, Jenkins jumps out, and the next thing I know he's opening my door to let me out.

I lean forward and look out of the opened door, not familiar with my surroundings.

"Where are we?" I ask, puzzled as to why we are sitting outside what looks like a dance studio.

"Your first appointment of the day, sir."

I pull out my phone and check my online schedule to discover a blocked-out chunk of time and all it says is *Private Appointment*.

"Ms. Donovan is waiting inside, sir."

I curse under my breath and step onto the sidewalk.

"What is this place?" I mutter to myself, squinting my gaze to protect my eyes from the dazzling sun and surveying the building that looks like a giant glass box.

What the hell has Arianna got planned for me?

"See you in an hour, sir." He closes the car door behind me as I walk up to the entrance then enter the building.

"Morning, Nathan." Arianna skips toward me, sounding chirpy, wearing yoga gear. "How are you this morning?" she asks.

"I was fine until five minutes ago. What am I doing here?" My voice is gruff and impatient.

"Yoga."

"Yoga?" I'm not doing yoga.

"Yes. Good for your heart, increases your flexibility, reduces blood pressure, helps you sleep better, and reduces stress." She claps her hands together, delight radiating out of her.

Is she joking? I don't have time for this Zen shit first thing in the morning.

"Go." She thrusts a gym bag into my arms, which I'm assuming is full of gym clothes. I hope none of it fits so I can get the fuck out of here.

"Changing rooms are in there." Grabbing my hand, she leads me to them.

"Arianna, I have a closing statement to prepare." I'm not doing this.

"You don't. Court was cancelled until late next week. In," she urges, pushing open the door. "No excuses."

"Arianna," I grit through my teeth.

"You said to book things that will help you relax. This is one of them. It'll be fun." Spinning around, she walks away with a light bounce in her step. "See you in there. Two minutes." Her voice is full of cheer. Then she's gone.

What the fuck is happening right now?

"Hey, man, class is about to start." A broad hipster-looking guy flies out of the changing room and disappears down the hall in the same direction Arianna did.

"Fucking man bun," I mutter and consider my options. "Fuck it." If yoga will help to promote a better sleeping pattern for me, then I suppose I could give it a try.

Within minutes I'm changed and in my new gym clothes, which sadly fit. Surprisingly, the shorts are much comfier than my tennis shorts and I quite like them.

I enter the room and I'm hit with three things all at once.

People. Lots of them.

Arianna. Who looks fuckable in those pink yoga pants.

And goats. Dozens of the hairy fuckers.

"I already registered you with the instructor," Arianna informs me as I try to pick my jaw up from the floor.

"Goats," is the only word I form.

"It's goat yoga."

"Goat yoga?" What the fuck is that?

This is not what I was thinking when I asked her to help me

find ways to relax. I feel tenser than a rubber band about to snap.

Stretching her arms out as if embracing the moment, she replies, "The goats improve mood and connect you to nature. It's fun."

"Fun?" My idea of fun was more along the lines of stripping Arianna naked then have her coming all over my tongue.

"Yes, fun. Lots of it."

A cheerful-looking woman at the front of class beckons me to her. "Mr. Hart, I saved you a spot up front."

I bet she fucking has. A tugging sensation pulls at my shorts and when I look down, I discover a goat gnawing at the hem of my new shorts.

"He likes you," Arianna says as the goat proceeds to shit on the floor.

Arianna sucks her lips into her mouth, and I can tell she's sensing how uncomfortable I am and loving every fucking minute of this.

"You're with me." The instructor appears and ushers me away. Drags me, more like.

"Have *fun*." Arianna gives me a finger wave, opening the door as if she's leaving. "See you soon." Where the hell is she going?

"You'll pay for this." I look back over my shoulder.

"Relax, Nathan."

And then she's gone.

What the hell was I thinking asking her to book ways to help me relax?

I think I hired a mistress of mischief, not a secretary.

* * *

ELI

goat emoji *poop emoji*

ME

Mature of you.

COLE

laughing emoji

MAX

If you don't marry Arianna, I will. Fucking epic.

* * *

MOM

goat emoji *poop emoji*

ME

Not you too.

MOM

I wish I had been there to see your face.

25

NATHAN

I walk out of the elevator and toward my awaiting limousine, narrowing my eyes suspiciously. "Good morning, Jenkins."

Although the surprising spring in my step I feel is justified because it's another day closer to the ball on Friday and I'm already wishing it was the big night because I want to spend more time with Arianna outside of work.

"Good morning, Mr. Hart." He opens the door and I climb in.

I pull my laptop out of my work bag, relieved that there will be no goat yoga today.

What the hell was Arianna thinking? My new shorts were gnawed to death by one of the goats that took a liking to me and stood on my back the entire time I did something called a cat-cow pose. When it screamed in my ear I almost shitted myself. Just like it did. All over my back.

Never again.

Although I did sleep better last night. Seven full hours of undisturbed sleep and I feel like a new man.

Just like yesterday, the car stops earlier than planned and Jenkins is opening my door before I can blink.

Is this fucking Groundhog Day?

"Where are we?" I ask tentatively, looking at the sign above the door we are sitting outside of, trying to figure out what the hell she has planned for me today.

"The Singing Bowl, sir."

"Do you know what's waiting inside for me today?"

"I'm afraid I don't, sir, no." His lips twitch.

Yes, he does.

"Ms. Donovan is—"

"Inside, yes, I figured." I walk up to the entrance and step inside and the same as yesterday, Arianna is waiting for me but today she's wearing one of her work dresses.

"Don't tell me, you're not staying?" I ask dryly.

"How did you guess?"

"What do you have planned for me today?"

"Laughter therapy."

This is bullshit. "I—"

I get railroaded, blindsided more like, by a jolly guy who is as wide as he is tall. "Fantastic. You're here, Mr. Hart. It's wonderful to meet you. I'm Rusty and you'll be with me today. This way." He leads me by my arm, clutching me tight, as if trying to keep me in place from fear I might run away. Which I want to do.

Rusty continues. "Now, laughter therapy is..."

I don't hear anything he says because I'm too busy staring at Arianna over my shoulder and throwing ninja stars at her. Not real ones, though in my head they are.

"See you in forty minutes." She winks then blows me a kiss as I disappear round the corner with Mr. Chuckles.

Fuck my life.

* * *

MOM

Laughter therapy? *laughing emoji* What next?

ME

Hell knows.

MOM

I like her. A lot.

I'm sure she does.

Not that I would ever admit it to anyone, but so do I.

26

NATHAN

"Anything evil planned for me this morning?" I ask. My question drips with boredom as I stride past Arianna's desk.

I do a shit job at hiding my intrigue, because yesterday's laughter therapy was the best thing I have done for a very long time. All day I felt lighter, uplifted even.

It's annoying as hell that she knows what I need.

"I made you an appointment for this afternoon," she replies, and I come to a halt. Turning on my heels, I make my way back to her desk.

She looks up at me with those big innocent eyes of hers. "You are having colonic hydrotherapy this afternoon." Her reply comes out easily and with a face as straight as an arrow.

"This is bullshit."

"No, it's to get rid of all the shit. Good for cleansing, improving your immune system..."

"Arianna," I warn as her face breaks into a grin.

"I'm joking. I booked a massage for you."

"With a sumo wrestler?"

"It's as if you're in my head, Nathan."

I lean forward. "You are screwing with the wrong man."

She drops her voice to an almost inaudible tone. "That so? What will you do to punish me? Spank me again?"

My cock springs to life, thickening in my boxers. "Is that a request, baby?"

"Might be." She sounds breathless as she pushes her chair away, leaving me standing with my cock at full mast.

I swear to fuck she exaggerates wiggling her ass for me as she makes her way down the corridor.

"I have paperwork for you to file," I shout after her.

"I'll do it when I'm ready."

Flirty firecracker.

27

NATHAN

Goat yoga, laughter therapy, and thankfully the massage with a sumo wrestler was a joke. Instead an actual masseuse appeared in the office and proceeded to pummel all the knots in my neck and shoulders away.

It was exactly what I needed.

It's finally Friday and the evening of the ball. Twenty minutes earlier than arranged, I rap my knuckles against Arianna's front door.

For days she's been fucking with me, I know she has.

I hate admitting it, but for the first time in forever, my muscles don't feel so tense and I almost feel... relaxed.

I will never forgive her for the goat yoga, but the cold-water therapy the masseuse suggested and massages are something I can totally see myself doing moving forward.

I smirk when Arianna squeals on the other side of the door and I hear her muttering words of annoyance as she gets closer to it. Opening it wide, she shoots me a nervous smile. "You're early."

"I am." I was eager to see her.

She looks down then slowly lets her gaze travel back up my body, clutching at the neckline of her black velvet bathrobe and I can tell she's nervous tonight. "You look..." She swallows; the V-shaped skin that's exposed on her chest flushes red. "...good."

I nod, acknowledging her compliment and wait for her to invite me in. Instead she continues to stare at me as if in a daydream, or something equally Arianna. Sometimes she's really organized and put together and other days she's lost in her own thoughts and distant. I can't seem to work her out, which annoys me because it's something I'm very good at.

"Can I come in?" I ask, motioning my hand inside her home.

She lays the palm of her hand on her forehead. "Of course, sorry, where are my manners? Come in." She steps back and holds the door open for me to enter.

When I'm in the small hallway, she closes the door and points to a brightly lit room. "Make yourself at home. I won't be long; I just need to pin my hair up, then put my dress and shoes on."

Better yet, just don't put the dress on. I'd rather she was naked. "Take your time," I reply.

"Give me ten minutes." She dashes off down the hallway with a midnight-blue painted ceiling, which I consider a bold choice. I walk inside the living area, to be met with the most unexpected décor.

Painted dark bottle-green walls with a flamingo-pink sofa covered in shocking mustard-colored scatter cushions invite me to take a seat. My senses struggle to take in the tropical maximalist decoration. Gold frames house pink hummingbirds, shocking blue peacocks, and lime-green parrots.

It's... fucking amazing. I lower myself onto the shocking fuchsia sofa and take in the exotic-looking room filled with giant fern and green houseplants.

I chuckle to myself at the pink banana ornament, then at the zebra one which is wearing a multicolored striped wooly sweater.

My girl is quirkier than she lets on.

Not my girl. Not yet.

Unless she gives us the green light to having some *fun* together, which I think she will. Having her in my life as more than just my secretary might just scratch my itch... temptation.

She's tempted, I know she is, because her flirting has moved up a notch. The laying of her hand on my shoulder, touching my hand when she passes me paperwork, the lightness in her emails, and eye contact. Fuck me, the eye contact. It's as if there's magnetics inside of her and I can't look away. Combine that with lip licking and the way she rolls her neck as if the tension is too much, and it points to one thing. She wants me.

We're great in bed together; how could she not?

I think, tonight, if I show her a little glimpse of my world outside of work, which isn't much, my family mainly, it might persuade her to take a step into the unknown with me.

For me, it's a complete black hole too. I've never had a relationship before. Hook-ups, yes, and one longer-term arrangement that suited both me and Kyla at the time. But a relationship? Would she want that with me?

Hell, it's what I want. I've made my decision.

Let's hope she wants that too.

I rest my back against the soft velvet sofa, a complete contrast to my, quite frankly, cold and unwelcoming black leather one in my penthouse, and inhale everything Arianna. It smells like vanilla and lemon and something else that's much fresher than that. Pine maybe? Hell knows. It's nice though.

My eyes land on the photo over the fake fireplace that's covered in more of her jewel-colored knick-knacks and I know straightway that it's her parents and sister. Emerald eyes and dark hair. Arianna looks just like her mom.

My fists clench in annoyance, angry for all the time she lost with them. What I wouldn't do to bring them back for her.

I face life-and-death cases every day. Some of those days it kills me hearing what others have suffered. Specializing in personal injury cases, I don't deal with small claims and someone who might have sprained a finger while tying their shoelace and want to sue the sneaker company. What I do is different. I represent people who have genuinely been screwed over and have lost their nearest and dearest or their health due to incompetence or the gross negligence of others.

Every year my brothers and I take on dozens of pro bono cases. It feels good to give back.

The sound of Arianna heading toward the living room makes me sit straighter in my seat and when she walks through the door with her head down and fiddling with a bracelet, my heart stops.

Fuck me. She's a goddess.

Wrapped in gold silk, hair pinned up, some strands left down at the front that frame her delicate features, accentuating her Bambi-size eyes, she steals all the air from my lungs.

"Could you help me with this?" Sounding flustered, she finally gives up fighting with the fiddly clasp and looks up.

My mouth goes completely dry, and I cough, willing my saliva glands to function properly. "You look beautiful." If this is what she bought with Joseph the other day, I'm promoting him to Arianna's personal shopper.

Her cheeks turn a soft shade of rosy pink before she asks, "Is my dress okay?" She looks down at herself as if unsure.

"Perfect." My brain is glitching again, something that only happens when I'm around her.

"My shoes are cute." She lifts her foot to show me the huge gold bow around the back of her ankle that matches the gold of her dress. "Thank you for all of this." She lays her foot back on the floor at the same time I walk to her to help her with her bracelet.

"You don't need to thank me for the dress. It was made for you." My voice is gruff but full of sincerity, and I love that the fire within her to stick thousands of dollars on my credit card wasn't a threat; she fucking did it and I'm happy she did. But how the hell will I get through the night with her looking this enchanting? She's a vision. I'm spellbound. "Here, let me." I point to her bracelet and take it from her.

As I lean closer, the whiff of her perfume invades my nostrils, making my pulse quicken.

Steadying my hands, I pinch the tiny gold clasp between my fingertips. It's fragile and soft, and I don't want to damage it. "Is this new?"

"It was my mom's."

"It's special." I pause before continuing. Knowing the delicate bracelet belonged to her mother makes me handle it with greater care. "Like you."

"She was but I'm not that special." She brushes away my compliment.

"You are undeniably special, Arianna." When I click the bracelet into place, I realize just how big my hands are compared to her dainty wrists, and how much I would like to wrap my hands around them and pin her against the wall like I did before.

I'm tempted, but I want to show her there is more to us than just sexual chemistry.

I brush my thumb lightly over her pulse point. I'm not ready to pull away, so I move my hand down to hers and link our fingers before lifting her hand to my lips, and as if captivated, she follows my movement and smiles when I kiss the back of it.

"You're very sweet when you want to be." Her voice is barely audible.

"Sweet?" I grin back at her, moving closer, my mouth hovering over hers.

"Yeah." She rises on her tiptoes and kisses me first. And it's so unexpected because she's been resisting me for weeks, driving me insane, but her making the first move breathes new life into any possibility of us.

Her lips feel soft, like what I imagine delicate dragonfly wings fluttering against my skin would feel like.

"I don't want to ruin your lipstick," I say, when all I really want to do is kiss her shiny lips for eternity and smudge it.

"It's clear lip gloss, it's fine." She cups my face with her hand and kisses me again, much firmer this time. "But it's time to go." I feel her smile against my mouth.

"Let's stay in." I run my nose along hers, making her giggle. I love that sound.

"You didn't buy this dress for me to stay in." Using the pad of her thumb, she wipes her shiny lipstick off my lips.

"I bought you this dress so I could take it off later." It's not a lie. "Admit that you want that too."

"I do." She nibbles on her bottom lip, teasing me.

I like how relaxed she is tonight, and I love how she's giving me little glimpses of her life, and more of her dazzling personality. Something she doesn't do often.

I understand why. I see it a lot in people who've been hurt in their past. Trust is a huge part of letting walls down, and I hope she's beginning to trust me, so I can finally start chipping away at the stone wall she's built around herself to let me in.

I think she will, because she's different tonight.

"Can I ask you something, Nathan?" Smiling up at me, in that dress and looking at me the way she is, she lights up the whole room.

I nod, scared what it might be. We've been playing a game of push-pull with each other and whatever I reply, I hope I don't make her flee again.

Clearing her throat, she asks, "Did you really mean what you said about burning the world down and"—she blinks once, then twice—"that you'd thought about settling down?"

"Meant every word." I cradle her face in my hand and brush my thumb across her cheek.

"Did you mean... with me?" She gulps.

"I don't know. If I'm being honest, I don't know what I'm doing or saying anymore." It's the only answer that makes sense to me right now, because if I go all in, I might scare her away. Maybe spending more time together will help both of us to figure this *thing* out. "This is new for me," I admit. Another first for me; I'm always prepared, but nothing could have readied me for Arianna arriving in my life like a fucking full-force hurricane, toppling me over.

"I don't know what I'm doing either," she confesses, looking at me with a worried expression. "You make me nervous."

"I think it's the other way around, baby." I place her hand over my heart to let her feel how fast it's beating.

"You do something to me too," she finally admits, repeating my sentiment from the other night.

I knew it. "Maybe we should embrace whatever is happening between us, then. No more pushing it or each other away and no more running. Sound good?" My face turns serious.

She agrees with a quick nod of her head, settling my nerves and filling my body full of hope.

"Got it?" I ask again, needing clarification and for her to say the words.

"Yes." Her bright eyes sparkle up at me before she lets go of my hand. "You look hotter than the devil himself in this tuxedo." Approving of my outfit, she straightens my bow tie, and I lift my chin to allow her to fix it as if we've done this a million times before.

I drop my voice and pull her into my arms again because it's where I like her being, then ask, "Does it bother you how hard I work?"

"No." She shrugs.

I slide my hand up the exposed skin of her back, desperate to take the fucking dress off so I can appreciate her beautiful curves once more, but know I can't as we have a ball to attend.

She's got pretty shoes she wants to show off as well as the dress she spent hours picking out, and who am I to be the one to stop her?

"Ready to have some *fun* together?" I ask, while my gut ties itself in knots of dishonesty. I want more. I just can't fucking bring myself to say it again from fear of being rejected.

"Sounds *fun*," she agrees, smiling, and I know she can see straight through me.

28

ARI

Nathan places his hand on the base of my spine as he ushers me into the ballroom. It's such a bold gesture in front of the most influential people in the city but I'm here for it. All of it.

Whatever is happening between us, it's like a runaway train, and I'm on it not knowing where we're headed.

Am I going to jump off? I guess I will have to eventually, but not now I've given in to this pull towards him. I can't stay away.

Which scares me to my core, because I'll have to tell him who I am sooner or later, but when? When will that happen? Will I trust my gut on the timing? Will I just know?

If I hadn't slept with Nathan all those weeks ago, my life wouldn't be this complicated. Yet, here I am. Maybe if I just asked him about my family's case, be truthful about who I am, would he help me?

No way. Not if it's questioning his father's ethics.

What the hell are you thinking, Arianna? Keep mum.

So I'll keep hiding who I am. For now.

And if we crash and burn—sorry, *when* we crash and burn—

then I guess I'll have to eventually deal with the consequence. Something I can't even think about now.

And as much as I keep telling myself that saying yes to Nathan and stepping into the wild unknown with him will get me one step closer to his father, it couldn't be further from my goal now.

I'm in so deep with Nathan because I like him. Really like him, and there isn't a goddamn thing I seem to be able to do to stop us from happening.

Of all the men in all the world, why does it have to be him that I see myself having a future with?

This is terrible.

And wonderful.

Why does he have to be so handsome, and have a brain that's as big as his dick, and why is he so goddamn irresistible?

He's the whole package.

My stomach feels like it's full of leaping frogs and I slow my steps down to steady myself.

"Relax," Nathan says, as if sensing my inner turmoil.

"I'm fine." I shake out my shoulders to ease the tension in them.

"You're as tense as hell." His lips find my ear. "Relax, baby, you're about to meet my mother." He chuckles when I groan, then plants a soft kiss on my cheek, which settles me a little.

Inhaling a deep breath, I prepare myself to meet the matriarch of the Hart family.

"Darling, you made it." A stunning, wide-smiled, gray-haired woman wearing a stylish black gown strides toward Nathan with her arms open wide.

"Mom." Nathan greets her with a kiss to each cheek and a one-armed embrace. Only one arm because his other is still wrapped firmly around my waist.

"How's Dad today?" Nathan asks, sounding sorrowful.

"Much the same," she replies with a sigh, stepping out of his hold, her voice heavy and weary. "He was sleeping when I left."

What happened to his dad? And why is he not here?

This is something I've yet to find out because no one in the office ever talks about him. I've asked; trust me, I've tried very hard to find out what happened to Nathan's father, but either no one knows or everyone has been asked to keep their mouths shut.

I'm thinking it's the first one.

I can't deny I'm slightly disappointed but also relieved that he's not here tonight because I'm not sure I'm ready to come face-to-face with him just yet.

Nathan's mother inhales a deep breath as if summoning all her willpower and paints on a smile and turns to me.

"And you must be Arianna." She reaches up to cup my face. "You are very beautiful." Her smile genuine, her eyes soften around the edges. "I've heard a lot about you."

"Have you?" I look up at Nathan in question. What the hell has he said about me?

"Oh, don't worry, dear, the boys talk to me. Nathan, not so much."

"Idiots." Nathan surveys the room, sounding annoyed, and it makes me giggle. He's such a grumpy bear when he chooses to be.

"It's a pleasure to meet you, Mrs. Hart." I hold out my hand for her to shake but she surprises me when she pulls me into a warm embrace, surrounding me in her exotic fragrance.

"Call me Michelle. Mrs. Hart makes me sound old." She stands back, giving me a good opportunity to get a full look at her. I'm not sure what age Michelle is but she's beautiful and I bet she was a knockout when she was younger.

"That's because you are old," Nathan says, deadpan, causing his mom to swipe at his shoulder playfully, and he doesn't even flinch.

"Excuse me, I'll have you know there's still life in this old gal yet." She straightens out her dress, then holds her head high. "Enough life in me to chase some beautiful grandbabies around the ranch. When will that be, Nathaniel? When am I getting some grandchildren?" She claps her hands together in delight. I can tell she's expecting some soon.

A fleeting mental image of me cupping my stomach full of Nathan's baby enters my mind and swiftly flies away again as quick as a blink. I shake my head to rid myself of the cocktail of emotions swirling through my conflicted thoughts.

Where did that come from?

Nathan grabs my hand and gives a squeeze as if urging me to move. "And that's our cue to leave. I hope you get stuck with Cindy Roberts all night," he says dryly.

Michelle gasps, annoyed at Nathan. "I wouldn't wish her on my worst enemy. She's the most boring woman here tonight. She could spend an entire night explaining the life cycle of a plant." She tries desperately to withhold a yawn of boredom.

"I know, enjoy talking about the speed a rose grows at." He takes a step away from his mom.

I chuckle, loving how they tease each other. It's refreshing, and such a special moment to witness between mother and son. I can't imagine living with five men was easy. Being outnumbered probably made Michelle grow a thick skin and the skill to beat them all at their own game.

Envy weighs me down. I wish I had family to tease me.

"See you at the table, darling." Michelle gives us a joyful finger wave and heads in the opposite direction from us, laughing as she leaves. "You're sitting beside me, and we can talk future grandbabies all night."

I file Michelle's mention of grandchildren away, but I'm amused that she knows how much it makes Nathan squirm like salt does to a snail.

At dinner the other night he said he wasn't sure if he wanted children. I wish he wasn't indifferent about that.

God, why do I care? It's not important right now; we aren't dating, we aren't anything, not really. Maybe we are, but a huge family is something I've always dreamed of having.

Since I was fifteen, life has been quiet. What I wouldn't do to fight over the last cookie in the jar again with Riley, who was the noisiest person I've ever met. Messy and clumsy, and boy, did we fight over the silliest things. If I knew then what I know now, I would have let her have the cookie. I'd have let her have every single one.

When I was fifteen and she was seventeen, we looked similar, and sometimes I find myself thinking about what she would look like now, what she would do for a living, where she'd work or if she'd have a family of her own.

I look around the shimmering room with golden chandeliers dangling from the ceiling. I know Riley would have loved this because she was a sucker for watching the Oscars. She loved the glitz and glamour and knew every designer dress the movie stars wore. She'd approve of my dress tonight; I just know it.

With our fingers threaded together, because Nathan hasn't let go of me yet, I follow behind him as he weaves us through a path of tables and dozens of people who all seem to know him.

He politely nods and shakes hands with everyone as he passes, and I do the same when he introduces me, not missing their looks bouncing between myself and Nathan as if questioning not only him being here but also that he brought a date.

It makes me feel special, because Nathan is a bit of an enigma and never does anything if he doesn't want to. Specifically, no dating. Yet here I am.

Bringing me here tonight is a big deal. Bigger than I considered at first.

I feel like a princess.

His.

A billion different emotions and thoughts whirl around my brain as we eventually arrive at our designated table on the far side of the room. The only thing I never expected tonight was Nathan introducing me as his secretary.

I saw straight through him back in my apartment.

He toned down his previous confession about settling down.

I guess we're both struggling with our feelings.

We're torn.

"Are you nervous?" Nathan asks as he pulls out a seat for me, then he sits in the one next to me.

"You introduced me as your secretary," I state, laying my purse on the table. It sort of threw me for a loop when he did that on arrival.

"And?"

"It's just, you know, I thought you might have said I was your date for the night."

Stop talking.

He pins me with a serious stare. "Would you have preferred that?" he asks seriously.

"I don't know," I answer honestly. Yes. No. Maybe. Definitely yes.

His voice low so no one overhears us, he says, "Because I will if you want me to, and if I kiss you again right here and now then everyone will know you're more than just my secretary. Is that what you want? Because I honestly don't care what anyone thinks anymore, but I know you had doubts and it's taken a while to decide about us, and the last thing I want to do is scare you and move things too fast. But Arianna, baby." He urges me to swivel around in my seat and he cages me in, his thighs on either side of mine. "I told you what I want and that is you. I don't think it matters how I introduce you."

My pulse is beating so hard with a mix of happiness and surprise, I bet the whole room can hear it.

He adds, "And I don't care if they know you're staff and we are dating. I made up a stupid law, rule, guideline, whatever you want to call it, in my head about not dating staff, and like my brothers have told me, it's a ridiculous one."

Nathan keeps saying things that feel like music to my ears. "So whatever you want, I'll do, but what we are going to do is enjoy the night as much as we possibly can because I'm going to be verbally teased at every opportunity by my brothers and mom. You'll have to dance with me to escape. And when you're on that floor with me everyone will know who you are to me. The only thing I'll be thinking the entire time is how soon we can leave so I can take you home and get you out of that pretty little dress. Something I'm dying to do, but not tonight, because I'm a gentleman and I want to show you that our connection goes beyond physical attraction and desire."

I feel disappointed by his confession but at the same time I love this side of him he's letting me see. He's considerate and patient, which makes me like him even more.

And he's not willing to put an exact label on us, which is refreshing.

Fun. That's not all we are, I know we're not.

Steady as a rock, he continues, "Instead, I'll donate money

tonight, then I'm going to take you home and kiss you goodnight on your doorstep then tell you how beautiful you are and how I was the envy of every man in the room."

I reach up and cup his face. "You're amazingly sweet when you want to be."

"You look stunning." He leans into my touch and kisses my wrist right over my pulse point that's beating faster than a marching drum.

"Oh, for fuck's sake. I might be sick." A gruff voice from one of his brothers breaks our tender moment; Cole, I think.

"You're going to make Eli sick." Max fakes a gagging noise, and I love how much they screw with each other daily. Their love for one another is tangible.

I say a quick hello and smile nervously. Nathan has me all flustered with how intense he is being tonight. I both love it and want to run from it all in equal amounts. It's overwhelming.

"Did you fall and bump your head or something?" Eli asks as he takes a seat opposite us, and Nathan covers his hand with mine then lays them on his lap.

Nathan replies without flinching, "I didn't bump my head."

"But you're definitely falling." Max sounds serious.

Max is clearly implying Nathan is falling for me, it's obvious Max can see what I feel.

"I think I need a drink," I say out loud, not meaning too.

"We all do." Eli signals to a waiter and the brothers continue talking amongst themselves again.

"Does me falling for you, scare you?" Nathan leans forward and whispers in my ear with strong determination. It feels like there is no one else in the room but us.

As if I'm a statue, I feel like I can't move or breathe. Nathan's words and confession are breathing new life into every cellular level of my body, lighting up my soul in ways I never knew were possible.

"Yes." Because I might be falling too and think it's naturally been happening like a snowball rolling down a hill. It's gained momentum, much bigger now, and it has been gaining speed and grown in size since the first night we met. "I'm petrified," I admit. "Working together complicates things." It messes with my original reason for joining Hart Law. I've made zero progress in my hunt to uncover the truth about my family's death. Now I've made the decision to leave it alone for the time being, I feel guilty because here I am, sitting cozy and falling for the man who I have loathed from afar because of his father.

It seems my judgment was unjust because the entire Hart family are nothing like how I imagined. My grudge sits with his father, not Nathan or his brothers, and I have to keep reminding myself of that.

It's him I want.

"We'll make it work, Arianna, and I don't give a shit what anyone at work thinks because—"

I don't let him finish. "I'm the best secretary you've ever had."

He moves closer to me, his lips twitching as if trying to hide his smile. "That's not what I was going to say."

I drop my voice, almost afraid of what his reply will be, but I ask anyway, "What were you going to say?"

"I was going to say"—he takes a second to consider his next words—"I don't give a shit what anyone thinks because for the first time in my life I'm putting myself before work." I get the impression he's stopping himself from saying more as he gives me a hard stare. "I care about you, Arianna."

"Those are some big words you're using tonight, Mr. Hart," I stutter, suddenly feeling hot all over in my thin silk dress.

Closing the small space between us, we move toward each other at the same time, and the air grows thick with anticipation, the sizzle of energy between us strong enough to set off a chemical reaction; his confession is potent enough to make me want to tear my dress off right here in front of everyone and ride him like a stallion until sunrise.

In harmony, we slant our heads, and our lips lock instantly. It's a soft kiss, but the way it makes my heart beat faster and heat burn in my core it feels like he's touching every part of me, reaching places I never knew existed.

Squeezing my hand, he brings an end to our kiss, then rests his forehead against mine.

"I'm not a sentimental man, Arianna, but when I'm with you, you do something to me." He uses the same words he did when he came looking for me in the records room.

"You do something to me, too." I hope he was joking about dropping me off later, because all I want is to feel the connection again that I've only ever felt with him.

When we slept together the first time, we were hotter than the sun, and we barely knew each other. Imagine what sex will be like together with emotion combined with the sexual tension that's been building for the last few weeks between us. It'll be scorching and we'll need the fire department to put us out.

A voice bursts our happy bubble. "If we have to put up with these two sickening love birds all night then I'll need something stronger than champagne to get me through."

"Cole, if I give you a hundred bucks, will you shut the fuck up?" Nathan snaps, finally unlocking his eyes from mine.

The shift happening between us is profound and powerful.

"Make it two hundred and you have a deal," Cole counters, completely unfazed by Nathan's outburst.

"You get fuck all for trying to negotiate with me," Nathan

bites back, and the table bursts into laughter. It's only then I notice another three women have joined us. Cole's, Max's and Eli's dates, I assume.

Nathan makes himself comfortable in his seat and throws his arm around the back of mine. Lifting his champagne glass, he points to my flute. "Cheers."

I pick mine up and *clink* my glass against his. "To fun," I toast, my lips twitching as I fight to hide the entertainment I get from playing along with his ruse.

"To fun." He winks, smiling wickedly against the lip of his glass before running his hand over the silk covering my thigh.

Fuck fun, we are so much more than that and he just gave himself away.

Which is what I should do too and tell him who I am.

The angel within wants so much to do that... *Hey, Nathan, I'm Arianna Donovan. Your father defended the man who killed my family and I've been working for Hart Law to seek justice for them and uncover your father as a corrupt lawyer.*

Yup, that's never going to come out in a way that doesn't make me sound like a devious bitch.

So I'll park that temporarily to come back to another time.

Fun?

Now, that I can do.

Fun without falling for him completely?

Shit, I'm in way too deep.

29

NATHAN

Arianna looks up at me with those beautiful green eyes I'll never be able to resist before she snuggles into my chest as we move slowly together on the dancefloor, enjoying the gentle pace of the song the orchestra is playing.

I was right; she is the most beautiful woman in the room tonight. She's also easy-going and surprisingly relaxed, which she hasn't been around me since she started working as my secretary, and she fits right in as if she has always been part of my family.

My brothers love her, which I knew since they were the ones who encouraged me to invite her tonight. They saw what I couldn't or wouldn't admit myself.

Arianna has spent the evening talking to my mother, who I know is just as smitten as I am.

When I confessed to her that I care about her, I couldn't help myself. It was as if there was a dam of words I was holding back that made my throat feel tight, but as soon as I started telling her how I really feel, a wave of emotion overtook me and I just couldn't stop myself. Which is new for me. And yet I feel at peace. Complete.

My brothers are right; I've turned into a sappy bastard, which is what they called me when Arianna excused herself to go to the restroom earlier.

With Arianna, everything feels different. She's different and has me questioning... my entire fucking existence. Which is what I have been doing—existing, not living life to the fullest.

Fun?

I want more. But I can't bring myself to tell her the full truth from fear of exposing myself completely.

I want walks on the beach, nights at the theater, a family perhaps. Fuck no, I'm not there yet. *One step at a time, Nathan.* Vacations, nights around a firepit. I want it all.

These new thoughts are so unexpected and what I always feared, yet I'm not scared or running away.

Maybe it's because she understands me, my work, and my commitment to my job, or maybe it's because she accepts me for who I am, flaws and all. And hell, I know Joseph calls me Mr. Crankypants, which I am a lot of the time, but in my defense, I spend the majority of my days in a state of permanent stress. Remembering every case inside and out, questioning witnesses, preparing closing arguments all while thinking on my feet and trying to maintain my composure is taking its toll.

I look down at the incredible woman who is wrapped around me. I must admit, having Arianna in my life makes me feel better. She soothes me in ways I don't fully understand.

Maybe I need a vacation. I can't even remember when I last took a day off and didn't check emails or prepare for a case.

There's no off switch in my life anymore and separating life and business has become a thing of the past. Every day seems to blend into one and before I know it, it's the New Year and I've said goodbye to another three hundred and sixty-five days. Somewhere along the line I lost myself.

Does she know what she's signing up for? Nights alone, missed dinners. Will she stick around if it all becomes too much... or not enough?

Can I have both?

"You're going to give yourself a seizure if you don't stop over-thinking us," Arianna pipes up. She tilts her head back, before flashing me a knowing smile.

"So you read minds now?"

"Just yours, and we'll work everything out as we go. No pressure."

"Could you be any more perfect?"

"Like I said, I'm not, but we'll agree to disagree on that one." Her voice is full of playfulness. "No more serious thoughts. Have you enjoyed yourself this evening?" She changes the subject.

"Yes, but I think I've spent enough money for one night." I pull her closer to me as we dance to the slow song the band is playing.

"Well, no one said you had to bid for half the auction items." She lays her forearms on top of my shoulders as we continue to move to the music.

"True." But after Arianna told me it was the charity she volunteered for and how underfunded they were following cuts to their funding streams, I want to help in any way I can. And I've already decided on Monday I'm going to set up a monthly donation and make them our charity of the year at Hart Law, something we renew every year.

"Thank you for bidding for all those items, but tell me, have you always wanted a private tour of Lucasfilm?"

"Nope, I'd rather eat a hornet's nest. But Eli will love it." He's a huge *Star Wars* fan.

"That's very sweet of you."

"Well, Eli had to leave early because there was an emergency with one of his clients, so it will more than make up for it."

"I don't think his date even noticed he'd left," she mutters.

I follow Arianna's path of sight to discover Eli's date, Fiona, I think her name was, slipping out of the room with Chase "Jerkoff" Torres.

"He's a shitty husband." Arianna's tone drips with disgust as she remembers the encounter she had with him the first night we met at the bar. "Where's his wife?" She surveys the room.

"Suzanne found out he wasn't being truthful about his whereabouts during the week and now she's divorcing his ass and taking him to the cleaners. Max is representing her." He specializes in divorce.

"Poor guy, I feel bad for him," she says with a sigh.

"Really?" I ask, surprised by her reply.

"Nope, not one bit." She shakes her head. "I hope Max squeezes every single penny out of him." Her chest shakes against mine with laughter, and I join in.

Arianna's laughter turns into a stifled yawn as if not wanting to give her sleepiness away.

"Tired?" I ask.

"It's been a long night; I'm ready to go home now."

"Let me say goodbye to Mom and then we'll leave."

"Okay," she agrees as I take her hand in mine, and we head off the dance floor.

"Ari." Someone from behind us shouts her name to get her attention, stopping us in our tracks.

"Julie." Arianna drops my hand before throwing her arms around a woman I know all too well.

Julie *fucking* Hanson, a journalist for *The Golden Telegraph*. She's a shit-stirrer and all-round thorn in Hart Law's side.

Max dated her for a while. It was a long time ago now and it didn't end well. We discovered she's pretty fucking handy with a golf club and Max never did forgive her for the damage she did to his 1940 Ford Deluxe Coupe. The one he saved every cent for from the age of sixteen, working for my father on the weekends to have restored.

Julie is a fucking tornado, out of control and completely unpredictable. I get that she was heartbroken when her and Max split, but while she thought they were going to settle down, get married, and have lots of babies—all the things Max did not want with her—Max was slowly moving her out of his apartment. In the end, when she refused to leave, we had to file a restraining order, one that has since lapsed.

I'm kind of wishing it was still in place. Six years wasn't enough.

"Nathaniel." Julie greets me with a tight smile.

"Julie." I give her a curt nod. "I didn't think vampires came out this early." She always did have a knack for sucking any good vibes out of the air. "Played any golf lately?"

Julie folds her arms around herself, tilts her head to the side, and rolls her eyes. "Very cute. It's been years, get over it."

Arianna watches our interaction, ping-ponging her gaze from me to Julie and back again as if trying to work out what the hell we are talking about.

"Not long enough." I push my hands into my pockets and kiss Arianna on the cheek. "I'll grab your purse. Meet me in the foyer, and don't say a fucking word to this one." I point at Julie. "She's a fucking snake." She's written numerous articles about us, each one factually incorrect. Who the hell knows what goes on in that twisted mind of hers.

"Nathaniel," Arianna scolds me, pinning me with an angry look. "Julie is my friend."

I tut, then lick my lips, annoyed that Arianna doesn't know how sneaky and vindictive Julie is. "If you class her as a friend, you need to find new ones."

Julie blows me a kiss then flips me the bird. "Love you too, Nathaniel."

"Classy as ever, Julie." I turn my back on her. "Five minutes," I tell Arianna, and I can feel the anger bouncing off my girl.

Fuck, now I'll have to tell Arianna about what happened between Max and Julie when Max never wanted anyone outside of the family knowing what went down between them.

Well, screw him. Arianna is one of us now.

A Hart.

She just doesn't know it yet.

30

ARI

"How do you know Julie?" Nathan asks as Jenkins drives toward my home in Nathan's limo.

"You were really rude to her, Nathan." The second I look at him, I know he's annoyed at me for questioning him.

Irritated, Nathan unties his bow tie then undoes the top button on his shirt, stretching out his neck from side to side. "If I tell you something, you must promise to never repeat it."

"You can trust me." Or maybe he can't; while I might have pressed the brakes on my personal investigation for now, against his father, I still want to eventually. According to Julie, her source and lead on the case is as solid as concrete and she reassured me tonight that the information is legit and that she will email it to me as soon as she has it.

I thought I trusted Julie but now I come to think about it, why did she give my old boss, Nick, a heads-up whenever a tabloid was about to publish a story on him and his, well... Mafia connections?

God, maybe I've put my trust in the wrong person. Now I'm questioning her loyalty and reliability.

I might have misjudged her.

Which is just awful.

I saw Nathan's attitude changing when he saw her, and I knew something was off.

Nathan wasn't just upset, he was angry, like a bubbling cauldron about to boil over.

I don't know who to trust anymore. I'm not sure I even trust myself.

Nathan runs his hand through his hair as if frustrated, then proceeds to tell me what went down between Julie and Max, from vandalizing his car to smashing his apartment up.

It seems I might have Julie all wrong. It was a long time ago, but after what he's said, I don't want to be on Julie's bad side. It sounds like she made Max's life a living hell. Sewing dead fish into the bottom of his curtains and stuffing his mattress full of fish guts was a terrible thing to do. She even tapped his phone and tracked him everywhere he went, turning up uninvited to every family event and court hearing he was in attendance of. When Max eventually moved on with someone new, his car was vandalized with blue paint, leading the insurance company to declare it a total loss. She tried to destroy everything of his as well as his reputation. However, attempting to set up Nathan's father by secretly filming him in his office and trying to make him have sex with her is as twisted as it gets in terms of revenge.

"And you're sure it was Julie?" I ask, completely shocked. It doesn't sound like the woman I've come to know.

"Oh, it was Julie, and I would never tell you not to be friends with someone or what to do, but that woman needs serious help."

"Maybe she got it." She sure seems stable to me.

"Don't be fooled by her blonde hair, calm voice, and dimples. There's a monster beneath that exterior, I promise."

Nathan's voice rises an octave, but as if to steady himself and the growing anger I can feel bouncing off him, he reaches over and takes my hand in his, using me to ground him. "Anyway, enough about her, I will not let Julie Hanson ruin our night."

I have so many questions whirling through my head now it feels like it might explode. But Nathan is right; I don't want to spoil our first official date together which made us look like a couple.

A couple.

That sounds wild.

And oh so right.

There's a shift in the air around us as he tugs at my hand gently, urging me to slide closer to him and tuck myself under his arm as he wraps it around me and kisses the top of my head.

"I've found it very difficult to keep my hands off you tonight, Ms. Donovan."

I hum, then slip my fingers inside the open neckline of his shirt. "You have the restraint of a gentleman," I say, keeping my voice soft and low. At least that's what he told me he was trying to be earlier. "But what if I don't want you to be a gentleman tonight?" I ask, undoing one of his buttons and then another.

"Arianna." The way he says my name sounds more like a warning.

"Nathaniel." I mimic his tone, teasing him, and glide my hand down his bare chest, drawing tiny invisible circles across it toward his nipple, where I pinch it between my fingers.

He lets out a strangled moan and before I know what's happening, he's pulled me onto his lap. "Straddle me," he instructs, and I can hear the desperation in the low timbre of his voice.

I shuffle myself on my shins on top of the leather seat and

push my fine gold silk dress up my thighs to accommodate his broad body.

Moving close, I drop my lips to his and take what I've wanted all night. The thing I crave. Him, all of him. I'm grateful that the concealed glass is doing its job by hiding our desperate kisses.

My pussy perfectly aligns with his thick, hard length, which I can feel beneath his pants, and he grunts when I grind myself against him, panting into my mouth as his tongue twirls around mine.

"Nathan," I whimper when he digs his fingertips into my hips, deep enough to leave bruises, sending waves of slick heat deep in my core.

He moves his lips to my neck, biting and nipping at my jaw, my ear, anywhere he finds as if desperate to devour me, before covering his mouth with mine again.

His fingers brush my skin as he slips his hands under my dress, then grabs my hips again to rock me back and forth, teasing my clit against his covered cock and the fabric of my now wet lace panties.

"I want you," he groans into my mouth when I rock my hips with more vigor, sliding back and forth to chase my own release. "But I told you I'm a gentleman and there is no way I am fucking you in a limo, Arianna."

"Forget being a gentleman, I want you to fuck me. Now." I reach down and unclip the hook and eye of his black dress pants, tugging at them, urgently pushing them down his hips.

He digs his fingertips into my skin much deeper this time, as if considering if he should be the gentleman he spoke of earlier or fuck me like I am telling him to.

"Stop thinking about it and just do it, Nathan." We've been teasing each other for weeks. We need this. "I want you inside of me." I need him, so much.

"Fuck it." Nathan kisses me breathless, and carelessly we struggle together, awkwardly shedding the fabric that's preventing us connecting again in ways I've been imagining for weeks.

"Jesus fucking Christ, take my pants off." He breaks our kiss momentarily, then lifts his hips to help me remove his pants, taking his boxers with them.

At the same time, I pull my dress up over my head and drop it on the seat beside us, then unstick my stupid bra from my skin, which is the least sexy thing I own and only bought to wear with the backless dress, exposing myself completely for him.

He drops his attention to my breasts, and his eyes darken as he takes me in.

Gently, he circles my pebbled nipple with the pad of his thumb, before rolling it between his thumb and fingertip, causing me to cry out with pleasure. "So beautiful," he declares before bowing his head and pulling my nipple into his mouth, licking and sucking at my sensitive peak.

I arch my head back, pushing my chest into his face, needing more of him. He flicks my nipple harder with his tongue over and over, and I'm panting, rubbing my pussy against him before he bites down firmly on my nipple, sending an electric current of arousal through my body.

Threading my hands into the back of his hair, I tilt his head up and capture his lips with mine. "I want you," I gasp, wanting everything with him, anything he'll give me.

I push myself up a little higher when he slips the soaked lace of my panties to the side, allowing him to line the angry-looking head of his cock with my entrance.

Looking down between us, he watches as I lower myself onto him. His lips twitch with enjoyment as I slide down the last inch of his length and let out a sigh of relief. It feels like years, not weeks, since we last had sex.

"Do you like my cock filling you up, baby?" he asks, his chest heaving in and out as if trying to control himself.

"God, yeah. I'm so wet for you." I reposition myself to accommodate him and gasp because I forgot how big he is.

"Look at how well your pussy takes my cock, baby." He pumps upward with the need to fuck me as my pussy aches and pulses around his hard dick. "You're so fucking wet. Now kiss me." He crashes his lips against mine, and at the same time we begin to move.

Rocking together, I ease myself up and down his huge length, taking him further into my body with every upward and downward stroke.

"Oh, God." My eyes roll into the back of my head as he thrusts up into me as if he can't wait for me to move faster.

"Say my name, baby."

"Nathan," I cry out as his thick cock teases my inner walls.

"Who do you belong to?" he demands.

Unable to control the volume of my voice, I shout his name, not caring that we're in the back of the limo or that the driver can hear us.

"Good girl." He nips at my lips in approval before laying a runway of kisses down my jaw, reaching the spot behind my ear that feels divine. "I'm going to fill you with my cum," he grunts into my hair.

"Yes," I hiss. "I'm on the pill, do it."

He places both his hands on the side of my face and stares into my eyes, tilting his hips, pushing himself into me and filling me completely with every delicious hard inch of him, and I can already feel the urge to come again.

Rapidly blinking, as if he's in distress or disbelief or hell knows what he's thinking when I told him to fill me up with his cum, whatever, I don't care, because right now having him fill me up with his baby doesn't seem like a bad idea.

It feels right.

I moan and frown at the same time, unable to read what he's thinking because his mood turned serious quicker than a hiccup.

"You're so fucking beautiful, baby," he says, running his thumb along my bottom lip.

My refined lawyer who only ever talks about work has turned into a sentimental man, and I'm totally here for it. I'm all in.

"Is this real?" I ask, my words coming out shaky.

As much as I want to believe it, my brain is taking longer to catch on, while my heart feels like it's spinning like a carousel inside my chest.

"You are it for me," he says confidently. "I fucking hated watching you leave my apartment, hated how it made me feel. I thought about you every fucking second of that day and every day since and I regret not asking you to stay."

"I hated leaving you that morning." I wished I had stayed, then maybe our time working together in such close proximity wouldn't have felt so painful. Close yet so far apart.

"You snuck out." He moves his hands from my face to my hips and lifts me off his cock then slams me back down as if reprimanding me for leaving.

"I didn't think you would want me around." It's partly true.

"I want you with me always. Don't ever sneak out on me again."

"Okay," I agree.

"Promise."

"I promise." I'm in so deep with him. How could I have been

so stupid to ever think he was like his father? It couldn't be further from the truth.

In this moment, something changes within me, a movement, a shift, a definite knowing.

My mission is no longer to find evidence or information on my family's case; it's to spend as much time with Nathan as I can. Learn everything there is to know about him, because what if I'm wrong and he's my true north?

It feels like he is. And I can't be the gatekeeper of secrets forever. I'll have to tell him. One day. Be honest. Bare my soul.

It scares me to think that he might not want anything to do with me once he finds out.

What then?

I can't even think about that now.

He growls, making his whole chest vibrate. Gripping my ass and hips in handfuls, he moves me up and down his cock, while I help him.

"Now ride my cock, Arianna, cover me in your cum."

I press the palm of my hand flat against the roof of the limo to give me the leverage I need to fuck him the way he wants me to.

Tilting my hips, clenching the inner walls of my pussy, I begin to move up and down his cock.

Pleasure dances over his face as he cups my ass and sits back to watch where we connect. On every downward thrust, I rub my clit against him, and he groans when I move faster, the tip of his thick crown teasing my G-spot with every punishing slap of our skin, my calves clamped tight against his thighs.

"You're so tight, baby." The sounds of our pleasure fill the small space of the car and I shudder when he slips his thumb between my pussy lips and rubs my clit.

"Nathan," I moan as he circles my sensitive bud, and then pinches it. "I'm... I'm gonna—" I stutter my words as my body shakes, my orgasm about to explode through every nerve ending.

"Come," he orders as he continues to swirl his fingertips over my clit.

Blazing-hot fire radiates through the apex of my thighs and my pussy, and I come. The power of my climax makes my body shake, the spasm of my inner walls clenching around him, and I let out a high-pitched whimper.

"That's a good girl." He nuzzles into my neck, his breathing shallow against my skin as he chases his own release and bites much harder at my skin than I expect, but it's a welcomed pain, mixed with the ultimate pleasure.

My inner walls flutter around him as the last waves of my orgasm spill from my body.

"Oh fuck, baby. I'm coming." He bucks up into me a few more times as he spills his hot seed inside of me, groaning as he leans his head back against the leather of the seat.

We stay like this for a while as we pant loudly together and come down from our high, the faint sheen of perspiration covering our bodies from the exertion.

"You're perfect," he murmurs. "So fucking perfect." His cock softens inside of me while my heart feels like it's beating out of my chest, already thinking about round two.

"Stay with me tonight." I press myself against his naked chest and rest my ear against his pounding heart, enjoying every beat, reminding me this is true and real.

"I already invited myself. There is no way I would have been able to kiss you goodnight on your doorstep and leave." He chuckles to himself, knowing how much of a lie that was, and I knew it too. "What did I do to deserve you?"

I look up at him which makes him bow his head so he can press a kiss to my lips.

I think it's the other way around because I feel like the luckiest girl in the world.

Or the unluckiest.

However I weigh it up, my scales are perfectly balanced; fair and unfair.

31

NATHAN

"Good morning, Joseph." I stride past his desk feeling better than I have in years.

Arianna and I spent all weekend together. She distracted me from work all of Saturday and Sunday and other than showering, she never let me leave her bed. I can't deny I was also on a mission to give her as many orgasms as possible so I guess we both achieved what we set out to do.

I did manage to persuade her to stay at my apartment last night because I needed a change of clothes and if I'm being honest, I didn't want to sleep alone at my place, which is the first time I've ever felt that way. While I'm still getting used to waking up with someone wrapped around me, sorry, correction, waking up to Arianna's lips wrapped around my cock, it feels like she's always been in my life and I don't want her to leave.

"Good morning, Mr. Hart."

"Am I not Mr. Crankypants today?" I ask, feeling mischievous for a Monday.

His mouth drops open in shock, his cheeks filling with color. "I... Eh..." he stutters.

I like screwing with him. I know I'm not the easiest person to work for, and I know what he calls me and why; I've just never let on that I knew.

"Leave him alone or I will call the goat yoga guy and book another session for you." Arianna appears as if from thin air. Who knows what time she left my apartment this morning? She was gone when I woke up and yet again my doubt about her skittishness swept in for a brief moment before I read the note she left for me on her pillow telling me she was going to her apartment because she forgot her work bag and that she would see me at the office.

She pushes a cup of coffee into my hand, looking beautiful from head to toe in a striking red dress and black heels. She looks fuckable. A vision of bending her over my desk later makes my cock twitch in my boxers. We are definitely doing that tonight once everyone has left.

"Morning, beautiful." I lean down and kiss her on the lips and feel her hesitation because I'm kissing her in front of Joseph and whoever is watching.

"Nathan." She bats her eyelashes at me, looking shy, which is most unlike her.

Arianna holds my gaze and mouths, *What are you doing?*

I don't care. I want everyone to know she's mine.

I wink and make my way into my office. "Arianna, please schedule lunch today for you and me at The Lime Leaf."

"So bossy," I hear her mutter behind me, which makes me smile. I pull my chair out, park my ass in it, then slide myself behind my desk.

Switching on my laptop, I pretend to focus on my computer screen as it boots up, but I listen in to the conversation between Joseph and Arianna as he hooks his arm into hers and leads her toward the kitchen, leaving a stream of really loud whispered questions from Joseph floating through the air.

When did this happen?

Are you going to marry him?

I want all the details.

I'm as excited about Arianna and me as he sounds, and he makes me chuckle to myself.

And even though there were many of the senior-level team who saw me kissing Arianna at the ball at the weekend, they would never say anything to anyone until I did.

That's what I like about my senior team. They don't gossip and gather around the watercooler fishing for the lowdown on who is doing what with whom.

They're professional and they respect my privacy.

Are you going to have lots and lots of babies?

My ears prick up when Joseph asks Arianna, and something shifts within me again.

I may never have wanted kids before but now I can see myself having a family—with her.

I want to ask her to be my forever.

What the hell is she doing to me?

32

NATHAN

For the last three months Arianna and I have been living in what she calls a happy bubble.

We cook our evening meals together between my place and hers, and we watch television series I've never heard of on one of those subscription channels everyone talks about at work, and in between that, I'm still working hard.

And I've yet to figure out how I take more time off, but I'm sure that will come eventually.

I'm still having weekly massages and both Arianna and I have started cold water therapy. On those days, I feel Zen-like as if I'm floating, and I don't know why I haven't tried it sooner.

I do know why I haven't met someone sooner; because I now realize Arianna was made for me.

Looking back, I can't believe how narrow-minded I was to think that having someone living in my pocket twenty-four seven sounded awful. Now that Arianna is in my life, eating, sleeping, and working together is perfect.

Our lives fit seamlessly together, and we just work.

I like having her in my home, and I love it even more that

she makes herself comfortable at my place and even invites her friend Maeve over for wine on the weekends.

Life is good and somehow, everything makes sense.

Like the stars have aligned or some cosmic shit I have no control over.

I'm all in with her.

A million percent.

"Nathan." She moans my name, arching her neck back as I slide slow, deep thrusts in and out of Arianna's wet heat.

"Come for me, baby," I breathe against her lips.

She gently brushes her fingertips across the skin on my back, causing goosebumps to rise across it as our tongues delicately twist around one another.

Our hot breath ghosts our lips, as our breathing grows heavier with each stroke.

She whimpers, tilting her hips to chase her release.

I take my time and in a slow rhythmic pace, we leisurely rock together, and I simultaneously tease her clit with my pelvic bone, beckoning her orgasm to make an appearance.

"Ah, Nathan," she cries as she slides her hand up into my hair and pulls the ends of it, sending shivers of pleasure down my spine.

I glide my hand up her thigh, up over her hip, cupping her ass, and lift her leg around my waist to pull her even closer to me.

In slow motion, our eyes lock, and inch by slow inch, we move together, and I take my time between careful thrusts, circling my hips.

Her mouth drops open as she lets out a long moan and I know she's almost there.

I hold myself deep, barely moving but filling her completely with my cock as her inner walls suck me into her body.

My cock swells, the familiar throb in my balls building as we climb.

And then we come. Together.

Her twitching, me jerking my release inside of her as the walls of her pussy flutter around me.

Then we kiss, and kiss, slowly coming back down from our high.

I love her.

I know I do.

She looks up at me with that just-fucked look about her and smiles.

"I'm going to order takeout then I'm taking you out tonight." I hope she likes my Saturday night surprise. I kiss her lips.

"Where are you taking me?" she whispers between kisses.

"Cirque du Soleil." I lean back and smile down at her.

She gasps, her eyes now the size of saucers. "Really?"

"Yes. Happy?"

"I think had I gone all the way to state championships in Beam I could have done something similar in my career."

"You think?"

"Yeah."

Well, this is news to me. But I think the scar along her shoulder has something to do with it. She hasn't told me how she got it, but I think it's connected to the car crash that wiped out her entire family.

"I've never seen Cirque before." Her mood is buoyant.

"Well, neither have I."

"I'm excited." She bounces her shoulders up and down against the mattress then hugs me tight.

I'm excited about doing everything with her.

This is just the beginning.

33

ARI

My eyes flutter open, then close again, my mind unable to comprehend why I feel so tired and why my body feels as if it's gone twelve rounds with a heavyweight boxer.

I grumble, my muscles aching and screaming at me to go back to sleep, so I turn over onto my side to be met by a wall of pure muscle and realize he's the reason my body feels like a punch bag. It's a pleasurable pain I will never complain about.

An instant smile shapes my lips and I softly chuckle to myself at how huge he looks in my tiny bed. You could fit my entire apartment into his bedroom.

Last night, after Cirque du Soleil, Nathan and I fucked like rabbits until I tapped out, unable to take any more. He's insatiable.

Nathan has stamina, that's for sure; buckets of the stuff.

I drape my arm around his waist and lay my leg over his. He must be just as exhausted as me because he doesn't even move a millimeter as I snuggle myself into his back.

Content, surrounded by his heady aftershave and everything him, I drift off to sleep to the sound of his steady breathing.

Yeah, this is the life.

* * *

When I wake up again, the sunshine is blazing through the bay window of my bedroom, and I groan as my sleep-filled eyes struggle to adjust to the dazzling San Francisco sun.

"Too bright," I mutter and give my eyelids a quick rub, then I stretch out my stiff body, pushing my hands above my head.

I look through the window at the summer sun. It's been much hotter than usual and at times I've questioned if I was designed for this weather. I much prefer snow to sun and would choose that any day of the week, specifically today when I want to curl up into a ball and hibernate for a month.

I glance at the open curtains I know I didn't open then snap my head to the side and realize I'm alone. A sense of dread overwhelms me until I spot something on the pillow, the indent of Nathan's head evidence he was here.

Pulling the comforter under my arms, I prop myself up onto my elbow and lift what looks like a letter off the pillow then smile.

My fleeting disappointment leaves me instantly when I stick my fist into my eye socket to give one then the other a rub and clear my cloudy vision so I can read the neatly penned letter, and I instantly recognize Nathan's handwriting. It is very distinguishable with loops and swooshes that all link together seamlessly. I swear he could be a font designer.

Good morning, beautiful,
    Fill a weekend bag, we're off to the family ranch until Tuesday afternoon.
    Pick you up at noon. Be ready.

Always yours, Nathan x

I read the letter again, much slower this time, and do a little inner squeal with excitement.

"His family ranch?" And is he taking Monday and Tuesday off? Well, this is a first.

This is huge for him. Time off is not something he does, and I might need to reschedule his calendar.

A sudden thought hits me like a cannonball to the gut.

Will his father be there?

Oh my God, I'm finally going to meet my nemesis.

With the roof down and the wind flowing through my hair, we drove for less than an hour, out of town and over the Golden Gate Bridge then onto the busy freeway, before heading to Nathan's family ranch just outside Mill Valley.

Off the main freeway, and down several winding roads later, camouflaged by trees and deep green foliage, his parents' ranch came into view as Nathan's Bentley Continental convertible, which costs more than I will make in a lifetime, rolled down the gravel driveway.

Nathan held my hand the entire drive here, and more talkative than usual, he asked me dozens of questions about the cases he's working on because he said he values my opinions. Then we moved onto small talk, which we do often, and shared more of our likes and dislikes, our favorite films and foods, before we moved onto places around the world we would most like to visit.

I was surprised when he agreed with me that Aspen in the winter sounded like fun, while Fiji was the ultimate luxury destination. Perfect for a honeymoon, I think is what he said. In fact, I don't just think he said that, I know he did, because I've mentally filed it away for safekeeping.

He let me choose what music we listened to on the way here, and I love that we have the same taste in music and that he even sang along to it. Outside of work he's very different and being around him feels natural, as if we've known each other for years. The man isn't an enigma to me anymore, because what I have discovered is that when he trusts, he trusts with his whole heart. He'd said he wanted fun, but I know for both of us this is growing into something neither of us could have predicted.

Everything he does has my heart fluttering in my chest, and when he pulled my hand onto his lap while he was driving then threaded his fingers into mine and kissed my knuckles, I about melted into my seat like a puddle of liquid gold.

He makes me feel safe, completely adored, and like I belong. Something I have never felt before. On the way here, he surprised me even further when he shared his love of tennis, which I already knew about, but what I didn't know was how good he was when he was younger. He was good enough to go professional and wishes he had seen it through.

I guess his father expected his sons to follow the same career path as him to continue the family business, which I kind of hate for Nathan.

What if he missed his calling to be a professional tennis player and could have been ranked number one in the world?

Now he'll never know, but what if that was his destiny and not the one his father chose for him?

I've spent my life wishing things were different, the list of what-ifs becoming longer as I get older.

What if my dad had taken a different route that night?

What if I hadn't made finals for the state championship on Beam?

What if we had gone for burgers and not pizza that night?

What if, what if, what if...

I let out a sigh as I wash the salad that Nathan's mother, Michelle, asked me to help with and look out across the sun-scorched pastures through the kitchen window.

"That does not sound like a good sigh." Michelle breaks through my wandering thoughts.

"I'm fine. Just daydreaming." My white lies are stacking up. I could build my very own pyramid with them all. "It's really beautiful here." That's the truth. Waking up to that view across the valley every morning must be so peaceful. What a way to start the day.

Michelle appears by my side and places more tomatoes on the work surface for me to wash then points to the hills in the distance. "Every summer, Daniel and I would walk up there and have a picnic as our reward when we reached the top."

"And you don't do that anymore?" I ask, unable to hide my curiosity, because Daniel, Nathan's father, is nowhere to be seen and Nathan and his brothers never speak about him in front of anyone.

She shakes her head and lets out an even heavier sigh than mine. "We haven't since Daniel got his diagnosis."

Like that woman from the restroom made reference to, his father *is* ill?

Why has Nathan never told me? Why has no one mentioned him?

"Diagnosis?" I ask, blunter than I intended.

Michelle turns away from the window and walks to the kitchen island before making herself busy. "Parkinson's disease was not something we factored into Daniel's retirement plan. Nor was the dementia. Or a memory care home for that matter."

"I'm so sorry, Michelle, I didn't know." I wish Nathan had told me that to prepare me.

"No one does." She rubs the end of her nose with the back of her hand nervously. "Not outside of the family anyway. It's something Daniel asked us to keep under wraps. He said he didn't want people's pity because he believes this is life's form of payback for all the cases he lost and all the people he let down throughout his career."

That's a terrible perspective because I've been doing a little digging of my own again; I couldn't stop myself. And according to Daniel's case statistics he only lost a handful of cases at most throughout his career, which is what made him the top lawyer in the city before Nathan took over the firm.

And I can't help but feel guilty for my plan to bring pain or discomfort to a man who is already suffering.

"I'm sorry." I say again, meaning it. No matter who you are or what you did in your past, no one deserves to face a disease that is cruel and indiscriminatory. That type of illness just takes and keeps on taking regardless of the kind of person you are.

"Thank you, Arianna." Michelle picks the dinnerware off the kitchen island and walks to the large pine dining table. She starts laying a plate down for each of us at each setting, as his brothers are here too and arrived long before we did. "Now..." She claps her hands together once she's finished and checks the condiments. "Salad dressing. That's what we are missing. Then I'll call the boys in."

I get the impression Michelle doesn't want to talk about Daniel and I take the hint.

"I'll go get them." I wash the last of the tomatoes and place them in a large bowl for Michelle to finish off the Mediter-ranean-style salad she's preparing before drying my hands on the towel.

"Don't let them talk you into giving them more time. They're pretty good at that," she calls to me as I make my way out of the kitchen door and out onto the wraparound porch.

"Okay." I take her advice, smiling as I skip down the steps onto the path that leads to the tennis court at the back of the house.

"And Eli is a terrible loser. Good luck." Her laughter spills out of the house, making me join in and raise my hand in understanding, not that she can see me.

I unhook my sunglasses from the top pocket of my plaid shirt and put them on before taking in the view, pushing my hands into the back pocket of my jeans.

The way the sun is touching the contours of the valley makes it feel like it's hugging them, as if to tell them to keep us safe down here.

A blissed-out breath leaves my lungs, and I pull fresh air back into them. "God, that's good." Unlike the stifling air of the city.

An array of banter from Nathan and his brothers floats into my ears as I move closer to the tennis court.

Prepared for an argument to give them more time, I'm surprised to find them all walking toward the house looking like they left a magazine shoot.

Like the ultimate quadruple threat, they turn heads wherever they go. And while they share strikingly similar features, each has his own distinct style, charisma, and allure that make each of them unforgettable.

And Nathan? He sticks out by a mile. He's charming, powerful, and commands every room he's in. And his crystal-blue eyes always make me feel like they see me, all of me, and they show me that Nathan accepts me for me, which hits hard because there's a part of me that I am hiding.

I shake my head when Cole pushes Eli roughly. They may

be grown men in the office, but outside of it, they behave like a bunch of frat boys.

As soon as Nathan spots me, he drops his tennis racket then whips his T-shirt off, exposing his never-ending laddered abs I'd happily climb all day every day.

"We're going swimming." His eyes sparkle with mischief as he flashes me a bold grin.

"Dinner is ready." I thumb over my shoulder in the direction of the house, screwing my nose up at his untimely suggestion.

"Fuck it." He races toward me and faster than a bullet out of a gun, he's fireman-lifted me over his shoulder and is running across one of the fields while I squeal in surprise like a captured piglet, making his brothers laugh their heads off.

"Put me down." I slap his ass, hard. It's a nice ass, and I much prefer this view than the one from the kitchen window, but what the hell is he doing?

It's so out of character for him.

I can't deny I love it though. I love how relaxed he seems today.

"No." He slaps my denim-covered ass in return. "And be quiet, or you'll upset the snakes."

"Snakes?" I shriek, looking around the grassland.

"Shush, no screaming. We're going for a swim whether you like it or not."

"I'm not swimming, I don't have my swimsuit on." I puff and pant even though I'm not the one running. "I didn't bring one with me."

Also, snakes!

"We're going skinny-dipping." He continues down the embankment.

"What?" I shout in astonishment, making my voice echo

around the valley. "What if someone sees us?" Panic crawls up my throat.

"There is no one around for miles. Relax, baby," he says, barely out of breath, which is ridiculous. He must be as strong as a bull if he can carry me and run at the same time.

"Have fun." I hear Eli shouting after us.

I push my hair off my face and lift my head to find them watching us with amusement.

"Your mother's going to kill us for not being there for dinner," I huff, struggling to get any words out because I'm folded in half.

"She won't care. Trust me." Nathan's steps become slower as he makes his way down the steep hill, and I throw my arms around his waist to stop me from bumping around.

"Nathan, put me down." Using all my strength, I squeeze my arms which are wrapped around him, causing him to let out a *humpf* noise as I try to push the air out of his lungs and get him to do as I ask.

"Fuck, you're strong. We're here." He comes to a standstill, then pries my fingers open before laying my feet on the ground.

"Oh my God, what the hell do you think you're doing?" I smack his shoulder playfully as I try to compose myself from his unexpected kidnapping, but he doesn't care; instead, he proceeds to toe-off his sneakers, before removing his immaculate white tennis shorts and boxers that highlight his deep tan.

"Strip," he orders confidently, walking toward the slow-moving stream below.

What the hell? He's serious about skinny-dipping. "Nathan," I call out, my hands on my hips, on the verge of having a tantrum, but he steps into the water.

"I'll come back there and strip you naked myself if I have to." He raises his voice above the steady sound of the moving water.

"Get in, Arianna." Spinning around, he beckons me to him before dunking his head below the surface and reappearing again, pushing his wet hair off his forehead.

Biting my lower lip, I consider my options. Run back to the house, jump in his car, and head back to the city—but then I'll get arrested for stealing his car—or go skinny-dipping and have some fun with a man I didn't think knew the meaning of the word.

"Oh, screw it." I borrow Nathan's slogan he uses when he takes a blind gamble and remove my clothes quicker than a blink.

"I'm difficult to resist, right?" Nathan says, sounding cocky and looking smug as hell.

I step into the much warmer than expected water, still wearing my bra and panties.

"I'm not happy about this." I only brought a few sets of underwear.

"I never would have worked that out," he replies deadpan, joking with me. "This might make you happy. Come with me." Standing up in the waist-deep water, he urges me to take his hand, which I do, never able to resist him.

It's like something weird happens when I'm around him. I just can't say no anymore.

I'm dick drunk, I'm sure I am.

I follow his lead up stream.

"Here." He points to a wall of stones that have been made into the perfect circular shape, holding in water that looks like it's steaming. "It's a natural hot spring," he says, sharing one of the hidden treasures around the peaceful ranch.

Nathan steps over the small wall and I copy him, dipping my foot in to test the water first to discover it's warm, really warm.

"This is amazing," I say, the corners of my mouth lifting with happiness.

"I thought you'd like it, but you have too many clothes on." A small bump forms between his eyebrows in confusion. "And as you can see, it's a clothes-free spring."

I play along. "There isn't a sign up stating the rules."

"It's invisible. Only people with the surname Hart can see it."

"That right?"

"Yes. It's right there." Using his pointer finger, he gestures to the grassy riverbank.

"Oh, yeah, I think I see it, now that you come to mention it." I stare into the void and play his stupid game. "That sign must also be visible for people with the surname Donovan because if I'm reading that correctly, it also says no grumpy bastards allowed, which means you gotta leave." Very slowly, to tease him, I undo my front-fastening bra, removing it completely. I drape it over the stone wall of the natural Jacuzzi before sliding my panties down my legs and placing them next to my bra.

He licks his lips, watching my every move. His jaw tics as if he's trying to contain himself and not jump my bones, which I sort of wish he would.

"At least I can remove my clothes, but you can't shed that grumpy ass of yours, so I'll meet you back at the house," I say, keeping a straight face as I lower myself into the water and take a seat on one of the large stones beneath. Sliding myself further into the water all the way up to my neck, I close my eyes and my muscles sigh with relief. It feels like I'm in a warm bath, which is much needed after our all-night sex marathon.

"You're a fucking tease," he mutters.

I open one eye and smile. "Takes one to know one, Mr. Hart."

I splash water at him. "Get in. Your dick is very distracting." I dip my gaze to his thick length hanging heavy between his thighs and lick my lips. That man sure does have a mighty fine-looking cock.

Nathan eases himself into the hot water then glides over to me slowly like a wolf stalking its prey.

"You good?"

"Better than good." I let out a dreamy breath.

"It's what you needed; you've been working too hard."

"So have you."

"We both have," he counters, staring me down. "This is the first day off I've had in months."

"Did you check your emails this morning?" He's like a teenager obsessed with social media, but his obsession is email checking.

His fingertips tickle my thighs as he moves up my body. "No." He doesn't blink, and I know he's telling the truth.

Just when I think he's going to touch my hips, his hands disappear from my body. Instead, he sits next to me then spreads his arms out on either side of him around the edge of circular wall.

If he falls asleep, I'm going to let him. His sleep pattern is much better, but he needs more. I copy him when he closes his eyes and use the sounds of the open space, the birds, the water, the wind, to help me zone out.

We sit in comfortable silence for a while, letting the healing power of the water soothe our muscles.

"Do you like it here?" His question breaks my meditative state, causing me to open my eyes, and I look around.

"I love it here," I admit. "I can see why your parents rent this place out for weddings throughout the summer."

"It hasn't been a working cattle ranch for years and Mom wanted to do something to keep herself busy once we left for college and while she waited for dad to retire. Weddings seemed like a great idea and she's booked pretty much all summer, except for this weekend."

I shoot my shot.

"I'm guessing that since your dad's diagnosis, your mom is spending retirement on her own instead of enjoying it together with him."

The silence stretches between us again before he asks in a low tone, "Did she tell you about Dad?"

"Yeah." My voice is quiet too, and full of sincerity. "I'm sorry, Nathan."

Time passes before he responds.

"Somedays, he doesn't recognize any of us, which is harder on Mom. She visits him every day at the memory care home. Some days he's great and some days are not so good." It's a long time before he starts talking again. "Me and my brothers see each other every day and have that built-in support, but Mom is here all by herself most of the time and I know she loves organizing the weddings with all the staff she hires, and she keeps herself busy, but it's not the same as having your soulmate by your side."

My chest grows heavy with sadness for the family as tears prick my eyes.

Nathan keeps opening up. "It seems so unfair, unjust almost. My mom and dad had plans to travel the world together once he retired. They had their flights booked to Singapore, but his decline was fast, and they never did make their first trip." As he runs his hands down his face, I can tell he's struggling with his father's demise. "I feel sorry for Mom more than anyone. She raised us single-handedly, drove us to every after-school club there was, spent almost every weekend alone or with friends while my dad worked long hours, and yet still she waited for him. She was always waiting. And now"—he looks off into the distance—"she's still alone, still looking after us and just waiting for him and his symptoms to worsen, which they seem to do with every week that passes. And she never complains."

"She's a remarkable woman." I've only met her a handful of times, and already I know she's made from resilience and strength and does everything with determination and grace.

"I never wanted that for my own family," he admits.

"Is that why you never got married?" I think the way Nathan lives his life is all starting to make sense.

Him showing me this vulnerable side no one else gets to see makes me feel special. The hard exterior he wears every day is to protect himself, I know this all too well, because I wear one myself. Around him, though, I've been slowly shedding it and letting him into my life, something I'm not particularly good at because I'm always waiting for the ball to drop, a moment when the tide turns.

That's what makes what is happening between us scary, because I'm falling so fast and hard but what if I end up alone again?

And while I want to still pursue the truth for my family, part of me doesn't want to know now, because I'll lose him if I do and I think Nathan might be *the one*.

He keeps sharing his innermost fears. "I didn't want anyone resenting me or waiting around like my mom has her entire life, and even now, fifty years later, she's still alone." He lets out a long exhalation. "The life I have"—he stalls again—"is not an easy one. It takes up all my time."

My heart aches for him. And why can't he see that he's the one who can break the chain? His future doesn't have to follow the same path as his father's.

I climb into his lap, straddling him, and clasp his face with both hands. "Your life is not defined by someone else's expectations." The weight of it must be crippling, but I know how much he loves his job. "You are the one in control of your life, only you." I give it to him in the simplest of terms. "Continue to do the job you love, but you don't have to take so many cases on. You don't have to take any cases on at all for the rest of the year if you don't want to. Work, yes, and assist other cases, but don't dig yourself an early grave trying to maintain what your father did. You don't have anything to prove to anyone. You have three other brothers to carry the burden. What your father did to build the reputation of the firm and make the Hart name everyone's first choice for a lawyer is incredible, but you don't have to run at the same pace he did and then regret it for the rest of your life. Bring in more support if you need to, or implement an executive management team, because I don't want you waking up one day in thirty years' time regretting that you didn't take that trip to see the Taj Mahal or sleep under the stars by campfire or learn Spanish. If you don't take your foot off the gas now, before you know what's happened, you'll be ninety years old, alone, moaning about taxes and wearing incontinence underwear."

"Incontinence underwear?" His features screw up in disgust.

"Yes, it happens to the best of us, Nathan, and while you're wearing them, you'll still be bossing everyone around and telling yet another secretary of yours she'll never last the week." I try lightening the tense mood.

"God, you made my future sound fucking terrible."

"You need to slow down. Or that will be your life." My green eyes hold his blue ones.

I rest my hands on top of his shoulders and wiggle in his lap, causing his dick to bounce to life. I glide his thickening length between my pussy lips to distract us from the heaviness of our conversation.

"You're annoyingly right sometimes, has anyone ever told you that?" he asks with a hint of mockery in his tone.

"Many times," I reply with a broad smile, and I move my hips back and forth, his cock now as hard as a rock.

"Will you look after me in my old age?"

"You're already old," I say, messing with him.

"Just the way you like me, right?"

I told him that one night and I think he loved it when I confessed that. "Yes." My reply comes out as a moan when the head of his cock rubs my clit.

"I'm still young enough to fuck that smartass mouth of yours out of your system though."

I rise up on my knees, repositioning myself, getting ready to take him. All of him, not caring that the rocks beneath are most likely scratching the skin on my knees.

He pumps his cock with his fist under the water a few times before lining up the tip to the entrance of my aching pussy, and I lower myself down onto him slowly as he holds the root of his shaft firmly.

"Prove it," I tease.

36

NATHAN

"Follow me." I gently tug Arianna by her hand, making her trail behind me as we walk across the field.

"Where are we going?"

"It's a surprise."

"I hate surprises," she grumbles.

"Stop complaining."

"I like complaining."

"Stop talking."

"I also like talking."

"Arianna."

She chuckles from behind me, teasing me. "I quite like the way you tell me off in that deep voice of yours. It's very authoritative. And I have nothing to complain about because I have a great view. You have a very nice ass, Mr. Hart."

"I much prefer yours."

"I'm a smartass with a nice ass." She lets out a soft giggle at her own joke.

"Precisely."

Following our dip in the hot spring, where Arianna

proceeded to fuck my dick raw, we then joined everyone for dinner, grateful that my brothers made excuses for our late appearance and told mom that I gave Arianna a tour of the ranch. After we finished, I told her I had something to show her.

The dry grass crunches beneath our feet as we make our way to the edge of the pasture.

"Oh my God, are we staying in that tonight?" She squeals and quickens her steps, holding her hand to her chest.

"Yes."

"It's beautiful, Nathan." She gives my hand she's holding a squeeze.

"It's the honeymoon suite, but since there is no wedding here this weekend, I thought we could sleep in the treehouse."

"It looks like the castle from the Harry Potter films." She sounds lost in pure happiness.

"Never seen them."

"You've never lived."

"I work."

"Too much grind, not enough unwind. C'mon, let's go." She starts running, and the rhythmic rustling of the blades crackle under our feet as they bend and spring back up. Her energy is infectious and she's so fucking happy that I find myself running after her, feeling like a fucking teenage boy all over again as we hurtle toward the suspended treehouse.

Running much faster now, I pray that our dull thuds from our feet against the soil below scare away any rattlesnakes who love the grassland.

Arianna lets out a whoop of glee, making it bounce off the crests of the valley.

I look up at the newly built two-story treehouse we call the watch tower because it's set higher than all the others and has its very own suspended walkway through the trees to access it.

Walking along the wooden walkway that leads to the main entrance, I use my head to point to the door as we arrive. "It's open," I tell her.

When she pushes it open, she gasps in awe at the oak surroundings my mother spent hours selecting. From the paintings on the walls to the furniture, every item in here, she personally handpicked it all. I guess it was a distraction for her at the time when dad took a turn for the worse.

"Look at the fairytale turret, Nathan." She looks upward wearing a massive smile. "I feel like a princess."

I wrap my arms around her and look up too, impressed by the beamed ceiling.

"Mom had some of the world's best treehouse carpenters build this. There's another ten for wedding guests. Each one is unique. But this one is extra special."

Arianna lays her forearms on top of my shoulders and drops her gaze back to me. "Thank you for this, it's..." She's speechless.

"We can stay here any time we want. Mom closes the ranch throughout the winter."

"I might want to move in permanently."

The warm lighting all around us makes it look like she's glowing with happiness.

I clear my throat. "You could always move in with me. Permanently." I don't know what made me say it, but the timing feels right.

She tilts her head to the side, her forehead creasing as she puzzles over my offer. "Are you being serious? I mean, it's a little fast is it not?" Her arms disappear from my shoulders and she begins pacing back and forth across the wooden flooring, every clunk of her boots mimicking the beat of my heart with worry.

Please say yes.

"We've been dating"—I go to correct myself because we

haven't mentioned dating as such—"I mean, sleeping together, having fun, whatever you want to call it, for months." It might not seem very long to some people, but to me, it feels like I've known her all my life.

It's not just fun for me anymore. She's it for me.

Fretting some more, she adds, "And you don't know me, not really, and then there's my apartment. I like it. I mean, it's okay but it's not where I want to stay for the rest of my life because I've been saving up to move to a better area, but moving in with you, that's huge." She threads her hands through her long dark hair as if anxious. "I would have to give up my apartment, and it was so difficult to find something I liked to begin with. I searched for months." Her lips press into a thin line of uncertainty, and I love that she seems to be having some sort of mini meltdown at my suggestion.

It's a big deal, I get it.

She finally comes to a standstill, shoves her fingertip into her mouth then bites her nail nervously, her eyes rapidly bounce about like a deer caught in headlights before they land on me.

I give her a little reassurance, a buffer, so to speak. "Keep the apartment, and I'll pay your mortgage loan, just move in with me, as a trial for a few months, to see how we get on." If she says yes to moving in with me, I'm never letting her leave.

"A trial period?"

"Yes. But if we have an argument, you can't run back to your old apartment. We stay up all night until we work it out."

She cocks her head to the side as if bewildered.

She takes too long to answer. Her silence is giving me anxiety, my mouth drier than a sponge.

"And this isn't a big deal," I lie and then try dumbing it down. "You practically live at my place already and it would make it easier for us to travel to work together. It makes sense."

"Easier?" she asks, looking petrified.

Fuck, maybe I blew it.

"Yeah, and it's not like you're my girlfriend or anything. We don't have a label for us, Arianna. The sex we have is fucking incredible. And it's not like you're catching feelings for me or anything." She doesn't disagree with me, which stings. "It's just easier," I say, annoyed because everything I just said is a complete fucking lie.

I know how I feel.

"Okay," she finally responds.

"Okay?" My chest swells with pride as satisfaction washes over me.

I move toward her and pull her close to me, holding her with firm possession. "You won't regret it," I murmur, my voice low in tone.

My life is suddenly starting to feel like it makes sense and I'm going to do everything in my power to keep her safe and happy. If I thought she was mine before, she damn sure is mine now. This is real.

"I'm going to look after you so good, baby." A sense of excitement overwhelms me, and I kiss her deeply, letting her know she's mine and I'm hers.

"Are you sure about this?" Her lips twitch nervously against mine, her voice a bit too timid, which unsettles my buoyant mood.

In my mind, nothing changes. She stays with me five nights out of seven and the other two I spend at hers.

What's with the hesitation?

"I'm certain. Organize a moving company for next week," I say, trying to reassure her.

"That soon?" She sounds almost disbelieving, her eyes wide as if she's panicked.

"And remodel my apartment in any style you want. I like yours."

Her brows dip and the space between them thickens. "Really?"

This is a much bigger step for her than I first thought.

"Make mine homier." I try again to convince her.

"Because yours is too fuck-pad-like at the moment."

"What the hell does 'fuck-pad-like' mean?" A low chuckle makes my chest rumble, my nerves now at about ten on the scale of vulnerability. I've never wanted to share my life with anyone.

"Your décor is like a one-night stand; it doesn't mean anything and has no significance."

"Jesus." That's fucking brutal. "Well, *our* one-night stand turned into something." I go to correct myself. "I mean, turned into the best sex of my life." Which makes her grimace for a fleeting moment and I wish I had the balls to admit to her that I have real feelings for her without scaring her off.

She's the most significant person in my life, my priority, but I get the feeling if I tell her that she'll bolt like a bull out of its pen.

"Same for me." Her body visibly relaxes with the sound as she considers my offer to move in with me, as if accepting we are what we are. For now.

"So it's a yes?" I ask again for clarification. My heart might stop beating if she changes her mind.

Biting her bottom lip, she stares at me for much longer than I want, which makes uncertainty prickle across my skin.

What is she so scared of? "Just think of it like a cab ride to work and sex on tap."

It's nothing like that and we both know it because we do everything together now from sunup to sundown and every hour in between.

"Okay," she finally replies.

I freeze, letting her words settle between us. An apocalypse could hit the world, and I wouldn't care as long as I'm with her.

A knowing grin shapes my lips, the feeling of happiness overwhelming me, and I lean in slightly, closing the gap between us, then place a soft kiss on her mouth. "It took you long enough to agree," I say, teasing her. "Tell me again, let me hear you say it." I need to hear it again for my own sanity.

"Yes, I'll move in with you." There's so much confidence in her voice, I almost suggest we call a moving company now.

I hope she hears every word I say next and mean. "I'm not perfect, Arianna, and I've never done this before." My voice is deep and raspy as I slide my hands up either side of her neck.

"I'm not perfect either, and I've never lived with my boss before."

"I fucking hope not, Nick Williams is a married man and represents clients I wouldn't touch with a ten-foot pole." A brief laugh breaks from her throat and I bow my head to kiss her tempting lips.

To me, she is perfect.

"You're amazing," I gush, unable to prevent my confession, because I've never felt this way about anyone before. She's thrown me for a loop but I'm here for the ride, all of it.

"Take me to bed and show me how amazing you think I am." She nips at my lips, and I lift her into my arms, her legs instinctively wrapping around my waist as I walk us up the stairs to the bedroom.

I don't have to be asked twice.

Annoyed that I can't sleep, while Nathan breathes in and out in deep slumber, I watch the shadows from the trees moving in the wind dance across the exposed wooden beams of the cozy treehouse.

I give into the inevitable and prop myself up slowly so as not to wake Nathan.

Leaning against the headboard, I grab my phone off the nightstand and, using facial recognition, I open my hidden photos folder and pull up every piece of evidence from my family's case I photographed and read through them all again for the millionth time.

It's pointless, I know this because I won't find anything new.

Because facts are facts.

Over dinner, I listened in awe as Nathan, his brothers, and their mother reminisced about the many clients Daniel had represented, the meaningful impact he made in the community, and the countless hours of pro bono work their family dedicates to each year. Their passion for justice and commitment to serving others is undeniable, and they spoke with a deep sense of purpose, wishing they had even more time to give back. It was clear that for them that the law is not just a job but a calling, one they use to help those in need.

They're good.

Daniel Hart is a great man.

This is the part I have been struggling with the most.

My duplicity in thinking otherwise.

The duality has felt like a deception. Every day. When Nathan asked me to move in with him, I knew I had to jump one way or the other off the fence I have been sitting on. I had my doubts for a moment. I think he felt it too, saw it in my face perhaps. But if anything, my family's deaths have taught me that life is too precious and can be taken from you at any time. Nathan's father had his health taken from him, which seems unfair given how many people he helped throughout his life.

It's unfair.

And he doesn't deserve the illness that was put upon him.

He was a smart man, top of his game, and legit.

Hart Law is legit.

I can now see what I couldn't see before.

I don't think Nathan's father was involved. I think it was all down to Kevin Taylor.

Because there is no evidence in the files to suggest Daniel had any involvement in fraudulent or corrupt activities in my family's case. In any of his cases.

Too clouded by my grief and with a need to blame someone, anyone, I failed to see the truth.

I flick through my photos on my screen one after the other, there are the documents, backed up by public records of evidence reports and the crash report, telling me I was completely off base.

I spent hours in the records room at Hart Law and I figured

out all is above board. Every fact checks out; no issues and everything is in order.

Except for the redacted letter, which still confuses me. The case was filed, thoroughly conducted, and the verdict was clear: not guilty.

There are no lies or secrets hidden in plain sight. Just facts and an outcome that has never sat well with me but one I must learn to accept.

Eventually I will find peace, but I've been unsettled for so long, it will take a while to shift that unease.

I close my phone down and place it on the nightstand, then slide back down under the comforter and make myself comfortable.

Working for Hart Law has given me the clarity and perspective I needed. Being here has reaffirmed that too. This sacred time with his brothers has been exactly what I needed.

It's time to let go of the past and move on, accept what has been.

And begin a new future.

With Nathan.

I turn on to my side to be met with Nathan's deep breathing, telling me he's in the heaviest of sleeps, something he's struggled with for as long as he can remember, though he tells me he sleeps better next to me. But I think it's the massages and more downtime that is helping.

I think I love him.

Worry works its way into my veins and I pray Julie never tells Nathan about who I really am and what my original intention was, because not only will it break Nathan, it will also destroy us, me, him, his family.

I don't want that.

Kevin's family is something I need to look into more, find out everything I can about them. That's where my focus lies now.

But learning more about Julie's unsettling behavior tonight at dinner where Max recounted in detail what she did on her path of revenge makes me feel uneasy. From fake news stories to using shady informants and paying wannabe actors to fabricate quotes and articles, it would seem that Julie's pillow talk was loose lipped in the afterglow, which left Max feeling cold and was ultimately what made him ask her to leave his apartment.

Like I said, the Hart family have standards.

But it made Julie wreak havoc on the Harts, which she is still doing. Max showed me a fake article written by her about a court case that never happened. Nathan said they never sued her because it would have attracted unwanted and negative attention, choosing to ignore it.

She's dangerous.

A dagger behind a smile. And I realize now she was very good at it with me. She used my weakness, and I think she saw me as an opportunity to get her revenge on Max.

I don't recognize the woman he spoke about tonight.

How could I when I've only ever been out for a few drinks and events with her? And thinking about it now, not many people were that enamored to see her, and all made excuses to be elsewhere. I've opened my eyes to what I had overlooked.

My grief has not only made me act out of character and make decisions that came from pain, but it made me gravitate toward someone who may or may not have my best interests at heart.

That's why I decided to drop an email straight after dinner informing her that I know I was wrong and whatever information she was still trying to find, to stop as we have been looking in the wrong place and that I am shifting my focus. I didn't tell her who I was focusing on but I made it very clear that the Hart family were not involved.

I'm done with her.

And now I have to move forward with my life.

I can't believe Nathan wants me to move in with him.

For me, it's bigger than the step the first man took on the Moon.

Not telling him who I really am is becoming the biggest elephant in the room. Maybe he doesn't feel it, but I do. That elephant is sitting on my shoulders every day.

I play every scenario out in my head and all roads lead to a shitty outcome, and I'll lose him either way. Deciding to keep mum is the only way forward.

I want to live with him.

It's so simple, really.

I read between the lines of what he said, and I know he's scared of getting hurt because we aren't just sex and a car ride to work together.

We are everything to each other but neither of us are willing to throw our hearts in the ring for them to be punched to death, so we'll continue to dance around the unspoken things, knowing we are more than we can admit.

Eventually, I must drift off and a woman floats behind my eyes. She's smiling and laughing one minute, then screaming the next... She's lost control... joy tangled with pain... pulled between extremes... And then, piece by piece, she begins to unravel before she dissolves into the dark, her voice a blend of agony and ecstasy before she reappears, rewrapping herself in layers of hope, acceptance, and new memories, rebuilding...

38

ARI

Nathan nuzzles into my neck from behind as we slowly wake up together in the treehouse. The warmth of him wrapped around me feels like I'm being swaddled in a giant blanket of comfort and safety, a cocoon that shields us from the world outside. "Mmm, let's stay in bed all day." His unhurried, lazy morning voice sounds a little slurred.

"I promised your mom that I would help her with breakfast this morning." My voice sounds groggier than his. "And she said she was going to dig out the photo albums of you as a baby."

He groans as if embarrassed about me seeing him as a little boy, but I can feel him smiling against my shoulder. Planting soft kisses down my neck, he stalls at the top of my scar that runs all the way to the bottom of my shoulder blade and I stiffen, which I know he senses immediately.

"I'm sorry," he rasps.

I don't reply. Can't.

There's a subtle shift in the air, an awkwardness that swirls around us.

"Will you tell me about it one day?" he asks, burying his nose in my hair.

I knew it's a question that would come sooner or later.

It's something I've put off explaining, and he deserves an explanation. If he's fully letting me into his life, I should do the same in return.

I can't bring myself to turn around and look him in the eye because his father is so intrinsically linked to my family. The more time I spend with Nathan and learn how difficult it has been since his father's health declined, the more it makes me want to dig a hole, bury my guilt for thinking he wronged my family and forget about it completely, because if they ever find out my true intentions at the beginning, it will cause even more pain for him and his family.

I can admit that I have my flaws, and often good people do bad things.

Kevin Taylor on the other hand, well, that's a different story. Daniel wasn't involved but Kevin still went free. I plan on uncovering what he did behind Nathan's father's back to exonerate himself. Nathan's family are good people, nice. I should never have doubted anyone to begin with.

There's a lot of peace within me now.

Peace with Nathan and his family.

Which is so unexpected.

Falling for the son of the man I've long believed to be responsible for the injustice done to my mom, dad, and sister was never supposed to happen. Yet here I am, torn between the weight of my past and the relentless tug of my heart.

My next words jolt nervously from my throat. "I was fifteen when it happened. My sister, Riley, and I had been at gymnastics practice. After, Mom and Dad took us to that great pizza place on Geary Boulevard to celebrate me and my sister making the finals for the state championship on Beam. Riley loved the pepperoni special that came with extra cheese and pepperoni." I smile, remembering how it was her favorite.

Except for the gentle brush of his thumb against the skin of my stomach, as if reassuring me he's here for me, Nathan remains as still as a statue behind me.

I close my eyes, and it takes me straight back to that night, every memory still fresh in my mind. From the sound of the engine to the pain in my shoulder, I remember it all.

And I can still smell that pungent smell of gasoline in my nostrils, something that to this very day makes me gag if I even get a faint whiff of it.

"We were out later than usual, and it was dark, foggy too. I remember Dad saying how bad it was that night." I take my time to get my thoughts straight. "And the next thing I remember was waking up and I couldn't move my arm. And Riley... she was outside of the car, just lying there, still in her teal leotard, and I couldn't move. I shouted to her; I kept shouting, but she was already gone." Tears escape my eyes, soaking the pillow below me.

"And there was this man who showed up and I begged him to help me, but he just ran off and after that I passed out from the pain in my shoulder." I wipe my nose with the back of my hand, unable to control my tears. "I didn't know at the time that the car was upside down and a piece of metal was lodged in my back." As if my scar remembers, a shoot of pain radiates through it. "The report said that even though Mom and Dad were wearing their seatbelts, they died instantly from blunt force trauma and internal bleeding. But Riley"—I suck in a stuttered breath—"she... she wasn't wearing her seatbelt, and she was thrown from the car." I shake my head against the pillow. "I miss her." So much. "I miss them all." Every day.

"Baby." He pulls me closer to him, sealing his front to my back. "I'm so sorry."

My heart twists in my chest. I hate people feeling sorry for me. I don't want their pity; what I want is my family.

I tell him what happened next. "With no family to care for me, after my shoulder operation I was discharged from hospital. I then went into a group home for a while, and after that I was placed in a foster home with a woman named Jean who became my foster mom. She took care of me until she died when I was twenty-one. She was older, only had one son, and her place was a rental, so when she passed away, I used some of the money I had saved from my wages to rent my own place. Although it wasn't my place because I shared it with five other people." It was chaos, and studying for my legal secretary certification while working full-time at Williams and Jones was exhausting.

I take my time to reply from fear of blurting out words about the role his father played in it, words I may regret. Instead, I say, "The man who killed them never went to prison. He walked free." Kevin Taylor is dead now. He had a heart attack while on vacation with his family. I know this because I know everything about Kevin Taylor. A wealthy influential businessman who probably paid the judge and the crime scene investigators a lot of money to clear his name and hoodwinked Daniel to make him believe he was innocent. That's the only explanation.

While my family lost their lives, he went about his without a care in the world. And I lost everyone I ever loved.

"Why was he not sentenced?" Nathan asks with his lawyer hat on, but his tone is gentle and full of concern.

"The jury and judge ruled it as an accident."

"And you don't believe them?" The serious timbre in his voice tells me he knows I don't.

"I never have." I feel unsettled every day about the verdict.

"I can investigate the case again. I would do that for you, Arianna."

I whip around in his arms as panic swirls through my veins. I don't want him to know it was his father who defended Kevin Taylor. Not until I find out the truth. "Promise me you won't do that." I stare up into his worried face. "I don't think I'm ready to know." It's a slight twist on the truth, because if I'm right then what happens to us? I lose him too; I just know it. And I've only just found him.

What a mess.

I blink repeatedly, a chill running down my spine at the thought of not speaking to him every day. Nathan Hart. The man who stepped into my heart and made a home there. Every smile, every touch, every moment with him feels like he's healing my heart and my soul. Every day with him gets easier and more incredible. And now, the thought of never seeing him again feels impossible, like asking the sun not to rise or the stars not to shine. It would tear me apart. Losing him is my worst fear and one I hope I never have to face. We belong together, and I'll hold on to him for as long as I can. Forever preferably.

"Okay," he agrees. "But if you ever change your mind, just ask."

A wedge of emotion fills my throat. "Thank you." I reach up and cup his face with my hand and brush my thumb across the scruff of his beard.

"I hate seeing you sad, baby." He kisses the tip of my nose and wipes away the tears that have run down my temples.

"Sometimes when I catch a glimpse of my scar, it reignites memories of the accident and reminds me of what I lost. I think that's why I don't like you touching it." I don't like touching it myself. "It's a tragic, permanent connection to their deaths, and my scar may be healed, but I am not. I never will be." That hurts my heart to say out loud.

A tremor of a smile touches his lips. "Your scar shows strength and survival. You overcame unimaginable loss. You're a testament to your family. Strong, and talented. The job you do now makes a difference to people's lives. We do, together."

I've never seen it that way before and my lips tremble at his heartfelt observation.

"Does it hurt? Your shoulder?" Using his head, he gestures to my back.

"Not anymore, but I sometimes still feel like there's metal in there. It's like phantom pain or something. And I get these weird shooting pains down my arm."

He pulls me into his arms again and wraps me in a huge bear hug I've come to love.

"I watch you sometimes clenching your fist and stretching out your shoulder," he admits.

"I think I do that out of habit more than anything else. But my physical therapist thinks I might have issues with compressed nerves in my shoulder, which means I sometimes get this electric shock sensation down my arm and into my fingers."

"We should get that looked at. You might have a brachial plexus injury, which can affect your neck down into your shoulder. You need to make massages and physical therapy a priority every week. That's an order."

"It doesn't help sitting at a desk most days."

"And you type faster than a hacker in a movie hunched over that laptop of yours." He offers a moment of light relief from me reliving the night that changed the path of my life.

"If it hadn't been for the accident, maybe I would have competed in the Olympics." That was always my dream. "When the doctor told me that I wouldn't have the same strength in my shoulder as I did before, I never went back to gymnastics." Not that I could have. I was moved to the other side of town. I withdrew. Barely spoke to anyone at my new school, except for Maeve, and spent every day praying it was all a dream, that maybe one day I would wake up to find them all sitting around the breakfast table arguing about what we were having for dinner. Riley hated vegetables, but Mom always insisted on making her eat them.

"Well, what you can't do in physical gymnastics, you more than make up for with verbal gymnastics. You're a fucking smartass, do you know that?"

"I am not," I disagree, half laughing, feeling better for sharing my story with him.

"Keep telling yourself that. Maybe I need to stuff your mouth full of my cock and make better use of it."

His cock jerks between our sealed-together bodies.

"Not happening." Feeling lighter, I grab his face and kiss him quickly, then leap out of his arms and the bed. "I have breakfast duties to attend to."

Nathan groans in annoyance then pats the mattress. "Get back here, now. Breakfast can wait."

"No, it can't." I pull on my panties then my jeans. "Now get up and come help. If you behave, I'll let you fuck my mouth."

Exasperated, he throws the covers back, revealing his hard cock. "Negotiating with you is like trying to haggle with a robot."

"Takes one to know one, Mr. Hotshot Lawyer." I yelp when he grabs me from behind as I wrestle with the arms of my plaid shirt, and he catches me off guard.

"Stop moving," he whispers in my ear, sounding serious.

I still in his embrace.

"Thank you for sharing your story with me, Arianna." The sincerity in his words is unmistakable.

I nod, unable to reply as guilt overcomes me, because I didn't share everything.

My new job started out with a mission and one outcome, but now it's turned into something entirely different.

"I've never done the commitment thing before. But after you shared your innermost secret with me, I might just want to share my life with you—completely. Every up and down, every trial and triumph, every damn millisecond of every day. You belong with me in my apartment." Opening up to me seems like a huge step for him. Us.

If only I could be completely truthful with him.

"Do you think if you like living with me, it will become a more long-term permanent thing?" he asks.

Does he mean give up my apartment, engagement, marriage... What exactly?

Holy fuckballs. Limo rides to work together and sex, my ass. This is a big deal.

"Are you still drunk from the wine last night?" I brush him off, nerves fluttering in my gut, and turn around to look at him as he drops his arms that were holding me in place.

He shakes his head, rushes past me, and smacks a kiss to my startled open mouth. "Just think about what that might look like long-term, baby," he says, cupping his junk confidently as he enters the ensuite. "You can pick your jaw off the floor now or you'll catch flies with it open that wide."

Catch flies? It's feelings I've caught, big ones, ones that feel a lot like love.

Nathan Hart wants to make us permanent, whatever the hell that means.

This is either going to go one of two ways for me. If I keep my mouth shut about my true intentions at the beginning, it will go beautifully, and if I don't, Julie might tell him, and it could be a giant-sized glorious disaster.

Think about it, he said.

Hell, I can't think about anything else.

39

ARI

I'm sitting at my desk, archiving Nathan's case files, feeling more contented than I've ever been.

Moving in with Nathan has been incredible and now permanent doesn't look so scary to me. It's been over a month since I moved in and with each passing day I fall more and more in love with him.

I've never said the words, I love you.

Neither has he to me, but I think he does.

Even his mom said that yesterday when she called to ask us to dinner tomorrow night, informing me that she'd never seen him like this before. She actually said he had hearts in his eyes that looked a lot like love which made him playfully end the call, but then he phoned her straight back and lied telling her his reception dropped out.

Chuckling to myself at the memory, I hum along to The Beach Boys, "God Only Knows," the song that's been swirling around my head all morning.

Just like Nathan, the beat is addictive.

A ding from my phone alerts me to new emails arriving in

my inbox and I sit up straighter, a knot in my throat building instantly when I see Julie's name flashing across the screen of my cell.

It's been months since I last spoke to her, because after I decided I was all in with Nathan, combined with Max's recount about how Julie screwed him over, and adding the fact Julie never sent me anything, I figured she was lying that she had anything concrete in the first place. My mind was made up and my decision was final; Daniel wasn't involved. And while I have been trying to dig for more information on Kevin Taylor, I have yet again come up short.

I think hiring a private investigator will be my best shot, but I have yet to narrow down my shortlist.

My fingers move fast across the screen, and I tap open her email and then the attachment.

I stare at my screen and reread the words.

Then again.

And again, making sure I understand, and I'm unable to believe what I'm seeing.

I hit print, then run to the printer before anyone sees it.

As I head back to my desk, the paper shakes in my trembling hands and I read it again.

Crash Report Summary
Case Number: 10CR07354

Weather Conditions: Clear night, no adverse weather conditions.
Road Conditions: Dry, no visible hazards or obstructions.
Incident Type: Two-vehicle collision with fatalities.

Summary of Findings: At approximately 11 p.m., a collision occurred between Vehicle 1, Toyota Corolla, and Vehicle 2, Ford F150, on Cabrillo Highway. Weather conditions were clear and road conditions were dry, with no visible oil spills, debris, or hazards present on the roadway.

Upon initial investigation, it was determined that Vehicle 2 driven by Mr. Kevin Taylor, traveling at a high rate of speed and in an erratic manner, crossed into the lane of Vehicle 1, causing a head-on collision. The force of the impact resulted in three fatalities in Vehicle 1: Mr. Robert Donovan, Mrs. Emily Donovan, and Ms. Riley Donovan and were pronounced dead at the scene. Another passenger of Vehicle 1 sustained injuries but survived the crash.

Vehicle 2's driver was uninjured but appeared to show signs of impairment, and preliminary findings suggest that a combination of alcohol and excessive speeding may have contributed to the cause. Further analysis is recommended to confirm the exact cause of the driver's behavior.

There are no witness statements but the evidence of tire marks and vehicle positions suggest that Vehicle 2's actions were directly responsible for the crash. No contributing external factors were found to be involved.

Conclusion: The crash resulted in the deaths of three individuals and the serious injury of the surviving passenger due to the reckless or negligent actions of the driver of Vehicle 2. The evidence points to a clear responsibility on the part of the driver of Vehicle 2, whose actions—likely influenced by speed and/or impairment—directly led to the fatal crash. Further investigation into the driver's alcohol/drug use is ongoing, and charges may be filed accordingly.

Is this real?

This is not the same crash report in my family's case file.

I throw my hand to my mouth to cover my dismay and slowly shake my head.

My lungs tighten as my breathing takes on a life of its own.

"I don't feel so good," I say to no one in particular. "I have to go."

Joseph jumps out of his seat and is by my side in a flash. "Do you want me to call Nathan?"

"No," I snap, not meaning to cause Joseph to jerk back in surprise. "I'm sorry, just, will you tell him I felt unwell, and I'll see him tomorrow or maybe the day after?" I need space and time to gather my thoughts. "I think I'm coming down with the flu and I should stay away from Nathan. He's in court for the next week and in the middle of a huge case. The last thing he needs is coming down with whatever I have," I lie.

"Do you want me to call you a cab then?" His voice is instantly full of worry at my sudden mysterious illness.

Which isn't a mystery. I just need to get the hell out of here.

"No, thank you," I say, lifting my purse off the floor in a daze. "I'll see you in a couple of days. I need to go to bed." I pull a tight smile and stuff the crash report into my purse.

I knew my life was going too well. I knew the ball would drop eventually.

I've spent a month of bliss in Nathan's arms, and now, if I decide to act on this information, that's all I might be getting.

The dates he organized, more days at the ranch, lazy evenings on the sofa; he even watched *Harry Potter* with me. I adore his family. I adore him.

More than that, I love him.

I know it now for sure, but what do I do with this information?

Who covered this up?

Was his father involved after all?

If so, where does this leave us?

The inevitable... I knew it... falling in love with a man linked to my family was stupid of me, and now I think I might finally have to face this head on.

My complicated life just got even more complex.

Rushing toward the elevator, I keep my head down to avoid seeing or speaking to anyone and say a swift goodbye to Joseph as I press the call button, then wait for it to arrive.

"C'mon, c'mon," I mutter under my breath and press it again impatiently.

The office feels like the full weight of its structure is sitting on my chest and trying to suffocate me.

Eventually it arrives and when I step inside, I break down just as the doors slide shut, and I press the ground-floor button to get the hell out of here.

My stomach in knots, I swipe away at a never-ending stream of tears running down my cheeks.

"This wasn't supposed to happen. It just can't be real." I yank the report out of my purse and stare at the blurry words.

Weather conditions were clear.

Road conditions were dry.

No visible oil spills.

No debris.

No hazards present on the roadway.

Alcohol.

Excessive speeding.

The words all blur into one big alphabetical jumble.

Is this the real report?

Was the other a fake?

Where did Julie get this?

She's unreliable. A fraud. That's what Max, Nathan, all of them told me.

Showed me, even. The fabricated articles she published to damage Hart Law's reputation. I read them all, and everything I've seen with my own eyes and know about Hart Law is lawful and goes against everything I thought I knew before I started working here.

Nathan and his brothers are kosher; his father, though, I've never met so how can I be so sure he is too? Maybe I wrote him off too quickly.

I'm now struggling to know what and who to believe, and how to separate fact from fiction.

I lay my hand on my stomach feeling like I am about to vomit my lunch back up and intake a deep breath to stop the squeamish feeling.

The weight of the decision squeezes my lungs, and I struggle to breathe.

My mission was always clear cut—loyalty to my family above all else.

But now there's him.

My Nathan.

The man I love.

The man I think meant he wanted to marry me when he said make us permanent.

It's what I want.

I still do.

I want to marry the man who let me cry in his arms on the night of my sister's birthday and made me believe in a love that went beyond my obligation to my family, but now, somehow, that doesn't feel right.

If I ignore this new information, I'll be turning my back on my family and if I expose this crash report, he will never forgive me and I'll lose him, and yet again, I'll end up alone.

There's no simple path.

I love them all and want the best for everyone, but whatever choice I make I betray someone.

What do I do?

I run out of the elevator and through the foyer, patting my face with the back of my hand to wipe away any evidence that I've been crying, in case I bump into anyone.

"I just need a few days," I whisper to myself and inhale a deep breath as I step outside of the building.

Fear wraps around me like a tight coat as I try breathing fresh air into my lungs, but all it does is make me feel as if I'm suffocating.

I need somewhere to think, to hear my own thoughts away from the noise so I can find my answer.

What if there isn't one?

40

NATHAN

ME

How are you feeling today, baby? x

ARIANNA

Much the same. x

ME

When are you coming home? x

ARIANNA

As soon as I am snot free. I don't want you
catching my bug, you're in court all this week
and next, and your work is important.

ME

I like how much you care about me and my
health, but I need you back under my roof and
in my bed. x

ARIANNA

I think I'll be better in a few days. x

ME

Let me come visit. Please? x

ARIANNA

I told you, I'm quarantining. x

ME

Well, if you need anything, just let me know, and I can think of about a hundred ways to make you feel better. *winking-face emoji* x

ARIANNA

I'm sure you can. Thank you for my flowers yesterday. They are beautiful. x

ME

Not as beautiful as you. I have to go back into court, verdicts in. x

I consider my next line, wanting to tell her how much I love her, but I know it's a dick move. I want to be looking into her eyes when I say it so she knows how much I mean it.

We haven't said those words to each other, but I know she loves me. I feel it, feel her pouring love into my body with every touch of her fingertips on my skin.

And the way she looks at me like I'm her whole fucking world feels fucking incredible.

She loves me, and I love her, it's simple.

ARIANNA

Good luck but I know you've got this. x

ME

Always the winner. Speak later. x

I close my messages app, switch my cell phone off then stretch out my neck, the tension there evident. My muscles have been throbbing since Arianna left the office the other day and had Joseph pass on a message that she was feeling sick.

All I've done since then is worry about her every minute of every hour.

She's been quiet. Too quiet. Distant, almost. Which is unlike her because she shares everything with me, even down to what brand of shampoo she's trying out to see if it will help with the volume.

I have no idea what the fuck that means, but it made her happy, and yet, for the last few days she's just not around. And I know she's sick, but she's barely replied to any of my messages, or picked up when I called, insisting that her throat hurt too much to talk.

Fuck it. I don't care how sick she is, my court case is over after today and if I get sick then we can spend the next week bundled up in each other's arms in her little apartment together.

Decision made.

I'm visiting her the minute I win this case and I'm out of court.

Knowing I'm going to see her in a few hours, my heart races and I already feel better.

Then I'll tell her how I really feel.

I never knew love could feel this good.

Get ready, baby, I'm coming for you.

41

NATHAN

Following a successful win in court this afternoon I had Jenkins drop me at my apartment where I had the quickest shower on record, changed, then drove myself to the pharmacy to buy some flu medication and throat lozenges for Arianna.

Hell knows what she needs, but I bought one of everything. Anything to help her feel better.

I may have sworn one too many times when I was stuck in downtown traffic on my way here, frustrated by commuters making their way home early. I fucking hate rush-hour traffic.

Living out on the ranch sounds peaceful and I can see why Mom bought the place years ago. It was a smart move; it's just such a shame she isn't living her best life with Dad and is now beginning her golden years by herself.

Me and my brothers visited Dad yesterday and I got the shock of my life when I saw him for the first time in two weeks. His decline in health was sudden, but once he was placed on the right medication to lessen his symptoms he plateaued for a while and I didn't want to believe Mom when she said Dad hadn't been great for the last couple of weeks, but she was right.

His mobility has lessened, he's more fidgety, which is what the doctor called dystonia, and he struggled to talk or hold a conversation yesterday which upset Cole.

Dad's deteriorating health has hit him the hardest, with him being the youngest, and he's the one who made us all go for tests to determine if we had the same Parkinson's disease and dementia gene. Part of me was curious and another part of me was quite happy to stay in the dark. Watching my father's health worsening has been painful for everyone.

Luckily for all of us, no one inherited it and when we told Mom, she broke down, relieved to hear the positive news. Something there hasn't been much of in the family as of late.

Much later than I planned, I finally pull up outside Arianna's apartment, the powerful hum of my Bentley Continental cutting through the quiet night. My heart pounds with anticipation—I haven't seen her in days, and every second apart has felt like an eternity. As I kill the engine, a grin tugs at my lips. She has no idea how much I've missed her.

To surprise her, I use the spare key she keeps at my place to quietly let myself into her apartment, closing the door gently so I don't wake her if she's asleep. The soft trickle of running water brings a smile to my face—it means she's in the shower and maybe, just maybe, she's starting to feel better.

I choose to let her be and head into the living room, settling in to wait for her.

Stacks of papers and folders, notes and files cover the coffee table and floor and I tut to myself, annoyed at her that she even brought work home with her.

I take a seat on the sofa and pick up a piece of paper with a printout of a case file number I don't recognize. As my eyes move down the photographed label, I spot the attorney and read the name. "Daniel Hart."

What the hell is she looking for?

I rack my brain for an answer, sifting through the dozens of photos and paperwork she's printed off and read the date on the file, and calculate it's a case from fourteen years ago.

A pile of papers fall off the table, scattering across the floor, and my breath hitches in my chest when I see a photograph of my father, me, and my brothers with red scribble notes underneath them that look like a list of questions.

Something isn't adding up here.

This isn't research for a case of mine. It's something she's working on herself.

I read the list of questions on the photograph of us, astonished by what I am reading.

Did the lawyer have ties to the defendant's family?

Were key witnesses paid off or threatened?

Who handled the evidence, and could it have been tampered with?

Did the insurance company play a role in covering up the truth?

Were there any past complaints or investigations into Daniel Hart, or Hart Law as a whole?

Has Hart Law been involved in other suspicious cases?

Did Kevin Taylor pay Daniel Hart as bribery to set him free? Was there a deal struck?

Did the judge have a history of questionable rulings?

Who else could have benefited from the verdict?

Was the crash report fabricated? If so, how much were they paid? Who worked there at the time of the accident?

"What the fuck?" Bile rises in my gut and bubbles like a volcano as I flick through more photos and scribbled notes until I come across two almost identical-looking crash reports. They contradict one another but I can tell one is a fake immediately from the non-government-issued paper, because the specific texture looks different and the watermark is in the wrong place.

"Three fatalities. Mr. Robert Donovan, Mrs. Emily Donovan, and Ms. Riley Donovan." I read their names out loud.

This is evidence from the crash that killed her family.

Which means my father defended the man she said killed them.

Has this been her plan all along? To expose my father for bribery and foul play?

My father is the most straight and honest person I know and would never do such a thing.

My jaw tightens and I let out a slow controlled exhale to contain the storm building within me when I read the email that stabs me through the heart.

I scan the lines of it, my focus now razor-sharp, and lock on to each word of the conversation between two betrayers. It's from Julie *fucking* Hanson informing Arianna that she found the evidence she had been looking for and that the crash report from her family's car accident was tampered with, and how she thinks my father paid the investigator to change it.

"Motherfucker," I grit out between my teeth, and every happy feeling I've felt since I met Arianna disappears like a ghost on the wind.

As I pull my phone out of the pocket of my jeans, my blood races through my veins, but I remain as calm as a monk in meditation while I photograph everything in front of me. From Arianna's theories to the coroners' reports and lists of journalist names and numbers who work at various tabloids, along with case files she must have acquired from our archive.

Arianna doesn't have a sore throat or a virus; she's got backstabber syndrome and has been planning my demise for months behind my back with her core mission to ruin my family and everything we took years to build.

No way am I letting that happen.

Her betrayal won't touch my father's respected name.

Overwhelming disappointment takes hold.

I've been sipping sweet poison straight from the source and I've been sleeping in my bed with a snake.

I'm disappointed in myself for believing that I could trust her and that she was the one.

For being too blind to see what was in front of me all along: a traitor.

She used me. Tricked me with her killer curves and tempting lips.

Everything was a lie.

She played me. Which means she never deserved me in the first place.

I take one hard look around and stand to my full height and stretch myself out before leaving as if I was never here.

Closing the front door as quietly as I can to remain undetected, I walk with purpose, not pain, toward my car and jump in.

My expression is neutral and stoic. I don't feel rage or sadness.

Heartbreak? Nah, not that either. This is my awakening because her disloyalty only proves that she wasn't made for me.

She lost me. I didn't lose her.

42

ARI

When I came out of the shower the other day, I got this weird feeling that Nathan had been in my apartment. It was as if I could smell his aftershave as his phantom fragrance filled the air.

I miss him, so maybe that's why I'm imagining things.

I still can't bring myself to call him—I feel awful lying about being sick when I'm perfectly fine health wise.

Heartbroken for my family, yes, but otherwise I am fit and well.

Guilt lingers—I should have told him the truth about who I am and if I don't return to work soon, he'll get suspicious.

Still, my guilt is different now. It's not just about deception; it's about what I've uncovered.

I've yet again dissected every piece of evidence surrounding my family's deaths, read everything twice, three times—sometimes more. I hired a PI, who agreed to help me as an emergency and worked tirelessly and solely on my case. It cost me some of my savings, but I don't care. It was worth it.

And now, I finally see the full picture. I know who is lying and who's telling the truth. Relief floods through me. It all makes sense.

And maybe it wasn't the outcome I wanted but I have to learn to accept the facts.

But first I need to tell Nathan who I am. If I want a future with him, I have to be honest. I can't hide who I am anymore.

Heart pounding, I grab my phone from the coffee table. My fingers fly across the screen as I message him, urgency fueling every tap.

> **ME**
> I'm coming back to work tomorrow. x

> **NATHAN**
> Fine.

> **ME**
> See you tomorrow. x

> **NATHAN**
> Looking forward to it.

No kisses? That's strange, he always puts kisses on the end of his messages.

> **ME**
> Everything okay? x

> **NATHAN**
> Never better.

> **ME**
> I could come home tonight. I'm not snotty anymore. x

> **NATHAN**
> I'm meeting friends for dinner. See you tomorrow.

Friends? What friends? And dinner? Nathan works every hour that's available to him. He never goes out with friends. His brothers? Yes, and me, but never friends.

ME

I could come with you. x

NATHAN

It's a business dinner.

ME

Okay. x

No reply.

Jeez. Mr. Crankypants is back.

And that's why I need to get back to work.

When I'm there, I keep him in check and he's way less of a nightmare to deal with.

A "human tranquilizer" is how Joseph described me.

I'm excited to see everyone again tomorrow, especially Nathan.

I've missed him, all of him, grumpy pants and all.

And I'm sure he'll understand when I explain my reasoning for getting the job at Hart Law in the first place and why I had my doubts.

I'm sure he will.

He's a reasonable man.

My man.

The man I love.

I wish it was tomorrow.

Then I can tell him that his father was not to blame for the injustice I thought was brought against my family, nor is Kevin Taylor. And that they were right about Julie all along. She's a fake.

"Morning, Joseph." I set my to-go coffee down on my desk.

"Morning, beautiful," he replies, not looking up from his computer screen. "You need to go straight to the boardroom, bosses' orders." He points to the closed door then does a mock salute. "Feeling better?" Looking up at me, he smiles, and I sigh with relief.

"Yes, I'm much better, thank you," I reply.

I love my job and I'm excited about seeing Nathan again.

I've missed him so much.

I know where I should be—here with him. In his apartment. Just everywhere.

Today's going to be a good day. Well, I hope so.

I hope he believes me.

Love conquers all, right? It just has to.

Drawing an invisible line in the air with his finger, he sweeps it up and down, motioning toward my deep purple dress, Joseph says, "I love that color on you, it makes your eye color pop." He pops the *P.* "You had better go, they've been waiting on you for twenty minutes."

"They? Who's they?" And why is everyone in the office before me today? I'm clearly losing my touch.

"The four of them. I don't know what's going on, but it seems important. They've barely said a word to each other since I arrived." Joseph picks up the ringing phone. "Good morning, Hart Law. Joseph speaking, how may I direct your call?"

I wonder what's happening today. Maybe a big case is coming our way and we're preparing for a storm.

Unplugging my laptop, I lift it from my desk and make my way to the boardroom, humming to myself as I push open the door.

My singing dies in the air when I enter the frosty room. The atmosphere is so tense you could cut it with a knife.

Max, Eli, and Cole are all seated around the table while Nathan is standing next to the window staring out across the bustle of the morning city below.

He looks... I don't know, I can't put my finger on it. Mad? Upset?

I can't work him out.

"What's happened?" I ask and pull out a seat to sit around the table as Max, Eli, and Cole remain silent and shift in their seats, looking uneasy.

I flit my eyes up to find Nathan's jaw tightening, but he doesn't speak right away.

"Is it bad?" I question, now really worried as the air turns heavier from the weight of unsaid words.

Nathan exhales sharply before answering. "You tell us— what's worse? Finding out that someone you employed has been plotting against you and your family from the very start? Or maybe it's the fact that she deliberately sought out the bar where the eldest son of the family drank, seduced him to gain his trust, and then set out to dismantle his business? Or perhaps it's stealing archived records from a case connected to her own family—does that qualify as 'bad' in your book?"

Oh no. This can't be happening.

"But maybe," he continues, turning slowly, his voice steadier and more controlled than I've ever heard it, "the lowest of the low is discovering that this employee used inside information—false information, I might add—from a woman who has been hell-bent for years on damaging the reputation of Hart Law—to try and take down a man she believed had bribed his way to an acquittal for a client she was convinced was guilty."

The thought of him believing I would betray him is the last thing I want.

It may have been my intention at first, but I never expected to fall in love with him.

Now, I know one thing for certain—I could never betray him.

"Nathan." His name comes out in a rush because I'm desperate to explain everything I've discovered in the last few days. "Please..." I plead.

He holds up his hand to stop me. "Let me finish." He unbuttons his dress jacket and sits down at the head of the table. It feels like he's a million miles away from me and slipping out of my grasp with every tick of the clock on the wall.

My eyes rove wildly, scanning the room for help from his brothers, but I know I won't get it as they remain as still as statues while my body trembles with panic.

"You," Nathan starts, leaning back in his chair, "Ms. Donovan, were planning to betray me, my family and more importantly, my father. Here at Hart Law, we are lawful. This"—he slides a piece of paper to Cole, who is sitting closest to me, who places it on the table in front of me—"is the crash report. The real one. Not the one Julie Hanson fabricated. You can tell from the positioning of the watermark, and the fact that it's on government-issued paper is a dead giveaway." He's too relaxed, too controlled, and his grip on the armrest of his chair tightens, and I know he's desperately doing everything in his power to settle his inner tornado.

I jump in. "I know all that, Nathan, please let me ex—"

He cuts me off. "I had an accident reconstruction specialist analyze whether the report aligns with the physical evidence and I'm sure you'll be saddened to learn, because you would have loved nothing better than to screw with my family and ruin my father's good name, that he confirmed Julie's was a fake. To get to us, she set you up, and you fell into her web of deceit."

I figured out that Julie had been lying to me all along. I studied the report against the real one, and the PI I hired confirmed it was a fake too. She fabricated the crash report, twisting the truth to serve her own agenda—revenge. All because she lost her job after Max filed a police report for the damage she caused to his car and home. Looking back, it was so obvious.

And then there was her connection to my old boss—a man I wouldn't trust to care for a guinea pig, let alone defend me in court. I should have seen it from the start. She played the part well—friendly, eager to get to know me—but the moment she learned about my family and how Daniel Hart had defended the man I thought was responsible for their deaths, something changed. She latched onto me, took me out for drinks, made it seem like she was on my side.

That's when she told me she could help me take the Hart family down. That we could get revenge. But it wasn't my revenge—it was hers. She persuaded me to get a job at Hart Law. She used me. And like a fool, I let her. Because I wanted that too.

Nathan's stare becomes razor sharp, locking onto me without blinking. "If you had come to me, been straight with me from the start, I would have investigated the case for you. And this is what I would have shown you."

Cole passes me another piece of paper.

It looks like the redacted letter from the archive file. Only this time there are no black lines disguising the words because it's the original and not a photocopy like there was in the archived case file.

I read the first couple of lines, and my chest tightens like someone is squeezing all the air out of my lungs, making them burn like the fires of hell, and I sob my heart out, my tears soaking the neckline of my dress.

"What you'll find there, Ms. Donovan, is a letter from Kevin Taylor to my father, confirming the funding that secured your placement in what was supposed to be foster care. But it wasn't foster care at all. Jean O'Neill was not just some foster guardian —she was a highly qualified child development specialist, privately employed by Kevin Taylor himself to care for you until you turned twenty-one. Jean's death was unfortunate timing because she made a vow to Kevin to take care of you past the time set at the beginning of your care, because she loved you like her own. I took a visit to your old neighborhood and asked around. You never went without. Your clothes, books, your first car. All provided for by Kevin." His voice steady, he continues shocking me with his words. "As you'll see from that letter, my father had planned to personally offer you a job once you were old enough. However, your determination and drive led you to secure one on your own before he ever got the chance because you were convinced that working within the legal system, you could somehow access records that don't even exist. No one hid anything from you. There was no bribery, extortion, or foul play involved with your family's unfortunate deaths. And my father and Kevin were both rooting for you to be successful and not fall between the cracks in the care system. Kevin, the man you've spent years believing murdered your family, was found not guilty because he wasn't guilty. It was an accident. The crash wasn't caused by negligence or malice, but by a perfect storm of conditions—dense fog, oil on the road, and your father driving twenty miles per hour over the recommended speed limit that night. He lost control and crashed into Kevin's car. And Kevin? He didn't flee the scene. He didn't abandon you like you've always believed. He went to get help."

I cover my mouth with my hand, in complete shock.

My PI uncovered great things about the random acts of kindness Kevin Taylor did throughout his life confirming I was wrong about him too.

I can't believe how badly I got it all wrong. I ruined everything, and I don't know how to fix it.

Nathan adds, "Kevin Taylor put people in place to take care of you, not because he felt guilty but because he cared about your welfare. The case file was labelled Attorney-Client Privileged because he never wanted you to find out what he did for you. It was his good deed, an act of kindness, and he expected nothing in return. He wanted to give you a chance at life, which you grabbed by the balls, and it got you to where you are today. I admire that about you, Ms. Donovan." Taking a moment, in slow deliberate movements he pushes back his chair and stands up. "But I will never forgive you for trying to take my family down. Now, if you'll excuse me, I'm due in court in an hour. Please leave the building immediately and do your best not to make a scene. I think we've had enough excitement for one day."

I hang my head in shame.

He stops next to me, the heat of his silent anger tangible, and he asks, "Just one thing before I go. Was making me fall in love with you some sort of sick game?"

I shake my head, unable to look him in the eye, and fix my eyes on the paperwork on top of the desk.

He's never told me he loves me, but I always knew he did. I felt it.

And now he thinks I double-crossed him and that my love for him isn't real, when it is. It's the most real and honest thing I've ever felt.

Calmly and deadly serious, he asks, "Do you have any idea what you've done?"

"I'm sorry." What else can I say? He's already made up his mind about me and whatever I say he'll never believe me.

He turns his back to me before reaching for the door to leave. "I'm sorry too, because you see, my brothers and I are no longer on speaking terms because I investigated the case and doubted my father a millisecond too long for them. The bond we have is broken, and it's what always mattered the most to us —law, legacy and above all, loyalty. We are bound by blood, and we fight for justice as a united unit, but you, Ms. Donovan, broke that, because I fight for the people I love, I fight for what I believe inside the courtroom, but you made me fight outside of it, and not only did I lose you, I lost them." A beat passes before he speaks again, his tone much lower now. "Did you really think I wouldn't find out?"

I push my chair back and rush to him, laying my hand on his shoulder to make him turn around, but he doesn't. "Please, Nathan, you have to believe me. I figured it out—I wasn't going to do anything, I swear. I swear on everything." My voice breaks, raw and desperate, tears streaming down my face. And I try to coax him again to turn around, but he still doesn't move. Doesn't flinch. Just stares ahead at the door. "I love you, Nathan. I love you more than anything. Please... please don't do this. Please look at me." A sob racks my body, my chest heaving. "I made a mistake, but I swear I wasn't going to do anything. You have to believe me. Please."

"I should be angry, but right now all I feel is disappointment. I knew something was off the first day you sat here in this very boardroom. I felt it but I just couldn't put my finger on it and I hate myself for the major lapse of judgment. You're fired." He opens the door, then slams it behind him before I can stop him, leaving me staring at the space where he just stood.

"I wasn't going to do it." My voice trembles, thick with desperation. I turn to his brothers, my vision blurred with tears. "Please, believe me. I swear on my life—I took the time off to go over everything, every piece of evidence. I hired a PI to help me. I know the truth. But I didn't know about Kevin looking out for me, but everything else... I see it now. I believe it. I do."

I clutch my chest as if I can physically hold myself together, my breath shuddering. "I wasn't going to sell my story. I wasn't going to tip off a tabloid because it wasn't the truth. I know Julie was lying. Please, why don't you believe me?" My knees nearly give out beneath me, but I force myself to stay standing tall, even as my heart fractures into a million pieces.

I look between them, pleading, my voice cracking. "Punish me if you have to." I'm already being punished; I lost the man I love. "Hate me. I deserve it. But don't take it out on him. Please don't make him pay for my mistakes. He had nothing to do with this." A sob rips through me, raw and uninhibited. "I love him and *you* love him. And I'm begging you, please... please forgive him."

Max runs his hands through his hair, looking tired and completely deflated. "I'll give you one chance to explain to us exactly what Julie said to you, and any other information she provided to you including what you know about her dealings with your ex-boss. Tell us everything. Then I want to know your exact intentions before you got the position here, and then what led to you changing your mind. You have ten minutes. I suggest you use this time wisely."

"Okay." I wipe my face with the palms of my hands and sit back down in my chair before telling them everything I know to ensure they mend things with Nathan. They have to; they're his best friends. Their bond is too precious to break, and I won't let that happen.

Nathan thinks I was going to betray him. I couldn't even if I wanted to because he would've given me the world, and that's the torturous reality I will have to live with.

This is one of the worst days of my life.

The first, losing my family.

The second, losing him.

44

ARI

Four weeks, three days, seven hours and twenty-three minutes.

That's how long it's been since I walked out the doors of Hart Law.

I miss the man I wanted to spend the rest of my life with.

I thought losing my family was painful, but this is a different type of pain I'm feeling. Guilt, shame, loss, hurt; they're all mixed together to create a cocktail of hate for myself.

I hate that I believed Julie was helping me for the greater good.

The day after I was fired, my belongings from Nathan's apartment were delivered to my place, each one packed neatly and labelled with what was inside.

From the handwriting on the boxes, I knew Nathan had personally packed each one, which made it even worse. Because what he really should have done is shred every piece of my clothing into tiny pieces and tipped my makeup all over them.

Except he didn't.

But it's what I deserved.

"Do you think she'll leave the bed today?" Maeve's voice

appears as she walks into my bedroom, and I have no idea who she is speaking to.

"She thinks you hate her." I figure out Maeve is on a call, which I'm guessing is to Joseph.

There's a beat of silence.

"Joseph says to tell you he doesn't hate you and that he wants you to come up with a plan to win Nathan back."

I pull the comforter I'm buried in further up over my head again and groan.

The bed dips to the side of me as Maeve sits down on the edge of the mattress.

"It smells like someone died in her bedroom." Her voice drips with disgust. "If we leave her long enough, she'll get bed sores and become a giant pile of puss."

"I *can* hear you, you know. I'm sad, not deaf." I flip the cover down from my head to my waist. "Can you please leave me alone?"

Maeve smiles down her cell. "Oh, we have life."

I let out a frustrated breath and stare at the ceiling, annoyed that for some unfathomable reason Maeve wants me to get out of my bed. How can I when my heart feels like it's bleeding out?

"I'll try," Maeve replies to whatever Joseph asks her to do.

"Try what?" I ask.

"To get you out of bed and into the shower."

"I had a shower three days ago."

"And that's the reason it smells like a morgue in here," she drawls.

I fly out of my bed to prove the point that I *can* actually get out of bed and that I am fine.

I'm not fine.

Far from it.

"Happy now?" I feel dizzy from a combination of getting up

too quick and being unable to eat anything substantial in weeks. Laying my hand on my forehead, I plonk my ass back on the bed. "I think that's enough exertion for one day." I admit defeat and climb back into my bed, which is calling my name.

"Gotta go." Maeve ends the call. "Nope, not happening. Up." She pulls the covers off me and throws them to the ground.

"Maeve," I shrill, sitting up. "Just…"

"Just, what?" She folds her arms in front of her and pops a hip. "What are you going to do? Rot away in this bed for the rest of the year, or get up and fight for what you want and believe in?"

"There's no winning him back, Maeve," I say through gritted teeth. That ship has sailed. More like it sunk with no survivors.

"You didn't even try."

"He told me that he would never forgive me."

"We all say things in the heat of the moment."

"There was no heat." He was as cold as an ice cube.

He was hurt by my cruel intentions, which I decided to put a stop to, but he didn't know that at the time and now all is lost.

I lost him.

I lost everything including my self-respect.

A deep emptiness crept in the minute I stepped out of the Hart Law building. It was as if I was moving in slow motion and completely disconnected from myself. Like I was watching myself from the outside. I don't feel like myself anymore. Everything feels wrong, and yet I can't find the strength to change my situation.

"I need to get a job," I say, defeated.

"The 7-Eleven down the block is hiring."

"Yeah, I could do that." My voice is heavy. My body feels numb and weary.

"Stop being an idiot. You are overqualified."

"I'm exhausted is what I am." And no longer the strong woman I once was.

"Well." Maeve sits down on the bed, takes my hand in hers and gives it a squeeze. "You might feel like that, but that's because you haven't eaten a vegetable or had a decent meal in weeks. Your hair is matted and it looks like a bird's nest."

I reach up and try pushing my fingers through it but I'm unsuccessful. "God, that is gross."

"And you smell really bad. I'm not just saying that." She rubs the end of her nose. "I think you should jump in the shower and while you're in there I'll change the linens. And then you and I are going to grab a bite to eat. If you lose any more weight, you're going to not only smell like a corpse but look like one."

"Do I really look that bad?"

"You have a cornflake stuck in your hair. And some weird-looking brown stain on your pajama top." She points to them both.

That's all I've been surviving on; cereal and chocolate. My skin must look terrible.

"I don't think I'm ready to face the world yet," I confess. I feel like everyone is looking at me as if I'm wearing my guilt like a flashing neon sign above my head.

"It's not the world. Just the coffee shop on Third Street. You can't stay in this cesspit for a minute longer or your neighbor will call environmental health to report the stench."

A genuine laugh bursts from my chest. I don't remember when I last laughed.

The last time I felt happy was the night before Julie sent me that fateful fake crash report that changed the next stage of my life.

"I blew it." Holding my head in my hands, I break down

again. All I've done is cry. There can't be any more tears left in me. "It's all my fault."

Maeve encases me in her warm arms. "You've survived worse than this," she whispers, then kisses the top of my head.

"I miss him." I soak her shirt in tears as she squeezes me gently. "My heart, it feels broken."

Maeve stays quiet and lets me get it all out.

After a while, she asks, "Will you come to the coffee shop?"

I lean out of our embrace. "Mmm," I grumble. "I don't think I'm up to it today."

"They have cake."

I consider her persuading offer. "Do they have banana bread?"

"Yes."

"You drive a hard bargain." I finally agree because if I don't, she's never going to leave me alone.

Maeve claps her hands together in excitement.

Something I also haven't felt in a while. Nothing feels exciting anymore and joy feels like an unachievable goal.

I need to start again because there is no me and Nathan anymore.

I fill my cheeks with air and drop my feet to the floor when Maeve stands up.

"We need to air out this room," she says, looking around before making her way to open a window.

We do, and maybe burn the comforter if it's as bad as Maeve says it is.

I catch a glimpse of myself in the wall mirror and gasp at my appearance. I look dreadful.

Spots.

Gaunt cheeks.

Puffy eyes.

Blotchy skin.

Tangled hair.

I'm ticking all the boxes I don't want to.

"I need a shower," I admit, finally seeing what Maeve does.

"Everything's going to be okay."

I suck my lips into my mouth to stop myself from crying again. "I need cake."

And I need to start looking forward, not back.

What's done is done.

It's time to rebuild my life without him in it.

Which sounds absolutely awful.

Impossible, even.

My cell alerts me to a text message. Half-heartedly, I pick it up off my nightstand and read the notification. "It's Max." I read his name aloud, confused as to why he's texting me.

It's the only contact I've had with any of them since I was fired.

Maeve stops what she's doing. "What does he want?"

I open the message to find out. "He wants me to call him."

"Do it, Ari."

45

NATHAN

"Eli tells me you haven't been home before midnight since you and Arianna broke up." My mother swans into my office and makes herself comfortable on the sofa opposite my desk.

"Eli needs a hobby," I mutter.

And we didn't break up. I fired her.

"Eli is worried about you." She drums her fingertips against the leather fabric and stares me down. "As are Max and Cole."

We've barely spoken to one another in weeks. No texts. No tennis on Saturdays.

It's all strictly business.

I lean back in my chair and rub my tired eyes. I'm exhausted but still can't sleep.

I miss her.

My girl.

But she's not my girl anymore.

What the fuck was I thinking?

I didn't want her to leave.

I didn't want to do what I did.

I should have listened to what she had to say.

But I did it to protect my father's reputation.

My brothers hate me for looking into her family's case.

Hate that I planted our brains with doubt about our father, something we all knew wasn't true but for a minute there, we questioned him, and ourselves, which we will never do again.

Scratch that—it wasn't us that sowed the seeds of doubt, it was Arianna.

"Go to her, Nathaniel."

"I can't do that." My brothers will never forgive me.

"They will forgive you," she says as if reading my mind. "Hell, I forgive you already. And I forgive Arianna because she didn't do anything wrong. She wasn't going to go through with it. As soon as she discovered the truth and worked things out herself because she's a smart girl, she halted whatever her initial intention was."

"She made me question... everything. Dad."

Our entire relationship was built on a lie. Turns out I don't really know her at all so how could I ever trust her?

"And if the roles were reversed? And if you had even the smallest niggle in your gut that made you want to seek justice for your family, would you follow the niggle or would you leave it alone?" She doesn't let me answer because she knows me better than I know myself. "You would follow your gut even if it didn't lead to the outcome you hoped for. Because that's what family does for each other. We fight for the people we love. Regardless."

It's what Arianna did.

She wanted to do right by her family no matter what. She took a risk that didn't pay off and something within me admires her for that. I love her for it.

"She loves you, Nathaniel."

I stay quiet, because when Arianna told me she loved me

that fateful day in the boardroom, I couldn't bring myself to look at her from fear of giving in, forgetting what happened and not letting go of her. Now I wonder if my silence was a greater betrayal than hers.

"Stop hating her."

"I don't hate her." I hate myself.

Hating her couldn't be further from the truth. I love her. I love her so damn much it hurts.

But love makes me weak, and weakness has no place in my world. She betrayed me, and I did what had to be done.

My chest tightens. I need to let her go—erase her from my mind like she never existed. And yet, the thought of never seeing her again burns more than the betrayal itself.

"This firm," my mom says, spreading her hands to gesture around us, "will be here for years—decades, even centuries. It will be passed down to your children, your grandchildren, and the generations after them. It will go on and on. But Arianna won't." She exhales slowly. "You, of all people, should understand that. Disease took away your father's chance at retirement and any enjoyment of life. Don't lose Arianna because you were too stubborn to admit to your brothers that you still love her. You don't need their permission, Nathaniel. And unlike the illness that took your father from us, you have a choice. You're not a cruel man. And love doesn't come easy. So grab it with both hands while you still can—because I lost the love of my life, and I don't want the same thing to happen to you."

"They will hate me." I refer to the tense relationship that's already under immense strain with my brothers.

"Do you love her?"

I nod.

"Even though she might have betrayed you but didn't, you still love her? After everything?"

"Yes." It's an unshakable feeling I can't ignore, no matter how much I try. It sits deep in my chest, pressing against my ribs, refusing to be silenced. I know what I want—what I've always wanted. But wanting something and having the courage to reach for it are two very different things.

Admitting I was wrong is a different matter entirely.

I swallow hard, my mother's words echoing in my head. *Love doesn't come easy.*

And yet, it's out there. She's out there.

Waiting.

Heartbroken, like me. I know because Joseph has been checking in on her, and she's spent the last four weeks in her bed probably dying inside like I feel I am.

"Well, I think you've got your answer because the same can be said about your brothers. Regardless of the decision you made to investigate the part your father played in her family's case, they love you and that will never change. Together, you four are unbreakable. Go to her. Fix it." She dares me to take the risk.

"I'll think about it."

"Well, don't think about it too long, or you'll lose her completely."

I tilt my head up in understanding.

"Now, switch that computer off and take your old mother out for dinner. I'm famished."

"You're going to get me drunk then make me spill my secrets, aren't you?"

"That's the plan." She winks cheekily. "A drunk mind speaks the truth. Liquid courage is exactly what you need."

I shut my computer down, grab my jacket, and offer her my arm, which she takes.

"You always have been the matriarch of meddling," I say with a hint of humor.

"I'm the cement that holds you boys together."

She really is.

If only she could cement my heart back together, maybe then I'd feel whole.

That's a lie.

I only feel whole when I'm with Arianna.

"Just a water, please."

"Not ordering something stronger? I thought we were celebrating." Julie arrives at the empty bar I arranged to meet her at wearing a smile as smug as a pirate plundering treasure.

I need a clear head for this conversation. "Water is fine," I reply.

"So if we're ready to expose Hart Law, are we doing it this week or next?" she asks.

I play along. "I was thinking next week? Does that work for you?"

"Absolutely." She motions to the bartender. "Martini with a twist."

I drum my fingers against the wooden bar top, nervous of being seen with Julie in such a public setting, but it's necessary. A means to an end.

"You look skinny," Julie says bluntly. "It doesn't suit you."

"I've had a lot going on."

"I hope you're not changing your mind, Ari. Daniel Hart fucked your family over, remember?"

"Yeah. I know. I'm tired, that's all," I lie. "I haven't changed my mind."

"You sure you're not pregnant? Fuck, that's the last thing you want to give birth to. Satan's spawn." Her whole face screws up. "Although imagine the amount of child support you could squeeze out of the Hart family."

My stomach twists like a nest of vipers curling round and round, making it feel like they are squeezing my heart. "I'm not pregnant."

"Pity." She shrugs dismissively. "You could have taken Nathan to the cleaners for child support."

I would never do that. She's disgusting.

"So," I start, confidence filling my veins, "I was looking at the crash report and it's fake." Fuck her for thinking she could fool me once with telling me she would help me and my family, then twice for sending me a fake report.

Julie stops stirring her martini with her cocktail stick and side-eyes me. "No?"

She knows it is.

"Yes. The watermark is in the wrong place, the font is incorrect and the one you sent me in the post that you said was the original is not on government-issued paper." And there was a spelling mistake in the word government in tiny letters along the footer. I got ninety-six percent in English, and I'm the one everyone asks to proofread their reports in the office. With the use of a magnifying glass, I caught Julie's mistake easily.

I knew all of that before Nathan laid it all out for me in black and white in the boardroom.

I add, "My family's car crash was an accident, Julie. I've read the case file." At least a hundred times. I sit strong and stand my ground.

"Arianna?" She uses my full name as a question.

"Yes?"

"Do you trust me?"

"Yes," I lie again.

"Then the report is real. Simple. I have a great contact, just don't ask who that person is." She taps the side of her nose. "I need to use the restroom." Sliding off her barstool, she grabs her cell.

As soon as she's around the corner I follow her, but I get the shock of my life when she's not inside the restroom but standing facing the wall at the end of the corridor where the restrooms are, so I hide myself and listen in.

"She's just told me she thinks the report is fake." She whisper-shouts to whoever is on the other end of the call.

Who is she talking to?

I edge myself a little closer.

"Don't talk to me like that. My contact did a great job to make it look real."

No, they didn't, it was a terrible job.

"Okay, okay, calm down, I didn't blow it. That dumb bitch believed me when I told her it wasn't. She's still going through with the interview next week."

She pauses for a beat as if letting the person talk.

Laughing manically to whatever the person responds with, she then says, "Once we get her interview we can create another dozen or so headlines and articles to back it up. She'll humanize the story, give a bit of legitimacy, then the readers will believe the others. Win win." She nods her head. "Yeah. I agree. This was much harder than hacking phones. Let's stick to that," she says brightly as if it's the most kosher thing in the world, when it's not. It's hideous.

They hack phones?

This is terrible and much more sinister than I realized. Julie is a snake and now I wish I had never met her. My hands are shaking, my mouth now completely dry.

"I'll keep her sweet, we'll get the story, and I'll sell you lots of newspapers, Buzz."

Bert, or Buzz as he's widely known, is the editor of *The Golden Telegraph*.

Turns out he's a snake too.

"I'm right, trust me. And I know it's becoming harder and harder. Fucking internet," Julie replies, spitting venom. "Since the invention of the fucking thing, I have struggled every day to get exclusive interviews and tell-alls. People share everything online first instead of selling their stories. It's a fucking travesty. Oh, hang on, I have an alert on my cell." Julie moves it away from her ear and must put it on speaker, though I can't see with her back to me. She continues talking. "It's Lexi, she said she got him."

"Hacking phones of the rich and famous has never felt so good." A masculine husky voice, which I am assuming is Buzz, fills the corridor, making me feel sick to my stomach.

Their morals are in the gutter.

"We're clever, right?" Julie asks, chuckling away.

It's horrible, evil, and downright wrong.

"It's the only way to get the inside scoop these days and that's why we do it all the time. Now, get your sweet ass back to my office and tell me all the ways you plan on ruining Daniel Hart and his firm's reputation. Then draw up a plan for who is next in this boring-as-fuck city."

"It's a shame I never made a copy of that video I made to set Daniel up." Julie kicks her foot against the wall in front of her.

"You're a pro at this now. You just needed someone like me to show you how to play dirtier," Buzz replies sinisterly.

Max showed me the video—the one she tried to use to

extort his father and get back at Max with. And Daniel? He never said anything remotely close to what she claims. In fact, the whole time in the video, he made it crystal clear to Julie that she was his son's girlfriend, that he had never strayed from his wife, and that he wasn't the least bit interested in some desperate, two-bit hussy. Daniel's words, not mine. I heard them on the video with my very own ears.

Daniel Hart is a loyal man. To his wife and his sons, and was dedicated to upholding the law.

"And that's why I faked the crash report. I'll finally get my revenge on the family for filing that injunction and getting me fired."

Julie is not only twisted, she's bitter, and while I wanted to seek the truth, she is willing to bend it into any way she wants to get her revenge.

"I lost everything, Buzz. He kicked me out of our apartment, did you know that?" she says, laying her forehead against the wall, sounding hurt.

"And that's why we wrote those stories about them sharing a girlfriend. It was a good place to start," Buzz says, confirming his part in helping Julie out.

Sounding smug as hell, she replies, "God, that was a good one, but my favorite was the one I made up about Max dating a supermodel who said his dick was tiny." I can hear the smile in her voice. "News flash. There was no supermodel. Now that I think about it, maybe it was the fake whistleblower story that was leaked." She wraps air quotes around her last word with her fingers. "About sexual harassment in Hart Law." She sighs. "If only that were true. Those fuckers are cleaner than a surgeon's scalpel."

"It's not your fault you and Max didn't end well." Buzz tries to justify her actions when in fact it couldn't be further from the truth. She had already started writing fake stories when she was dating Max; now she works under Buzz, I think he's even worse than her.

I don't trust any of them and will never believe anything I read in the tabloids.

"I may have done some things to his car and apartment that ended up with him placing an injunction against me, Buzz," she admits. "It was just a little scratch on his car, I don't know why he was so upset." She twirls a lock of her hair between her fingers. I get the impression she believes her own lie.

I've seen the photos. She totaled his vintage car with a golf club.

"Well, we all do things we regret," he replies, sounding genuinely sympathetic.

"Oh, I don't regret any of it." Julie shakes her head. "So, we're still on for exposing Hart Law next week." Changing the subject, she gets down to business.

"Yes. We'll publish end of week, double-page spread and front-page exclusive. What about Kevin Taylor's family? What do we have on him?"

"Nothing, but it doesn't matter. The public will believe the headline because I've been planting seeds of doubt in the minds of our readers for years about Hart Law and their legitimacy. This story will seal their fate and they'll have the authorities all over their archive files, questioning procedures, and before you know it they'll not have any clients because no one will trust them and they'll fall out of favor with the public. I guarantee they'll fold before the year is out once we release this."

Julie hasn't been plotting against them for a few months, it's been years, and she's using my story as the big finale.

What a bitch.

"I like your plan, Julie. You'll get a raise for this."

"It was nothing really. Arianna working at Williams and Jones was a gift. Inviting her out for a drink that night after work turned out perfectly for us, Buzz, especially when I discovered Daniel Hart was the one who represented the man she thought killed her family—that's all the connection I needed. She was my in, she trusted me, and I used that. She made it easy for us to figure out a way to spin the story, to create that report, and together, we will build a stream of articles that will ruin him. And Nathan Hart? That man has never let a woman into his life before her. I bet he fell in love with her. We probably broke him too. Two birds, one stone."

"Thank you, Ari." Buzz's slimy buoyant voice slices my heart open.

They used me.

I've been a pawn in their big game.

"Right, I gotta go, Buzz. See you back at the office. And I have an idea for who we target next. She's a big celebrity."

"Atta girl."

I tiptoe quickly back to my seat and push the bile that I can feel rising in my throat back down.

Julie appears looking happy with herself while I die inside some more.

"Sorry, I need to get back to the office, Ari, but I'll be in touch. We'll do an interview, photos, the lot. Stay by your phone. Have my drink." She points to the martini I wished the bartender had now laced with poison.

"Thanks." I pull a fake smile, my fist itching to have a conversation with her face.

"Thanks for being a friend, Ari, you're a trooper. I think it was fate that I met you."

No, it wasn't.

Admitting to Buzz on the call that she used me feels like she stabbed me with a knife I handed her myself. She's vile. Dangerous. I feel like such a fool.

"We didn't do this together, Julie. It was all you." My stomach rolls in waves, my ears ringing, drowning out everything around me, and it takes a massive amount of effort to sound calm.

"Whatever, that's a matter of perspective." She dismisses me, looking smugger than the devil sealing the deal, then she leaves.

Waiting several minutes to make sure she's gone, with trembling hands, I pull my phone out of the inside pocket of my coat, hit stop on the voice record button then pull up one of my contacts and call it.

Max picks up instantly. "We got her. We heard everything."

"Thank God," I reply, clutching my hand to my chest, nervousness flowing through my body like blood through my veins, and I look down at the secret microphone placed between my cleavage.

Max knows the guy behind the bar and had the place tapped within an inch of its life, ensuring we heard her regardless of where she was situated. The plan was to talk to her to get a confession; instead, she hung herself and played right into our hands.

I'm not the one who's the dumb bitch.

"You heard everything?" I clarify.

"We got more. Phone-hacking is a serious offense, Arianna."

"It's the worst."

"I'm sending you copies of the voice files by email and I'll make another copy as a backup."

"Okay." I'd already thought about that.

"You got her, Ari."

"*We* got her, Max." It was a team effort. Max and his brothers came up with the idea of luring her out and making her talk because she considered me a friend. She took the bait.

And what kind of friend would falsify information surrounding the death of an entire family? She is not my friend. She never was.

"Thank you for doing this for me."

"I did it for all of you." For Nathan.

"Are you okay?" he asks, his voice full of genuine concern.

"I need a stiff drink," I admit, still feeling shaky. My legs are bouncing up and down with jitters.

But most of all, I need to see your brother's face again. I miss him.

"I'll buy you one when I see you next."

That won't be any time soon.

47

NATHAN

"I think I did something really stupid, Dad." I close my eyes and talk to him even though he's fast asleep.

It's so peaceful at his memory care home during the afternoon, but I wasn't expecting my dad to be sleeping today.

He had therapy this morning and I'm guessing he's tired.

"I lost her. I messed up." I close my eyes and rest my head against the back of the chair. "I should have listened to what she had to say but she thought you did something. Something illegal, and now I can't see past it."

How can I ever trust her again?

"I'm so tired and I wish you were still working behind the desk I now do because I know you'd tell me what to do."

I'm lost.

Have been for weeks.

On days like today, I know I could have asked him anything.

"And I lost my case yesterday." My chest feels compressed, like it's being squeezed in a vice grip. "Well, I didn't lose it, I just couldn't make the pharmaceutical company increase their payout." I feel terrible for Sabrina. I promised I would get her more.

Without Arianna in my life, I can't think straight. My apartment still smells like her. The office. My bedroom. My limo. The ranch. Everywhere I go. It all reminds me of her.

Food has lost its flavor, not that I can eat, and while I'm starving, I feel sick to my stomach.

"Mom says I'm lovesick." I keep my voice quiet so as not to wake him. "She thinks I have a broken heart."

I do, and I don't want to feel like this anymore.

"I don't hate her." Can't. "I love her, Dad." I even boxed up her belongings and moved her out. Why the fuck didn't I listen to her? I should have listened.

"I don't know what to do anymore." I'm torn between my family and her.

I love both.

"Tell me everything, son." Dad's croaky voice cuts through my muddled thoughts, making my eyes snap open. His lips lift at the sides. "I can still help."

I lean forward and rest my hand on top of his, then tell him everything.

"Go to her, Nathaniel." His answer surprises me.

"Even after what she did?"

"Intended to do," he corrects me, his words long and drawn out. "She didn't do it. She knew. She figured Julie out. Now she knows the truth." My father's mind is still sharp sometimes and I know he's in there somewhere, not often these days, but he's still here and I hate what the diseases are doing to him. I want more good days for him. "If you had doubt"—slowly, he speaks —"you would have done the same for your family."

"Mom said the same. Eli, Cole, and Max are barely speaking to me because I looked into the case, Dad. I doubted you. Arianna's doubts became mine." I cough to clear the emotion building in my chest. "They won't forgive me. I will never forgive myself."

"I forgive you." His three little words come out strong. "They will forgive you over time. They are good boys. Call your brothers. Make it right with them." His eyes turn watery. "Forgiveness will heal. And we learn from our mistakes, Nathaniel. She will too."

"Mom said forgiveness is a choice."

"Your mother is a smart woman."

"She is." I smile and give his hand a squeeze.

If only their love story could have ended differently.

"Choice is not always easy, but it can be powerful. Go to her. Fix it." His eyes droop closed as if he's drifting off again.

"I love you, Dad."

"Love you, son."

48

NATHAN

I have no idea what it could be, but it's the first time in weeks my brothers have written in our group chat, which dried up the day Arianna left the office.

My patience is on a knife edge. It has been for weeks. I feel like a shaken bottle of champagne about to explode.

A link to a news article followed by dozens more appear in the chat one after the other, making me clutch my cell in confusion. I tap open each one and skim read them.

ME

What is this?

ELI

Arianna helped us to get this information. She helped us set Julie up.

MAX

As repayment and to apologize. To fix us.

COLE

Forgive her.

ELI

We spoke to Mom.

COLE

We can't go on like this. Not talking to you every day is killing me.

"It's killing me too." Max appears in my office doorway, snapping my attention off my phone and onto Eli and then Cole behind him.

It's Saturday; what the hell are they doing in the office?

"I messed up. I won't let that happen again." I hope they believe me.

"It's what we would have done, too," Eli admits.

"You were right to go through the case again," Cole explains further. "It confirmed how great Dad is."

I lift my chin. He really was a great lawyer. I just hope he's as proud of us as we are of him.

"Go to her. Fix it," Max states.

My eyes widen in shock. "That's what Dad told me to do too."

"He told us, too." Max's lips twitch at the corners.

"He remembered?" I'm surprised by that, but his moments of clarity have been growing by the day due to the new promising medication he's been on for a few weeks and it seems to have started working.

Mom was so happy when she called me the other day to tell me he remembered her birthday. It's the small things that mean the most.

"We good?" I ask, my brothers standing in a semi-circle on the other side of my desk, and I remove myself from it and walk to them.

"We're brothers, we'll always be good." Max lays his hand on my shoulder.

"I've got somewhere I need to be."

"Yes, you do." He winks.

49

ARI

It's The Connecting Kids Foundation fundraiser day.

Forty-eight hours of agonizing anticipation have passed since I met with Julie in the bar and I've been patiently waiting for the outcome.

Today that ended.

As Max had promised, he moved quickly. This morning, a damning exposé broke—not just in one paper, but across national tabloids and news channels, both online and off—unveiling the shady dealings of Julie and her team at *The Golden Telegraph*.

With phone-hacking making the headlines, dozens of people have been posting their stories online all day using the hashtag exposingthetruth with calls to shut down the newspaper and charge everyone responsible.

Separate articles were published about Julie and the several injunctions against her, as well as police reports and charges previously filed against her. For Buzz, it was even worse: extortion, bribery, phone-hacking, fake news; the list keeps on growing.

Max kept his promise to keep my name out of everything and only made reference to the fake crash report she created amongst a long list of other documents she forged.

In comparison to the phone-hacking and everything else she did, the fake crash report is insignificant.

Significant for me, because it would have made me look like a fraud had I taken it to the police.

She was happy to throw me under the bus and let me die there for all she cared, as long as it got her the outcome she wanted—to destroy the Hart family.

I'm glad I am here at the fundraiser day to help distract me. It's been a long and busy day. Not only did people turn out in their droves to support the foster charity I volunteer for, but they also dug deep into their pockets to help us support foster kids who need it the most, meaning we can now hire two full-time trauma therapists and child psychologists, who are much needed and long overdue.

I take a seat on the bench at the far end of the garden within the grounds of the group home overlooking the city, remove my sandals, and give my toes a wiggle. Having been on my feet all day looking after the stand selling lemonade, which the kids made themselves, my feet are throbbing.

Feeling more like myself than I have in weeks, I let the sun kiss my skin and consider my next move. This coming week I need to get myself a job. I can't live on my savings for much longer because I need the money for a deposit on a new house I still plan on buying in the future. The prospect makes my heart feel heavy.

I was naive to believe I'd end up living in a luxury penthouse with the man of my dreams—the kind of life anyone would trade a kidney for.

"It's a beautiful view."

My heart cartwheels in my chest as the sound of Nathan's voice cuts through the air.

I snap my head around to discover he's behind me and I about melt into a puddle, like butter in a hot pan. He looks delicious in a dazzling white Henley and black jeans that more than likely cost more than my monthly rent.

What the hell is he doing here?

I stay glued to the seat, while he walks toward the bench, and I follow his every move as he sits next to me.

"San Francisco at dusk is always beautiful," I say, keeping our conversation neutral.

"I wasn't talking about the landscape, Arianna." Our eyes lock and I realize he was talking about me.

He still thinks I'm beautiful.

When all I have felt is ugly inside since he fired me.

I've never been fired from a job before.

Never loved anyone the way I love him.

"How are you?" he asks, his brow creasing, giving me a once over, but he doesn't let me answer. "You've lost weight." He tuts, his voice deep and low.

"I don't have an appetite." Heartbreak does strange things to your mind. I keep forgetting to eat. When I do, everything tastes bland and flavorless.

"Me neither," he admits.

I can tell he's not sleeping well either. The shadows beneath his eyes speak of sleepless nights and heavy burdens.

Fumbling with something inside the pocket of his jeans, he finally pulls out his phone, then holds it in front of my face. "My brothers told me you helped them with this."

I nod, unable to speak as he scrolls down pages and pages of headlines about Julie and *The Golden Telegraph* scandal.

"I wanted to ask you myself and personally thank you."

"You don't need to thank me. Julie hung herself."

I hope she loses everything the same way I have.

I pick at the skin around my nails. "What are you doing here, Nathan?"

"I was invited."

"Why?"

"Because I'm setting up a college and career prep center with the charity."

"That's you?" I overheard Martha and a few other trustees discussing it earlier.

He nods. "I'm donating laptops, implementing job interview workshops, and setting up a fund to help buy work clothes. I'm also starting a mentorship program for older foster youths aging out of the system. They'll come work at the firm."

"Nathan." My sight blurs with tears, clouding my vision. "That's so kind."

"I don't think I was very kind to you. I'm sorry I didn't give you an opportunity to explain yourself, Arianna."

"And I'm sorry I doubted your family." The lump in my throat the size of a football swells until it spills over, hot tears tracing paths down my face. "I knew who you were that night at the bar, Nathan." My voice trembles, thick with regret. "And I swear to you, it was never my intention to seduce 'the boss' just to get close to you. You have to believe that."

I might have told myself that's what I was doing at the time, but I was lying to myself. I liked him the minute I laid eyes on him.

I take a shaky breath, wrapping my arms around myself as if that could keep me from unraveling completely. "I liked you. God, I really liked you. And I hated myself for it. Because you were funny, handsome, and so damn smart. You weren't the man

I thought you were—you were better. And it terrified me because it wasn't supposed to happen like this."

I glance up at him, searching his face for anything—understanding, forgiveness, anything at all—but he's unreadable. My chest tightens, but I push forward.

"When I started at Hart Law, I had the wrong intentions. And I owe you an apology for that. I am so sorry, Nathan. I never believed Julie. I knew her crash report was fabricated but you never gave me a chance to explain that day in the boardroom." My voice cracks, and I swallow hard, trying to keep myself together.

"For as long as I can remember, I was so sure Kevin Taylor being acquitted was wrong. I was so sure of it. Because how could life be so cruel? How could it take away everyone I ever loved away from me and leave me completely alone in the world? I was fifteen, lost, and scared. My parents didn't have much, but they made sure Riley and I had gymnastics. We had dreams, Nathan. We wanted to win competitions, compete in the Olympics, do it for them, to make them proud, because they were. That night... that night we were celebrating because we made the State Championships. And if we hadn't, we wouldn't have been out so late. I felt responsible. Like it was all my fault, and I was looking for answers, anything to shift the blame, I guess."

A breath shudders out of me, and I tighten my arms that are wrapped around me as if desperately trying to contain the pain from spreading. "I will never forgive myself for doubting the verdict. For doubting Kevin. He saved me, and now I will never get the chance to thank him or your father for what they did to put Jean in place to take care of me." My voice barely rises above a whisper. "And for that, I am so truly sorry."

Tears sting my eyes like sharp needles piercing them as my

throat burns, my words coming out forced and fast. "I'm sorry for breaking policy and stealing and photographing files from the archives. But most of all, I'm sorry for falling in love with you. Because I know I hurt you in ways I will never be able to make up for." I wipe at my face, but the tears keep coming and I stand up, shove my feet into my sandals and get ready to leave. "In the beginning, I wanted justice for my family. That was all that mattered. I thought the verdict on the lawsuit was wrong. But *I* was wrong. In the end, I fell in love with you. With your family. Because you're good people doing incredible things for others."

I take a step back, because I need to get out of here from fear I'll shatter completely if I reach for him and he pulls away. "I just hope that what I did to help you bring Julie down was enough for you to see how truly sorry I am. But if you can never forgive me, I'll understand."

Willing him to believe me, willing him to see my heart laid bare before him, I apologize. "I'm sorry, Nathan," I whisper. "I don't know how many times I've said it, but even a million times wouldn't be enough." I turn away from him, breaking my heart all over again and walk out of his life.

"Come back here, Arianna," he orders with quiet authority as I take another few steps.

That's not what I was expecting him to say and whip back around to face him.

He stands to his full height and walks to me confidently and firmly says, "No more apologizing."

"Okay." I nod, agreeing to his request, but I'm not sure if I can stop myself.

"You helped bring down an entire publication today, an organization that has been led by ego for far too long. You played a part in shaking things up and for that I am so proud of you." Another step closer to me until we're standing toe to toe. "You were brave."

I didn't feel brave when I was doing it.

He cups my face with his hand, and I lean into his touch, loving the warmth of his hand on my skin again. "Arianna, I want you to know that if I was in your shoes, and if there was any doubt in my mind about the circumstance in which my family died, I would have done the same as you."

"Do you think so?" I don't think that's true.

"I know so. You and I are similar in a lot of ways. We both fight for the people we love."

"I never wanted to come between you and your brothers." I feel terrible about that.

"What you did for us, and so many others set off a chain of events that will bring that tabloid to a close before the day is over. The police have already begun making arrests. Phone-hacking is a serious crime, Arianna, and it's because of you that it's finally ending. People's privacy is safe now—all thanks to you."

I still can't believe I thought Julie was good in the beginning. My desperation clouded my judgment.

My heart beats faster when he brushes his thumb over the skin of my cheeks.

Unwavering, like he's memorizing every detail of my face, he says, "I forgive you, Arianna. I know your actions were motivated by the love for your family. There is no doubt in my mind that I would have done the same." He places a knuckle under my chin, lifting my face gently to meet his gaze. "I miss you."

"I miss you too," I whisper.

He clenches his jaw in the same way he always does when he's fighting his emotions. "Come home."

Is he serious?

He finally makes his throat work. "I love you. I won't pretend I don't." His hands find my waist and he pulls me closer. "You're coming home—where you belong. I can't live without you, I won't."

"I can't either. I love you, Nathan, I have from the start." I've been his from the first night we met.

"No more secrets, Arianna."

"I've told you everything." I've nothing left to hide. "This is me."

With strong athletic arms, he presses me firmly against him and then he's covering his mouth with mine and we lose ourselves in each other. His kiss scorches my skin as our tongues collide, greeting each other like long-lost lovers and finding their way back to one another.

Threading my hands into his hair at the back of his neck, I close my eyes and immerse myself in everything him, from his scent to his touch and warmth, as I melt into him.

Nathan skims his hands down the curve of my back, making us hum into each other's mouths in appreciation, our connection much needed.

Throbbing between my thighs drowns out everything around us as he fucks my mouth with his tongue. Thrilling sparks of energy dash between us and I can't believe this is actually happening.

"We should stop," I pant heavily, hearing the faint laughter of people in the distance.

"I don't want to," he mumbles against my lips, and covers his mouth with mine in what feels like the ultimate kiss of all kisses.

This kiss is different. It feels full of hope, love, and a future together, dissolving all the pain we've felt for the last few weeks as if mending our hearts. Our tongues dance together in perfect rhythm, licking and tasting each other.

For the first time in weeks I feel happy as joy flows into my heart like a warm river melting away the cold weight of loneliness, filling me with light and hope once more.

When I open my eyes, I find him looking right at me, pinning me with his powerful gaze. He threads his fingers into the hair on the back of my neck, gluing our lips firmly together, and we get lost in our forever kiss again.

He bites my bottom lip, sucking it into his mouth, becoming rougher, as if it's a promise of what's to come.

Unhurried, we finally come apart and he trails soft kisses down my neck before he nuzzles into me. It takes my breath away.

"I love you, Arianna." His hot breath dusts my skin.

"I love you so much." Tears flow down my cheeks, a mix of happiness and relief.

"I've missed you so much. I need you naked, baby," he mumbles between kisses.

"Then take me home."

"I like the sound of that."

50

ARI

Moving down the bed on my knees, I slide myself between Nathan's thick thighs, then slowly lay a path of soft kisses across his hip.

He lets out a low moan as his eager cock becomes harder and thicker with every one of my kisses.

I never believed in second chances until him. I also didn't know that love could be as powerful and deep as ours.

I am certain that my family guided me to him—I feel it in my very soul, an unshakable truth as undeniable as the dance of the sun and moon across the sky.

We found each other.

He is my unwavering compass, leading me home—to where my heart truly belongs. With him.

I open my mouth, lay my tongue out flat and lick up his thick, hot length from base to tip, making him flinch, his cock twitching in appreciation and leaking like a tap.

"Baby," he groans, threading his fingers into my hair, thrusting up into my mouth to fuck it.

Running my wet tongue up and down his shaft, I take him

fully into my mouth and swirl my tongue around his crown, sucking him harder as I lick along his thick vein on the underside of his shaft.

"You're so good at that, baby." His voice is dangerous and low. He bucks his hips, pushing, thrusting, making tears run down my face.

He grins down at me then holds the base of his cock and slides himself out of my mouth. Tapping the head against my lips, I push my tongue out to taste the salty precum beading at the tip. I moan with excitement, pleasure zooming through me as my body comes alive, every nerve tingling with anticipation at being with him again.

"Suck me," he commands, stroking himself back and forth.

I stick my tongue right out and let him rub himself against it before I suck him back into my mouth, gagging when he hits the back of my throat.

He clenches the sheets between his fingers, bucking his hips against my lips, unable to stop himself.

I circle the head of his cock with my tongue and find it difficult to breathe around his thick length as saliva spills from my lips because I'm struggling to swallow.

"I need to be inside you." He pulls himself out of my mouth and grabs the base of his cock, squeezing hard as if to stop himself from coming.

He's panting hard, his chest moving in and out, and every inch of him is covered in a faint sheen of perspiration. Looking down at me with hooded eyes, he slowly sits up, urging me to do the same before kissing me breathless.

He slips his fingers between my pussy lips then slides a finger inside of me and with his other hand he reaches up and wipes away my tears that slide down my face from deep-throating his cock.

A guttural moan rumbles from his throat, and he finger-fucks me, teasing my orgasm to make its appearance. He circles his thumb over my clit, while sliding his thick fingers in and out with intention.

"You're so wet, baby," he whispers as I rock my hips and ride his fingers. "Now turn around on your knees," he demands, removing his fingers from my pussy, and I whimper from the loss. It felt so good.

I do as he asks, turning around, and he moves behind me.

My back to his front, I ready myself for him.

"Hands on the mattress, Arianna," he whispers in my ear, sending shivers down my spine, and I get down on all fours, fully exposing myself to him, and wiggle my ass in the air.

He slaps my ass cheek, hard, which makes me arch my back and call out his name and silently pray he does it again.

Instead he pulls my ass cheeks apart and sticks his face between my thighs, then licks my pussy front to back. His rigid tongue plunges inside of me, over and over again, my orgasm building, weaving its way through my body.

"Nathan, I'm coming," I cry.

I feel him grinning against my pussy and he stops what he's doing, and I almost sob as my orgasm disappears. "Not yet. Turn over."

I quickly do as I'm told and lay back on the mattress, opening myself up for him because I'm so desperate to come.

"Good girl." He leans down and kisses my clit and I jolt as a shot of electricity shoots through my sensitive bud.

Leaning back, he lifts my legs up and places them on top of his shoulders. Lining the head of his cock to my dripping entrance, I push myself onto his dick at the same time he slams himself inside of me.

"You are so tight like this," he grits through his teeth, digging his fingers into my hips, fucking me steady and fast with his powerful thrusts.

He gives me the permission I seek as he punches all the air from my lungs as he fucks me until I'm thrashing, panting with need, and I can no longer take the pressure building in my core. "Now you can come."

And I do, I come all over his dick, shouting his name, clawing at his arms, urging him to keep going. Stars explode behind my eyes as he controls my overly sensitive body, every nerve ending connecting with his again. I shudder as my orgasm hits me like a ten-ton truck, bursting into a shower of gold heat through my entire body.

It's the most pure and true love and pleasure I've ever felt. Because it's with him.

Every beat of my heart belongs to him. Every minute of every day is his. Forever.

Emotion builds in my chest as he drives into me and stares at me, unblinking.

His balls slap against my ass over and over again, and I dig my nails into the skin of his arms, my ankles clamped around his neck as he fucks me up the bed.

"I'm coming, baby. Gonna fill you full of my cum," he rasps, driving into me faster.

God yeah, I want that. "Come."

Our breathing grows louder, as if in time with his power thrusts that have become filled with desperation. I clench my inner walls around him as the thick veins in his neck pound, the skin of his neck becoming red and angry looking as the pressure builds in his body.

Nathan roars my name then tells me he's coming as he spills himself inside of me, filling me with his cum, which I hope makes a baby. Our baby.

He moans loudly, holding himself deep inside my body, pouring every last drop, before sliding back and forth as if drawing out his pleasure, his cock twitching and pulsing.

"Holy shit," he hisses, and he takes a few moments to recover before he removes my legs from his shoulders and slowly slides himself out of me.

He lies on top of me, with his arms on either side of my head, and presses his firm body against mine.

"This is it—just you and me, forever," he says, before kissing my lips.

We stare at each other, which is all we ever seem to do, memorizing every freckle, line, and expression.

"There might be more than just me and you soon, if that's what you want."

"That's what I want." His voice turns serious. "With you."

I grin up at him, in shock at how quickly everything has changed for both of us. "I want that too."

His cock grows hard against my hip as he rubs his wet crown back and forth, ready to go again, because we have all the weeks we lost to make up for. "Want to start now?"

"Yes." I think I died and went to heaven.

51

NATHAN

It's been almost three months since Arianna moved back into my apartment. In that time, she's decorated the bedroom and living room and is currently underway with a full remodel of the kitchen.

I haven't asked her what color she finally decided for the cabinets because she's been swaying back and forth for weeks between bottle-green, navy-blue or pink. Which I'm not keen on.

She did such a great remodel in the other rooms though; I should trust her on the bold choices she seems to be able to pull off with ease.

Fuck it, if a pink kitchen with gold hardware makes her happy, then I'll be happy too.

We've settled comfortably into working life together. However, what is different is that she has made me have more time in my schedule to prep between cases, and she makes sure I don't take too many clients on at the same time. She also has me leaving the office before ten most nights, which means I'm getting more sleep.

Well, maybe not, because we fuck, a lot.

But the best part is not working on weekends because I implemented a team of lawyers who buffer me from weekend calls and emergencies.

On Saturdays we do date nights at the theater or dine out after spending most of the day on the beach after playing tennis with my brothers in the morning. And on Sunday mornings we laze about and spend hours between the sheets then enjoy the afternoons with my brothers and mom at the ranch.

I share everything with her, but there is still one important part of my life I want to share with her.

It's someone she's been keen to meet but I only wanted her to come here when she felt the timing was right. Today is that day.

"Dad, I want you to meet someone." I lay my hand on his shoulder.

Even though we found the best memory care home in the city for my dad, I still wish he was at home with my mom.

He requires full-time care and that would be too hard on my mom. This way he gets the therapy and dedicated around-the-clock specialist care he needs.

"Your dad is on form today. Watch yourself." The nurse winks, chuckling to herself, which means he's having a good day and causing mischief. "Just call if you need anything." Cynthia leaves the room, and I quickly thank her.

Arianna sits next to my dad on the chair beside him and nervously plays with her fingers in her lap.

"Who's this, now?" My dad's voice is sounding fainter and gruffer with each week that passes, and I hate how his muscles are becoming weaker, and his head is slowly becoming more tilted to one side.

"This is Arianna, Dad," I say and settle myself beside her in the other chair.

"Hello, Mr. Hart. It's lovely to meet you." She lays her hand over my dad's. "I've heard so much about you and all the wonderful things you have done to help so many people."

His lips twitch, and I can tell from his expression he likes her. How could he not? She's perfect.

"Arianna. Now that is a pretty name." His words come out slow and drawn out. "I think I knew an Arianna once." Confusion lines his brow.

I've spoken about her before. Sometimes he remembers her, sometimes he doesn't.

I know he doesn't remember our conversation from all those months ago when he told me to go to her. It's like it has just all gone. *Poof.* Like a puff of smoke.

"Did you know an Arianna before, Dad?" My dad's mind comes and goes. On good days when his mind is really clear, we talk about old cases because he loved his job and I know if he could, he would still be fighting cases and running circles around me and my brothers.

I'm so relieved I'm on speaking terms with my brothers again. For a moment I thought I'd lost them but like Mom said, we love each other regardless.

"Mmm," my dad hums as if deep in thought, and he takes his time to reply. "From a case, I think."

"My name is Arianna Donovan. Do you remember Kevin Taylor?" she asks, smiling and leaning closer to him, her voice full of hope.

His eyes look away and then at me and back again, and I can tell he's trying to figure something out. "I do," he eventually replies. "Car crash. It was a terrible accident." He struggles with the last two words of his sentence. "You're Arianna?"

My chest fills with emotion, because I wish that things could have been different for him. He was the best lawyer in the city, and he helped so many people. He deserves a better ending to his life.

"Are you happy, dear?" he asks, concerned about her welfare. "Did Jean look after you well?"

It doesn't surprise me that he remembers the case. Today, which is a good day, he's remembering everything but then when he goes to sleep for the night, it's like his mind resets and the next day won't be so good.

"She did and I wanted to thank you personally for helping Kevin organize my care. I'm very grateful." Arianna's eyes turn watery, and I lay my hand over hers, which is rested on top of my dad's.

"Arianna is amazing, Dad."

"I'm a legal secretary," she interjects, trying to hide her tears, sounding brighter than she looks.

"Are you Nathan's secretary?" He shifts his attention to me and then back at Arianna, struggling to move his neck. "I hope you keep him on his toes, Arianna."

"She does, Dad," I assure him. Having her in the office again has been incredible. We work well together, she makes my life ten times easier, and hell, she just gets me and the job I do and never complains.

"Good," is all he says, and while it's slow, it's firm.

"We're getting married." I rub my finger across the top of Arianna's four-carat diamond solitaire.

She was adamant she wanted something smaller but there is no way I was having that; I don't do anything by halves. The bigger the better. She's mine and off limits, and I wanted to show the world who she belongs to.

"Well, now, this is a turn up for the books." My dad chuckles before coughing a little. "Who is giving you away, dear?"

He knows that Arianna's father is no longer around, and I hadn't even thought about it.

"I was thinking Max could, if that would be okay with you?" She asks him for his approval.

"Now that is a good idea. I would, but you see I'm sort of stuck here now." His voice trails off.

I suddenly feel like I can't breathe. He's a shadow of the man I once knew.

"Well, if we could wheel you down the aisle in this fancy chair of yours and bring the service to you, would you do it?" Arianna asks hopefully.

I swear to fuck I haven't cried in a very long time, but I'm on the verge now.

My father smiles wider than the moon, and it sparks something in me—pride, relief, maybe even hope. If he can still smile despite everything, then I have no choice but to be strong.

"Do I have a suit, Nathaniel?" he asks, sounding determined.

"Yes, Dad." He won't have one that fits because he's lost a lot of weight, but I'll have someone here this afternoon to measure him if it makes Arianna happy.

"I know we set a date for next year, Nathan, but could we make it happen quicker?" Arianna questions, lifting her shoulders to her ears in excitement.

I just hope Dad has a good day for the day we set, but that's something none of us have control over.

"In weeks or months?" I ask.

"Weeks," she replies, sounding hopeful.

How the hell are we going to do that? Knowing her, she'll have everything booked by sunset today.

I guess she senses that my dad might not have much time

left either but that's something I can't even think about now, and I just want to focus on soaking up each day he has, whether those are good or bad.

She lets go of my dad's hand then turns to me. "Let's do it, Nathan."

"Let's do it," I agree, feeling excitement bubbling in my chest.

Arianna leans closer and shocks me to my core when she whispers in my ear, "I forgot to take my contraceptive when we broke up and so when we reconciled we made something beautiful together, Nathan. A happy accident. I'm pregnant."

I try my best to school my emotions but fail. "I'm going to be a dad." I swallow hard, because I once believed that I was meant to live my life alone, choosing work above everything else, but now I know that's not true. With unwavering belief, I know her family has been watching over her, guiding her to me since the beginning.

And now, she's giving me a life I never dared to dream of; a family and a place that's not just a penthouse, but a home, where we will grow, laugh, and love each other in the best way possible, because she taught me how.

My Arianna. My destiny.

* * *

MORE FROM VH NICOLSON

Another book from VH Nicolson, *Lincoln*, is available to order now here:

www.mybook.to/LincolnBackAd